A RELUCTANT QUEEN

THE LOVE STORY *of* ESTHER

JOAN WOLF

THOMAS NELSON
Since 1798

NASHVILLE   DALLAS   MEXICO CITY   RIO DE JANEIRO

Published in Nashville, Tennessee, by Thomas Nelson. Thomas Nelson is a trademark of Thomas Nelson, Inc.

Thomas Nelson, Inc., titles may be purchased in bulk for educational, business, fund-raising, or sales promotional use. For information, please e-mail SpecialMarkets@ThomasNelson.com.

Publisher's Note: This novel is a work of fiction. Names, characters, places, and incidents are either products of the author's imagination or used fictitiously. All characters are fictional, and any similarity to people living or dead is purely coincidental.

Library of Congress Cataloging-in-Publication Data

Wolf, Joan.
  A reluctant queen : the love story of Queen Esther / Joan Wolf.
    p. cm.
  ISBN 978-1-59554-876-4 (trade paper : alk. paper)
  1. Esther, Queen of Persia—Fiction. 2. Bible. O.T. Esther—History of Biblical events—Fiction. 3. Women in the Bible—Fiction. I. Title.
  PS3573.O486R45 2011
  813'.54—dc22   2011009289

Printed in the United States of America

11 12 13 14 15 16 RRD 6 5 4 3 2 1

FOR MY DEAR FRIEND, EDITH LAYTON FELBER.
I MISS YOU.

About Language

The languages spoken by the characters in this book would have been Persian and Aramaic. What you are reading is a "translation" into modern English.

CHAPTER ONE

485 BC

Esther rose early as usual. She dressed in her brown robe and overtunic, fitted her veil over her long black hair, and went out to the courtyard behind her uncle's house to begin making the day's bread—more than she and her uncle needed because she gave some to the old women in their community every day. By the time Mordecai came into the courtyard, she had kneaded the dough and set the loaves out to rise.

"Tired, Uncle?" Esther asked in a teasing tone as she saw

Mordecai yawn. "The Great King's feast kept you up late last night."

Mordecai smiled ruefully. "Far later than I care to be out, chicken. But I had no choice. All of the palace staff was invited and the Head Treasurer would have noticed if I did not appear for the king's birthday."

He took a seat on the bench at the small table in the courtyard and Esther began to assemble their breakfast. The plates contained dates and figs and slices of yesterday's bread, which Esther had warmed in the outdoor oven. She fetched cups of water from inside the house, Mordecai said the blessing over the food, and silence fell as they ate.

Esther waited until her uncle had finished before she spoke again. She and her friends were all curious about the new king, Ahasuerus, who had only recently arrived in Susa, the capital of the Persian Empire. It had been a huge surprise two years ago when the old king, Darius, had chosen him over his other son, Xerxes, and it made him an intriguing figure. But the real reason for the girls' interest was the gossip they had heard in the marketplace that the king was the most handsome man who ever lived.

Unfortunately, the Jewish girls who made up Esther's circle would probably never have an opportunity to see this paragon for themselves, but they hoped that Esther's uncle might have seen him at the feast.

"Did you get to see the king, Uncle?"

Mordecai pushed his plate a little away from him. "No, Esther, I did not. We menials were crowded into the Apanada, while the king and the Royal Kin dined inside in splendor. But I must say that we were treated well. There were huge quantities of meat and fowl: horses, camels, oxen, donkeys, deer, ostriches, geese; the countryside must have been decimated to provide so much food. The wine served was from Damascus, I was told, and everyone assured me it was excellent."

"Did you at least take a cup of water?" Esther asked.

Mordecai gave her a stern look and did not reply.

Esther wasn't surprised. The Jewish community to which they belonged held strictly to the Mosaic dietary laws. Even a cup from a Persian kitchen would be unclean for Mordecai.

Esther thought about how thirsty her uncle must have been and sighed. His look grew sterner. "The Law is the Law, Esther. Except if you're that weasel Ezra and his friends. They were eating and drinking without a thought for what it means to be Jewish." His lip curled in disgust. "They were as drunk as the Persians by the end of the evening."

This was one topic that Mordecai could hold forth about for a long time. The Susa Jews were broken into two sects. The smaller one, to which Mordecai belonged, held strictly to Mosaic Law. The other sect, comprised of most of the wealthy Jewish merchants in the city, had assumed many of the ways of the Persians among whom they lived.

Esther nodded impatiently.

Mordecai continued, "It's a disgrace. That the descendants of Abraham and Moses should turn their backs on the Torah and seek to become like these pleasure-loving Persians! It was Nebuchadnezzar who forced us out of our homeland of Judah and dragged us into years of subjugation in Babylon. Now these traitor Jews seek to imitate the very people who enslaved us? Bah! It is disgusting."

Esther tried her best to cheer him. "You taught me the scriptures, so I know that such a thing has happened many times before, and we always survived. We are God's chosen people, Uncle. No matter how many may turn away from the Covenant, we will always triumph in the end."

He grunted, looking only slightly mollified.

Esther attempted to steer the conversation back to their original topic. "Even if you didn't get to see the king last night, I'm sure you will see him soon. After all, you work right there in the palace. And he is going to reside in Susa now, isn't he?"

"Yes, it appears he has decided it is time he took up the reins of government here in the capital. He's been Great King for almost two years, but first there was that rebellion in Egypt that he had to put down, and next he decided to go to his summer palace in Ecbatana to escape the summer heat. But I understand that he has come to Susa for good."

Esther reached across the table for her uncle's empty plate and put it on top of her own. "There is still a chance that

Rachel got to go with her brother to the procession through the city yesterday. Ahasuerus was riding in his golden chariot and she might have gotten a good look at him. I know that Sarah and Rebecca weren't allowed to go. Nor was I." This last statement was accompanied by a faintly reproachful look at her uncle.

Mordecai regarded her with a trace of amusement. "I am asking myself, why would a group of nice Jewish girls be so interested in the Great King of Persia?"

Esther grinned. "Because he's supposed to be so magnificently handsome. We want to know if it's true or not."

Mordecai's thin, intelligent face became instantly grave. "I hope you have enough sense not to be swayed by a good-looking face, Esther." His voice was as severe as his expression. "That's what happened to your mother, and look what it brought her."

"It's just a game we're playing, Uncle Mordecai. We're not really interested in the king." Her voice softened. "I will never run away from you, dear Uncle. You have always been so good to me. And I love you."

Mordecai looked away, both embarrassed and touched by her statement. She waited for him to resume the conversation and finally he said, "I may not have seen the king, chicken, but I do have some exciting news to tell you about the feast."

Esther's interest sparked. "You do?"

"Yes, indeed. It was quite an extraordinary thing. None of

us in the Apanada saw it, but we heard about it as we were leaving. Soon all of Susa will hear about it, but here is a chance for you to be first with the news to your friends."

Esther's eyes widened and she leaned forward. "What happened?" she breathed.

"The king sent for his wife, Vashti, to show herself at the banquet."

Esther's mouth opened in amazement. Persian women were kept sequestered, allowed to see no males but their husbands or blood kin. Such a summons would be unthinkable in Persian society.

"Before all those men?" she asked.

"Yes." Mordecai raised his graying eyebrows. "*And* unveiled, because he said he wanted them to see how beautiful she was."

Esther gasped. "A Persian woman would never do that!"

"Exactly. She refused, and apparently that made the king angry. I'm sure he was drunk. All of the Persians had been drinking for days."

"What happened next?"

"The king issued a royal decree, right there in the banquet room. He was angry, but I've heard his anger runs cold, not hot. So he issued this decree, with perfect clarity, stating that Vashti's refusal to obey her husband's request was a violation of her marriage vow and a dangerous example to the women of Persia. Therefore she was no longer his wife."

"But he put her in an impossible situation! It would have

been wrong of her to show herself, and it was wrong of her to disobey him. How could she choose correctly?"

"It was a diabolically clever move," Mordecai said with a tinge of admiration in his voice. "Everyone knows he never wanted to marry Vashti. Now he is rid of her."

"I think it was a horrible thing to do." Esther glared at her uncle. "Poor Vashti. How she must feel!"

Mordecai shrugged. "I think Ahasuerus means to rule. Vashti was pushed on him by his father, and now that Darius is dead, Ahasuerus wants a fresh start, unencumbered by a politically connected wife."

"How terrible it must be to be a Persian woman. To be unable to walk to the market or visit friends, to have to cover up your face and hide inside a harem and never get to see the men of your community." She shivered. "I thank God, Uncle Mordecai, that you brought me up to be a Jew."

"You always were a Jew, Esther," Mordecai assured her. "Your father might have been Persian, but a Jew is defined as the child of a Jewish mother. Among our people, the father's blood does not count."

Mordecai rose from his bench. "Now I must wash and go to the palace." He gave a grim little smile. "The place will be buzzing with speculation and gossip. Everyone will want to know what is going to happen next."

Esther watched her uncle depart, but instead of removing the breakfast plates, she leaned her elbows on the table and rested her chin in her hands. The morning sun was warm, not hot, and it felt comforting on her shoulders and head.

Poor Vashti. Her mind turned to what she had said to her uncle about being glad she had been raised as a Jew.

Her life might have been very different had that not happened. When her mother had been only a little older than Esther was now, she had eloped with a Persian cavalry lieutenant. After her father had been killed in battle, her mother's brother, Mordecai, had taken her mother and Esther home to Susa; Esther had been two years old at the time. Her mother had died when Esther was only six. Since Mordecai had not remarried after the death of his wife, for many years it had been just the two of them in the tidy, mudbrick house in the Jewish quarter of Susa.

Esther knew nothing about her father except that her mother had loved him enough to turn her back on her own family and community to follow him. When Esther was small she had once asked Mordecai to tell her about him, and her uncle had shown that stern face she always obeyed and commanded her never to mention her father to him again. She had never done so.

But sometimes she thought about this Persian father of hers, who had stolen her mother's heart and then died tragically at a young age. Her mother must have been brave. Esther knew she could never do such a mad thing. She was comfortable in her familiar surroundings: her small, tight community;

her friends; her beloved Uncle Mordecai. She was fifteen and knew that one day she would get married. She liked her best friend's brother, Abraham, and she thought he liked her. But she was in no hurry to leave home. No hurry at all.

That afternoon Esther joined the other women from her street for their weekly visit to the local market. All of the Jews in her community patronized this particular market because it was the only place in Susa that offered meat and fowl that had been ritually killed and dressed by a trained Jewish butcher.

Esther's clothing was nicer than the clothes she wore to work around the house; today she wore a long white tunic encircled with a narrow leather belt, and over that a shorter robe in green that opened at the front. Her long black hair was braided, wound into a bun and covered by a light veil with a simple gold fillet. On her feet she wore soft leather sandals. It was a style of dress adapted to the hot climate of Persia, and most inhabitants of Susa, male and female, wore some variation of it.

Esther walked through the familiar narrow streets of her neighborhood chatting to her neighbor, Naomi. Naomi had always looked out for Esther, inviting her over to spend time with her own children so Esther would not be lonely. After the initial polite greetings, Esther related the tale she had heard from Mordecai about what had happened at last night's feast. Some of the other women overheard what she was saying, and by the time they reached the market everyone had the news.

The Jewish women kept together as they made their way from stall to stall. The market was both noisy and colorful: the cries of the vendors, the chatter of Aramaic spoken with the accents of countries from all over the empire, the stalls heaped with colorful produce from the countryside, even live lambs and bullocks for slaughter. Esther and Naomi were examining a display of delicious-looking pomegranates when they heard someone call Esther's name. Both women turned their heads.

"Rachel!" Esther said in surprise. "What are you doing here?" Rachel was Esther's closest friend, a small, dark girl with the long-lashed eyes of a deer. Since her father was a rich merchant, the servants usually did all of their household shopping.

A young man stepped up to stand beside Rachel. "She has a nice piece of gossip that she can't wait to tell you, that's what she's doing here."

"Abraham." Esther smiled up at her friend's tall, well-built brother. "Did she make you bring her?"

"She did," he replied.

"We went to your house first and when you weren't there, I remembered this was your market day," Rachel explained.

Naomi commanded, "Come away from the stall, girls. We

are impeding people who wish to buy." She shooed the young people out of the way, then turned to Rachel. "Now, what is this gossip that is so urgent you must seek Esther out at the market to tell it to her?"

"The king has put away Vashti!" Rachel said, looking around to see the effect her dramatic revelation had on the others.

Naomi's face broke into a small, satisfied smile. "Oh, that. We already know all about that from Esther."

Rachel's face fell and she turned to Esther, her brown eyes bright with accusation. "Your uncle told you! Why didn't you come right away to tell me?"

"I was going to come to your house after I finished the marketing," Esther apologized.

"Isn't it dreadful?" Rachel demanded. "He put her away for not obeying his command to show herself. How could she be expected to do that?"

"Uncle Mordecai thinks he wanted to get rid of Vashti for political purposes."

Abraham nodded agreement. "It's politics, all right. The court is divided into the party that wants to go to war against Greece and the party that doesn't. Vashti's family evidently belonged to the wrong party."

Esther shivered at the thought of how terrible it must be to have your whole life ruled by the vagaries of politics. "I'm glad *I'm* not a Persian woman," she said.

"Me too," Rachel agreed.

Naomi looked from one girl to the other. "A Jewish woman can be divorced against her will, girls. You must know that."

"Yes, but that can only happen if the wife has committed adultery," Rachel replied.

"That's not true," Naomi said. "A Jewish man can put his wife away by simply giving her a bill of divorcement. The marriage is immediately dissolved, even if the wife doesn't agree."

Rachel frowned. "But doesn't he have to give a reason?"

Naomi patted her arm. "Believe me, Rachel, if a man wants to get rid of a woman, he will find a reason."

Rachel was horrified. "But . . . if the wife is forced to leave her husband, where does she go?"

"She goes home to her parents. Where else can she go?"

The autumn sun was warm, but Esther suddenly felt chilled. If her future husband should grow tired of her, could he divorce her because she was half-Persian? She pulled her robe closer to her body. It was as if the tightness and security of her little community had suddenly been breached and the world was a less kind and stable place than she had thought.

That evening, over supper in the courtyard, Esther asked Mordecai if what Naomi had said about Jewish divorce was true. He confirmed that it was.

She toyed with her bread, her eyes avoiding his. "What if that should happen to me?"

"It won't happen to you, chicken. No man would ever want to put you away."

"You say that because you love me, Uncle Mordecai."

"Esther, look at me." He waited until her eyes were looking directly into his. "Do you trust me?"

"Of course I trust you."

"Then know that I would never give you into the keeping of a man whom I did not think would take care of you for the rest of your life. Do you trust me to do that?"

She smiled. "Yes, Uncle Mordecai, I do."

"Then finish your dinner," he said with mock sternness, and obediently she took a bite of her fish.

CHAPTER TWO

I t was one of those beautiful spring days in Susa where the sun was bright but not hot and a cool breeze still blew from the mountains. Esther had taken the house oil lamps out into the courtyard to clean them, and she was wiping down the simple clay containers and humming a tune when she heard Rachel call her name. She looked up and saw her friend and Abraham standing in the doorway.

"Come out, come out," Rachel called. "I'll move these lamps. It's too nice a day to be indoors."

"Let me move those lamps for you." Abraham hurried to

the table and, as he took the lamps from the table to put on the ground, Esther went into the house for refreshments. When she came out again carrying a tray with cups of pomegranate juice and honey cakes, Rachel and Abraham were sitting at the table, waiting for her.

Esther served the refreshments, then sat down herself and took a long, thirsty drink of the juice. She put her cup on the table and smiled at her friends. "How nice of you to call on me."

Abraham smiled back. "I should be at work with my father, but something happened that Rachel insisted she must share with you. So I brought her."

Esther briefly lowered her eyes. Abraham was finding many reasons to come to her house these days. She said, "It is always nice to see you, Abraham."

She turned to Rachel, who was clearly bursting to speak. "So, Rachel, what is your news?"

"The king has announced that he is going to hold a contest to find the most beautiful woman in the empire to be his wife." Rachel managed to look both excited and disapproving at the same time. "Isn't that disgusting?"

"A contest? What kind of contest?"

"He has sent out a proclamation to all the countries in the empire that they should send beautiful young virgins to the harem in Susa to be candidates for his hand. He said that the one who pleased him most would reign in place of Vashti."

Esther pictured the capital city being inundated day after day with waves of beautiful young girls hoping for a chance to be queen. It was the maddest idea she had ever heard.

She said, "This king certainly has a strange way of dealing with women. He chooses them and gets rid of them as if they were horses."

Abraham chuckled. "It does sound rather like a horse fair." His arched black eyebrows rose a little higher. "I am sorry to have to inform you girls that the proclamation my father and I saw posted specified that only girls of the Achaemenid clan may apply for the position of queen." He shook his head with mock sorrow. "Neither of you will be eligible."

Esther laughed. "Oh, Abraham, you just broke my heart."

He grinned back at her and she felt her cheeks grow a little warm. Abraham had a nice smile.

Rachel's long-lashed eyes had been darting between her brother and her friend. She said, "Oh well, I suppose if you are a Persian woman and have to be shut up anyway, you might as well be queen and get shut up in a palace."

Esther's tender heart was touched. "That may be true. Poor things, what a life they are forced to lead."

She and Rachel looked at each other in mutual recognition of their own superiority to the pitiful Persian women who had not been lucky enough to be born Jews.

Even though the Jewish women of Esther's community con-demned the Great King's way of searching for a new queen, they were nevertheless extremely interested in the process. Within a month of the king's proclamation, girls began to pour into Susa, hoping to be found beautiful enough to enter the Great King's harem and compete to be queen. They came from Mesopotamia, making the easy journey by ship down the Tigris or the Euphrates; they came overland, from the courts of the satraps in Cappadocia and Lydia, Baktria and the Hindukush. And, of course, there were the girls from the Achaemenid aris-tocracy whose families lived right around the capital.

Mordecai, who worked in the finance office of the palace, obliged his niece and her friends by gathering as much informa-tion as he could about the seemingly endless stream of hopeful candidates. But Mordecai had more on his mind these days than the king's potential marriage choice. The unrest between the Jews and the Edomites in their homeland of Palestine was increasing, and all the men of Mordecai's community were worried that, should fighting break out, Ahasuerus might not side with the Jews.

Cyrus and Darius, the two Persian kings who had preceded Ahasuerus, had a history of supporting the Jews. Cyrus had even given his permission for the Jews to rebuild the Temple in Jerusalem. But no one knew where Ahasuerus stood.

One Sabbath afternoon, after Esther and Mordecai had returned from the synagogue gathering in Rachel's father's house, Mordecai shared his concerns with his niece. The brutal summer heat had begun, so the two were sitting in the common room of their own house, which, like most of the houses in Susa, was protected from the merciless sun by a roof of palm covered over with three feet of earth.

As women were not allowed at the synagogue meeting itself, Mordecai told Esther about the discussion the men had held after their reading of the Torah. The conversation always changed when the women came in with the food, so Esther never knew what had been discussed by the men until she reached home, where her uncle had formed the habit of sharing everything with his niece.

Mordecai was a teacher by nature, and once he had discovered how quick Esther was, how curious and intelligent, he had made her his pupil. They had progressed from him reading the scriptures to her, to him teaching her to read them for herself.

Today, though, Mordecai was focused on political matters. Esther could see that he was deeply disturbed and she listened intently as he spoke.

"You know about the land the Edomites stole from us when we were driven into exile in Babylon," he said.

"Yes, Uncle. You look worried. Has something happened?"

"Yes. I have learned from my friend Araxis, one of the palace scribes, that the Edomites have sent a letter to the Great King asking him to confirm their rights to southern Judah."

"To *our* land?"

"Yes. Our land." Mordecai pulled at his beard, something he always did when he was upset. "Then, to make matters worse, some mad prophet is going around Jerusalem trying to stir up our people to go to war to take it back."

Now Esther understood why her uncle looked so concerned. "War in Palestine? That would not be a good thing for anybody!"

"It is the worst thing that could happen. Should war break out, and the king decide to send troops to pacify the region, we don't know which side he will favor. Darius would have favored the Jews, but no one knows about Ahasuerus. If he should choose the Edomites, we could lose half our country!"

Esther slid forward on her stool, leaning toward Mordecai. "Do you think the king would send an army? Would he not let the two sides fight it out between themselves?"

Mordecai shook his head. "Palestine lies directly on the route into Egypt. No Persian king wants unrest in Palestine." Mordecai slapped his hand against the arm of his chair in frustration. "This king is so hard to figure out, Esther. He went to war against Egypt when that country rebelled against Persian rule, and he put the rebellion down quickly and efficiently. But he is outraging the party at court that wants him to continue the war against the Greeks by refusing to do so." He looked at her somberly. "I don't know what he will do, and the not knowing makes me nervous."

"Ahasuerus was supposed to be a good king in Babylon, wasn't he?"

"He was a very good king. Darius sent him there when he was only eighteen years old, fully expecting him to fail. But he surprised everyone. The people in Babylon loved him. And he has brought back a contingent of his councilors from Babylon to whom he appears to listen. Darius' people are furious because they are not the ones who have the king's ear."

Esther shook her head. "It all sounds complicated, Uncle. The Babylonian party, the Persian party, the Greek War party, the anti-Greek War party. It must be hard to keep it all clear in your head. But surely you must know someone in the palace whom you can approach to find out how the king stands on Palestine."

"I don't," was Mordecai's grim reply. "I work in the Treasury, chicken. I am too far removed from the political scene to be acquainted with anyone who might know the king's mind."

Esther let her eyes run around the simple room, with its ceiling supported by plain wooden columns and its white-washed mudbrick walls. She had arranged some bright ceramic vases on a small wooden table to give the room color, and an old Persian rug added its faded tints as well.

As she regarded the parchment roll her uncle had brought home from work, she had a thought. "Why don't we Jews imitate the Edomites and send our own letter to the king? They have written that they want their rights to our land confirmed, then we should write that the land is legally ours and it should be confirmed to us."

Mordecai smiled. "My clever girl. That is exactly what we have decided to do."

"You should make me part of your council, Uncle."

Mordecai laughed, as she had intended. He stood up and stretched. "The sun has gone down. Perhaps we might find a breeze in the courtyard."

Esther rose easily to her feet and followed her uncle outside.

Summer in Susa was not pleasant. The sun burned relentlessly over the plain upon which the city was situated, and no breeze arrived from the surrounding mountains. In the summertime, Susa baked.

The Great King had gone to his summer palace of Ecbatana, taking with him most of the court, so the issue of Palestine was set aside for the moment. Life in the Jewish community went on as usual, although most of the socializing took place in the evening, when the heat abated a trifle.

Abraham had continued to accompany his sister on her visits to Esther and, by August, she realized that he might want to marry her. This idea was strengthened when Rachel told her she was going to be betrothed to another of the young men in their congregation.

Esther was surprised and said so.

Rachel laughed. The girls were sitting in Rachel's court-yard, which was much bigger than Mordecai's. A few other community families were there as well, but Rachel had taken Esther aside to give her the good news.

"How can you be surprised?" Rachel gave Esther a quizzi-cal look. "We're both of the age to be married. We've spoken about it."

Esther put her hand over Rachel's as they sat side by side on a small wooden bench in the corner of the courtyard. "I know, I know. I suppose I kept thinking it was still in the future . . ."

"I thought Jacob would ask for me." Rachel sounded pleased with herself. "He always talked to me at supper after synagogue." She looked into Esther's eyes. "Do you think he's handsome?"

Jacob was not quite as tall as Esther, but then Rachel was small. And his ears were big. Esther looked back into her friend's eager eyes and said, "He's very handsome, Rachel. And nice too."

Rachel beamed.

Abraham chose this moment to come into the courtyard from the house. Both girls looked at him, then Rachel said mischievously, "Perhaps you won't be far behind me, Esther."

Abraham was far more handsome than Jacob. But Esther felt herself shying away from the thought of marriage. Her life with her uncle was so comfortable, so safe. She wasn't sure if she was ready to give it up.

Mordecai had evidently been thinking about marriage also, because as soon as they returned from Rachel's he suggested that they go out into their own courtyard to cool off before they went to bed.

"I thought Rachel looked happy," he remarked as they took the chairs best positioned to catch the tiny breeze.

"I think she is happy, Uncle Mordecai. She is looking forward to having a house and family of her own."

"Are you looking forward to being married, chicken?"

Esther didn't answer.

"Abraham's father as much as told me tonight that I can expect an offer for you."

"I don't know what to say."

"You have turned into a beautiful young woman, Esther. If you don't wish to marry Abraham, there will be others. I can promise you that."

Esther was surprised. Her uncle never complimented her on her looks. He told her often how smart she was, but never once had he said she was pretty. She met his eyes briefly and saw that he was serious.

"Tell me what you want, chicken," he said gently.

"Wouldn't you be lonely without me, Uncle Mordecai?"

"I will miss you very much. But I have always known that you will marry, Esther. That is where your future lies, with a husband and children of your own." He smiled at her. "I will be their eccentric grandfather."

She laughed shakily. "I know I must marry. But . . . I'm not sure if I'm ready yet. You see, I have my own house here with you, Uncle Mordecai. And we have such a nice life! I would miss my studies—"

He cut in. "There is no reason to stop your studies. Abraham would never ask that of you."

Esther knew that. She was reaching for excuses, that was all. "If I wait a little, do you think I will be too old for suitors?" she asked.

Mordecai smiled. "Esther, you will never lack for suitors, believe me. And if you want to spend a little more time with your old uncle, you will make me very happy."

She grinned at him, relieved by his reply. "I do like Abraham," she said. "Do you think he will be willing to wait?"

"Didn't Jacob serve seven years for Rachel? Believe me, chicken, Abraham will be happy to wait."

CHAPTER THREE

The coming of autumn brought the king and his courtiers back from the mountains and trouble back to the Susa Jews. A week after the court's return, Mordecai came slowly into the house after work and shocked Esther by the grayness of his face.

"Sit down, Uncle, and I will bring you a cup of water," she commanded.

He obeyed without protest, which worried her even more. When she handed him the cup, she saw that his hands were shaking.

She sank on her knees in front of him. "Are you ill?"

She struggled to keep the fright from her voice. What would happen to her if she lost Mordecai? For almost all of her life he had been her rock, her protector, the person who loved her most in the world. She had a few memories of her mother, but the person who had always been there for her was her Uncle Mordecai.

"No, chicken, I'm not ill. I've just had a bad shock."

She took the empty cup from him and put it on the floor. Then she held his cold hands in her warm ones.

"Can you tell me what happened?"

"First we must send for the men of our community so I may speak to them. Can you run across the street and ask Naomi if her servant could pass along that message for me?"

Esther jumped to her feet, found Jacob, and came back to tell Mordecai that he would go. "You must eat, though, Uncle, before you have this meeting."

He shook his head. "I couldn't swallow a morsel." He waved his hand toward her usual stool. "Sit and I will tell you what has caused my distress. Talking will help me to collect my thoughts."

She leaned forward to listen.

"Haman, one of the men who came with the king from Babylon, came into my office today. It doesn't matter what he wanted, but in the course of our brief conversation I discovered that he is not a Babylonian, as we all thought, but an Edomite.

An Edomite, Esther! And he has the ear of the king—is one of his most trusted advisors, in fact. I was horrified."

The first of the men Mordecai had summoned knocked on the front door and Esther went to let him in.

When the meeting finally adjourned, Esther came in from the kitchen to find Mordecai looking as pale and worried as he had when first he came home. Although Esther had been brought up to feel both religious and racial ties to the Jewish homeland, her immediate worry was more for her uncle's health than it was for war in a faraway place.

"There is no sense in making yourself ill about something you have no control over," she urged, as they sat at breakfast the following morning. "War has not broken out in Palestine. War may never break out there. Nothing you do can change what happens, Uncle Mordecai, so don't worry about it so much."

He shook his head. He had hardly eaten a thing. "I have a terrible feeling about this, Esther. I cannot help it. Something dreadful is going to happen to the Jews. It is like God is sending me a . . . a prophecy."

The weeks went by and cool air finally began to blow down from the mountains, and the streets of Susa, almost empty in the heat of summer, became lively again. The markets were crowded with people, the king's cavalry rode through the city on an almost daily basis, and the sun's warmth felt good, not oppressive. It was Esther's favorite time of year.

Then one night Mordecai had a dream. Esther heard him yelling from his sleeping room and she grabbed her shawl and ran next door, afraid that he might be having a heart cramp. "Are you all right, Uncle Mordecai?" she called from the doorway.

She could hear him panting as if he had run twenty miles. She lit the oil lamp and went in to check on him. He was sitting up, his eyes wild, his body bathed in sweat.

"What is wrong?"

"A dream," he gasped. "A terrible dream."

Relief surged through Esther. A dream would not kill him. She knelt next to the raised pallet that was his bed. He was shivering, and she took the shawl she had thrown over her nightdress and wrapped it around his shoulders. "You're all right, Uncle Mordecai. You're safe. You're here with me."

In a flash of memory, she recalled the times when she was a child and he had come to comfort her from a bad dream with the exact same words she had just spoken to him.

He breathed in deeply several times, trying to gain control of himself.

"Do you want to tell me about it?" she asked.

He croaked, "Yes, I think so." He cleared his voice, waited a moment, then went on. "I think it is important, Esther. I think this dream was sent to me by God. I need to say it out loud before I forget any of it."

"All right, then. Tell me."

He gazed in front of him, as if he was seeing something she could not. "I saw the earth spread out before me and it was shaking with booming thunder and earthquakes. Then two huge dragons appeared and began to fight each other. As they struggled, I saw the entire world dissolving into hatred and evil, and I knew"—for the first time during this recital he looked at her—"I *knew*, Esther, that the whole of the Jewish race was doomed to destruction." He shook his head, as if to clear it. "I cried out to God for deliverance, and God answered by sending a great healing river over the earth, and the sun broke through the darkness, and I knew that my people would be saved."

Esther was stunned. It was such a fantastic dream. Dragons fighting? The world delivered over to hatred and evil? Where had such a dream come from?

Mordecai said, "God sent me this dream. He sent it to warn me. Those dragons, Esther . . . those dragons had eyes that looked just like Haman's."

Suddenly Esther felt chilled. She wished she had her shawl back.

"Are you sure?" she whispered.

"Yes. We must find someone to counteract Haman's influence with the king! We must find someone to represent Jewish interests."

"But who?"

Mordecai looked at his niece. Esther was kneeling in a pool of lamplight, and the removal of her shawl showed the long line of her throat and the swell of her chest under the thin linen of her nightdress. Her black hair was loose and flowed over her shoulders and down her back. Her large eyes were filled with concern for him.

"Here." He removed the shawl from his shoulders and handed it back to her. "I am fine now and you must be chilled."

She took it and wrapped it around her shoulders.

"Would you like me to fetch you a cup of milk?"

"No." He reached out and flicked her cheek with his finger. "Go back to bed. I have disturbed your sleep enough, chicken."

Esther thought that he was looking better. His shivering had stopped and his voice was stronger. She stood up. "Do you really think the dream came from God, Uncle?"

He looked up at her. "Yes, Esther, I do."

In the days after the dream Mordecai was deeply preoccupied and spoke very little. Esther tried her best to find out if something was bothering him, but for the first time in all their years together she felt as if he was withdrawing from her. It made her uneasy.

Then, the following Sabbath, Mordecai asked her to

remain after the meal so that he and a few of the men from the community could speak to her.

"Have I done something wrong?" she asked in alarm.

"No, Esther. You have done nothing wrong. We just wish to speak to you."

So Esther stayed while the other women left, Rachel throwing her a curious glance before she went out the door. The table that earlier had contained the food still stood in the middle of the floor, and the two men who had remained sat opposite Mordecai and Esther, with the table between them.

Esther was frightened. Something unusual was about to happen, and she was not comforted by the somber looks on the bearded faces of Rachel's father, Jojachin, and the community's priest, Shimeon.

Mordecai spoke first. "We have received bad news from Palestine, Esther. The prophet Obadiah has been whipping the people of Jerusalem into a frenzy about the Edomite's theft of southern Judah. If he succeeds in rousing them to arms, there will be war."

He stopped and Esther nodded that she understood. What she didn't understand was why she was here.

Mordecai went on, "We need to place someone in the palace who will be able to represent Jewish interests to the king."

Esther struggled not to look as mystified as she felt. She nodded again.

Suddenly, Mordecai raised his hands to his face. "You tell her," he said through his fingers to the priest. "I cannot."

Shimeon gave Mordecai a sympathetic look, then turned to Esther. "Esther, we have decided that our emissary to the king must be you."

Esther stared. She could not possibly have heard aright. "I am sorry," she said. "Will you repeat that?"

"I said that we have chosen you to be our emissary to the king. We have decided that you must enter the competition to be the king's wife. If God wishes you to have this position, then the king will choose you." Shimeon lifted his bushy eyebrows a little. "Who better to have the king's ear than his wife?"

Esther's heart gave a thud. She looked from Shimeon to Rachel's father, Jojachin, who sat beside him. They seemed perfectly serious. Then she turned to Mordecai, who was sitting beside her. He had uncovered his face and was looking haggard. She said, "This is impossible, Uncle Mordecai. You must realize that. The king's proclamation made it quite clear that only Persian aristocrats could apply. As you have always told me, I am a *Jew*. I cannot be considered."

Mordecai's voice was husky. "The Persians count their lineage through the father, not through the mother as we do. Your father was an Achaemenid, therefore, in the eyes of the Persians, you are an Achaemenid too."

Esther's heart felt as if it was thundering in her chest. It was unbelievable, but they were serious.

Mordecai went on, "I was furious when your mother ran away with a Persian noble, and I have always tried to ignore his very existence. But it is in my mind now, Esther, that God allowed that marriage for a reason."

"What reason?" Esther asked, dreading the reply.

"You have the two things necessary to become queen. You have extraordinary beauty and you are an Achaemenid. Believe me, Esther, it is excruciatingly painful for me to ask this of you, but I have come to believe that God has a purpose for you. I believe that God has chosen you to be His instrument to save His people."

Esther raised her voice. "This is all because of that mad dream, isn't it? Well, I am not going to allow myself to become incarcerated in a Persian harem because you had a dream, Uncle Mordecai. I am not!"

Rachel's father leaned toward her. "You have the right to refuse, certainly, but we have discussed this at length and we have prayed about it. I beg you to consider your decision, my dear."

Esther stared at him. "Would you ask your daughter to do such a thing?"

He smiled a little. "Rachel has not the qualifications. You are the only one who does, Esther. That is why we are asking you."

She shook her head. "You are wrong. They will never accept me if they know my mother was a Jew."

The priest answered, "We understand that. Our plan is to keep your Jewish blood secret. We will say that your mother was a Babylonian. That will not hinder you from being a candidate."

By now anger had completely washed away Esther's fear. "No one is to know that I am a Jew? That is your plan?"

"That is right."

"Suppose we imagine that the unlikely happens and the king actually chooses me to be his wife. How am I supposed to represent Jewish issues to him if he doesn't know I am a Jew? Or am I supposed to reveal myself on my wedding night? I hardly think such a revelation will so endear me to my husband that he will listen to my advice. In fact, he will probably put me away even faster than he got rid of Vashti."

"I told you she was smart," Mordecai murmured, a flicker of life in his shadowed eyes.

The priest held her angry eyes with his grave ones. "You cannot tell anyone, Esther, not even the king. I will give you permission to ignore Mosaic Law and follow Persian ways. Remember, Moses lived as an Egyptian until the time came for him to answer God's call. So will it be with you."

"I am no Moses!" Esther cried.

"Perhaps not," Shimeon agreed. "But you may be called by God in a different way." He leaned forward, bringing their faces closer. "Listen, my child. God gave you the gift of great beauty. Extraordinary beauty. It was given to you for a purpose,

Esther, and we believe that this mission we have asked you to undertake is what that purpose is.

"Will you at least think about it?" Shimeon concluded, extending a pleading hand in her direction.

All Esther wanted to do was to get away from here. "I will think about it." She turned to her uncle. "Right now I just want to go home."

"Of course I will take you home, chicken," he said, standing as well.

Don't call me chicken! Esther longed to shout those words at him. How could he have done this to her? How could he have put her in such a position? She had thought he loved her, but he had betrayed her. This was all his idea. She knew that, even though no one had said it. This idea belonged to Uncle Mordecai.

Ignoring all protocol, Esther stood, turned her back on the men, and walked to the door.

Esther felt as if an earthquake had hit her. She did her household chores, fixed her uncle's food, answered his attempts at conversation with short sentences, and all the time her brain was in a whirl of anger, outrage, and fear.

Uncle Mordecai had betrayed her. He, who had told her she could wait before she decided to marry a man of her own people, a man who cared about her, was ready to sacrifice her to the horrors of a Persian harem. He actually wanted her to be chosen queen. To sleep with an uncircumcised pagan, a man who had no respect for women and would most certainly have no respect for her.

It was impossible. They were asking too much. She would not do it. She could not do it.

She was sitting by herself in the courtyard on the second night of sleeplessness, watching the first light of dawn brighten the sky, when she began to think of what it would mean to refuse to do her uncle's bidding. Tiredness swept over her like a heavy cloak. She had never felt so weary in all her young life. Could she bear to continue to live her ordinary life, knowing that she had failed to answer the call of her community in their time of need?

Her eyes fixed on the sky, just where the light was starting to peek over the horizon. *Father in Heaven*, she prayed. *What am I to do? Shimeon our priest is a very holy man, and he wants me to do it. Uncle Mordecai is a very holy man and a brilliant man as well. Would he have asked me to do this if he did not think it was Your will?*

Slowly the sky began to lighten and a thought for escape began to form in Esther's mind. If God was looking for a savior for His people, He would not look to a simple Jewish maiden. He would surely have someone else in mind. However, the men had become so enamored of their idea that they would not even try to search for the true savior if they continued to think that she was the one.

Their idea of getting her into the harem would never work. Esther had her mother's polished bronze hand mirror, so she knew what she looked like. She knew she was pretty. To be honest, she was probably the prettiest girl in their small community. But the Persian women who would be presented as candidates to the king would be soft and lovely, with skin like ivory and eyes like does. Their hair would be curled and they would smell like exotic spices. They would know all the protocols of courtly behavior and would fit into their place as smoothly as rare silk from Damascus.

They would not have a heavy mass of black hair that was straight as rain and impossible to curl. They would not have skin still browned from the summer sun and hands rough from outdoor work. They would not have muscles in their shoulders and arms from carrying heavy buckets of water. They would all be far more beautiful and presentable than she.

She would never be accepted into the harem—the Head Eunuch would take one look at her and send her straight home. Esther smiled as the idea grew in her mind. This was a way she could make everyone happy. She would tell the men that she agreed to the scheme and she would tell Uncle Mordecai to present her as a candidate for the contest. She doubted she would even make it in the door.

Her smile broadened into a grin. She would be returned to Mordecai, and her old life would go on as usual, and everyone would be grateful to her that at least she had tried. The sun was brilliant now in the eastern sky, and Esther rose to her feet and stretched her arms over her head, rising up on her toes as far as she could go. Maybe she would marry Abraham after all, but in her heart she was still angry with Uncle Mordecai for putting her in this position.

The sun rose even higher in the sky and soon Mordecai came out into the courtyard looking for her. She turned to him with downcast eyes and said softly, "I have been thinking about your request, Uncle Mordecai, and I have decided that I will obey your wishes and those of the synagogue council. I will seek to become a candidate for the king's hand."

Mordecai reached out and took her into his arms. "I am glad, Esther," he said.

CHAPTER FOUR

Esther spent the three days she had left at home cleaning. She was determined that she would leave her
uncle with a house that shone like a jewel. When
Mordecai protested that her labor was unnecessary, she raised
her voice to disagree and he let her alone. Once the house
had been cleaned to her satisfaction, Esther set about getting
a woman to come in to cook and clean for her uncle. Again
Mordecai protested, and again he rebounded off the hard shell
of Esther's determination.

The hard work had kept Esther too busy to think much,

which had been her plan. It seemed sudden when she discovered herself riding through the streets of Susa in a covered box on her way to an appointment with the powerful Head Eunuch of the king's harem. Mordecai had made all the arrangements through Filius, the Deputy Treasurer, for whom he worked. As the synagogue council had planned, no one in the palace knew that she was Jewish. Their story was that Mordecai was introducing her as a favor to a friend.

The box was enclosed by a curtain, so Esther saw nothing until her uncle pushed it open and assisted her in descending. She glanced around at the cobblestone courtyard where she stood and then to the towering sinister bars that formed the Harem Gate. A tall, golden-skinned young man was standing beside Mordecai. Esther cast a quick glance upward and saw that his expression was haughty and that he had no beard.

He must be a eunuch. Esther had known that the Persians gelded the men who were to guard their women, but she had never seen such a creature before. He was speaking to her uncle in a slow, careful voice. "You are Mordecai, from the Treasury?"

"Yes. And this is Esther, the daughter of my friend; she has an appointment to see Hegai."

"I am Hathach," the eunuch replied. "I will take her to Hegai, then I will come to your office to let you know if she has been accepted or if you must come to collect her again."

"Thank you," Mordecai said, and turned to Esther. "I wish you good fortune, my dear."

I can't do this. She stared over her veil at her uncle and she knew he must see her terror. *Please,* she begged him with her eyes. *Take me home. Don't let me do this.*

But he was smiling at her, his face under perfect control.

"This way, lady," the eunuch said, and took a step toward the Harem Gate. She had been told that no man was allowed to enter through that gate save the Great King. The thought struck her that this might be the last time she would ever see her uncle.

"Good-bye," she whispered.

He didn't reply, but for the first time his face looked old and drawn. She waited a moment, but he made no motion toward her. He was not going to take her home.

Esther stiffened her back. *So be it. They have all left me on my own and I will just have to take care of myself. This Hegai will never accept me into this horrible harem.*

However, despite her brave thoughts, she felt her stomach heave as she followed the tall eunuch through the Harem Gate. She repeated to herself the prayer she had been saying ever since she had agreed to this masquerade. *Father in Heaven, let me be rejected so my uncle will realize how impossible this plan of his really is. Let me be rejected so the way will be open for the true savior of our people to show himself.*

Just inside the gate was a ceramic-tiled waiting area. They passed through this into a large columned courtyard, with a lovely marble fountain. A number of beardless men sat on the stone benches that surrounded the fountain, laughing and talking among themselves. Esther peeked at them out of the side of her eyes as she followed her escort through the courtyard and into a garden. Next they arrived in another lovely open-air garden, where Esther had a glimpse of several unveiled women walking amid the autumn flowers.

The women all turned to look at her as she followed Hathach across the garden. "Are those some of the candidates?" she asked him.

"Yes." Clearly Hathach was not inclined to talk.

They stopped at a large, carved wood door. Hathach's knock was answered by a small boy with jet-black curls and large blue-green eyes. Esther looked at the beautiful child and was horrified to think that he may have already been gelded.

They stepped into a small reception room with the most magnificent rug Esther had ever seen. The little boy went into the next room and returned to announce, "The lady may enter. You are to return in an hour, Hathach, to hear what Hegai's decision is."

A strange calm descended upon Esther. She was here and soon it would be over. She glanced around the room, which was furnished with silk divans and elegant, low wine tables. The rug was even more magnificent than the one in the first room. Then another door opened and a man came in. He was tall and heavy, his nose slightly crooked, his lips full. His skin was not young, but it was beardless. He was dressed in a long embroidered robe made of fine wool dyed to a rich shade of blue and girdled around his ample middle by a soft leather belt.

This must be Hegai, Esther thought. The eunuch's gray eyes were unreadable as he looked her up and down. He spoke in a soft tenor voice that sounded odd coming from such a large man. "So you are Esther, daughter of Zopryas."

"Yes," Esther returned clearly. "I am she."

"You may remove your veil, Esther."

Esther did as he asked and stood in silence, straight-backed and rigid, as he cupped her chin in a soft, well-tended hand. He turned her face from side to side, then tilted it up so she had to look at him. Color burned in Esther's cheeks, but she met his eyes directly and did not look away.

"Your face is lovely." Hegai's voice was matter-of-fact. He ran a finger along her cheekbone. "There is a pleasing sweetness in the curve of the cheeks. And the eyes . . ." He nodded approvingly. "They flash like black fire. Magnificent."

He sounds as if he's discussing a horse, Esther thought, which probably made her eyes flash even more. He motioned for her to take off her head veil, which she did, revealing the waist-long fall of her hair. The eunuch looked at it and raised an eyebrow. "You do not curl it?"

"It won't curl," Esther said shortly.

"Hmm." He took a strand between his fingers and rubbed it. He gave her a disapproving look. "You have not taken care of it. It is dry and dull."

This interview was going exactly the way Esther wanted it to. "I come from a home where the women are expected to work. We don't have the time to pamper ourselves as the wealthy Persian ladies do."

Hegai frowned. "Filius assured me that you were an Achaemenid. The Great King is not interested in any women who are not of the aristocracy."

Esther produced the answer her uncle had told her to give should this question be asked. "My father was an Achaemenid, a cavalry officer. We have a villa in the foothills outside Susa, but we are not wealthy."

"Your skin is in deplorable condition. It is sunburned and dry."

Esther had to force back a smile. This was going better and better. "I am outdoors a lot."

Hegai's crooked nose quivered as he took in that piece of information. "Without a veil?"

"Yes." She said this emphatically. "It is difficult to work when one's face is covered."

"Filius told me you were recommended to him by a clerk in his office. A Jew."

"He is a friend of our family."

Hegai shook his head, as if he could not believe what he was hearing. Esther chose this moment to call attention to her hands by raising one to push the piece of hair Hegai had touched behind her ear.

A large, well-kept hand reached out and captured hers. "What have you done to your hands?"

Esther regarded her rough hands with complacency. "As I said before, in my family the women have to work."

Hegai looked horrified and Esther was so delighted by his patent disapproval that she smiled.

This was a mistake. *You can warm your hands at Esther's smile*, her Uncle Mordecai had often said. And now the Head Eunuch stood in silence, her hand in his, his eyes focused on her face.

He said slowly, "Your skin and your hair can be repaired and made beautiful. Your bones are already beautiful and it is the bones one cannot change."

Esther's smile vanished.

Hegai kept looking at her, then he nodded. "I do not think the Great King will be displeased with the results."

Esther snatched her hand away and stepped backward. Her heart jumped in her chest. "What do you mean?"

"I mean that your face has passed the test, Esther. Now we must examine the rest of you."

Never, for as long as she lived, would Esther forget the scalding humiliation of the following hour. If Uncle Mordecai had known about this, he would never have sent her. He would never have let her be handled like a piece of merchandise, prodded and poked and stripped naked in front of an expressionless eunuch who never said one single word the entire time. The worst moment came when he inspected her to see if she was indeed a virgin. She wanted to scratch his eyes out.

What followed was just as bad. She was taken back to Hegai, who told her that she was indeed a fortunate girl, that despite her flaws she had been accepted as a candidate. "Hathach will inform your friend, who will inform your family. I am certain they will rejoice at the news." He gave her a narrow-eyed look. "Although, I must confess it amazes me that they sent you here in such a deplorable condition."

Esther was speechless.

He crooked his finger. "Come, Esther, and I will take you to your room."

She couldn't move. *This can't be happening. They are going to put me in the harem. It's a mistake. I can't let them do this. God did not want this. I'm sure He didn't want this. How could He? I must tell Hegai the truth, tell him who I am so he will let me go.*

She had almost opened her mouth to speak when she remembered: If she confessed that Mordecai had lied about who she was, Mordecai would be in serious trouble. He would certainly lose his job. He might even be punished in other ways. She couldn't take that chance. Angry as she was with him, she knew he had done this because he truly believed in his mad dream. He truly thought she was going to save the Jewish people from destruction.

I have to stay, she realized despairingly. *I have to stay until the king picks a wife.*

Hegai, realizing she had made no move to follow, turned around. "What is the matter?"

"Nothing." She took a long, steadying breath. "I am coming."

Father in Heaven, she prayed, as she followed Hegai deeper into the maze of corridors that was the harem, *I beg You to help me. I have no one else. No father, no uncle—no one to turn to except You. Please help me to get through this ordeal. Give me strength to bear what must be borne. Give me the strength to keep Uncle Mordecai safe.*

Chapter Five

Esther looked around her room. It was small and windowless. The walls stopped a foot short of the ceiling, providing the only possibility for the movement of air. Two small chests were pushed against one of the walls and a lamp, a charcoal brazier, and a table comprised the remainder of the furnishings. A small, polished bronze mirror hung on the wall over the table, upon which were arranged a variety of combs, colored ribbons, jars, and bottles. The heavy scent of some kind of musky perfume hung in the air.

Esther felt she would suffocate if she had to sleep in here.

Hegai said, "We had to send the king's entire harem to Babylon to make room for the new additions here. The girl who was previously in this room was dismissed by the king yesterday, which is why we have space for you."

"Dismissed?"

"Yes. The Great King is granting each candidate a separate interview. This has been going on for months, and so far he has rejected every one of them." Hegai looked put out. "We have sent him some extremely beautiful girls, but Ahasuerus is fastidious."

"What happens to the girls after they are rejected?" Esther asked with apprehension.

"They are sent to another part of the harem to wait until we can send news to their families to come and collect them."

"They do not remain in the harem, then?" Esther was anxious to have this point clarified.

Hegai looked down his nose. "Achaemenid girls do not become concubines."

Esther smiled in relief. It would be all right. This fastidious king would want nothing to do with her. Once her interview was over, she could go home.

Hegai pointed out the cupboard where the sleeping mat was kept, then told her that the Mistress of the House would come shortly to attend to her.

After Hegai had left, Esther looked slowly around the room again. She inhaled deeply, as if trying to convince herself that there was air enough in this enclosed space for her to breathe. Then she raised her hands in the ancient Jewish attitude of prayer and looked upward.

Father in Heaven, help me to get through this ordeal. Give me the courage to keep my purity, even though I must live in this unclean place.

Her prayer was interrupted by the abrupt opening of the door. An immense woman surged into the room and Esther dropped her arms and backed up, overwhelmed by the vast amount of space the woman was taking up.

"I am Muran, the Mistress of the House," the fat woman announced. "And you are Esther?"

"Yes." Esther's back was against the wall.

The Mistress's eyes slowly scanned Esther, from the top of her head to the tips of her shoes. The woman's flesh breathed out a sweet floral scent that overpowered the musk perfume that already hung in the air. Esther thought that never in her life had she seen such enormous breasts.

"Hegai tells me that you need a lot of work, that your hair and your skin are a disgrace." The Mistress stepped forward, lifted a lock of Esther's hair, and rubbed it between her fingers in exactly the way the Head Eunuch had done. She even went so far as to sniff it. Then she clicked her tongue in disapproval and asked, "Why are you wearing green?"

Involuntarily, Esther glanced down at her best robe, which she had always thought was pretty. "I got a good price on the wool."

"You should never wear green. It makes your skin look sallow."

Esther's chin lifted infinitesimally. "Perhaps my skin *is* sallow."

The woman's eyes, buried in pouches of fat, were coolly critical. "It will look less sallow in a color other than green."

Esther wondered why on earth they had taken her if she was so far below their standards. She longed to ask this question, but knew that it would look odd coming from someone who was supposed to be thrilled that she had been accepted.

Muran sighed. "Hegai was right; you need a great deal of work. Come with me now and we shall begin with a bath." The Mistress turned, maneuvered her huge bulk through the narrow doorway, and Esther followed.

Esther had never had the experience of being submerged in water, and the thought made her nervous. All Persians were fanatical about personal cleanliness, and they expected all the various races who lived in their cities to be clean as well, but only the very rich had built-in baths. And, since Persians also believed that rivers were sacred, no one was allowed to bathe in them. In a city surrounded by rivers, most of the population of Susa laboriously washed and cooled themselves with a basin and a washcloth. The use of river water was permitted only after it had been removed from its natural flow.

Esther followed Muran down several corridors, all of which looked alike to her, until finally the Mistress opened a door and ushered Esther into a large mirrored room. Gold and silver stools lay scattered about the ceramic brick floor and the warm moist air was scented with roses. A tall, blond, blue-eyed young girl came forward as soon as Muran entered and asked, "May I be of assistance, Mistress?"

"Yes. This is Esther, a new candidate, Luara. Make her ready, please."

Luara bowed to Esther from her waist. Then, as Esther stood stiff and silent, the girl slipped a long linen robe over her head. Esther was soon profoundly grateful for this modest covering, as Luara next began to remove Esther's clothing. The experience of being stripped naked twice in one day turned her scarlet with outrage and embarrassment.

"Very well," Muran said, her small eyes glittering. "We shall now begin your treatment. Come with me."

The first thing Esther saw as she entered into the main room of the harem bath was a magnificent marble fountain in the middle of the room. Several girls clad in robes like hers were sitting on the edge of the fountain, trailing their hands in the water and talking to each other. Other girls were taking baths in the huge marble basins that were set up against the blue, yellow, and green enameled brick walls.

The sound of feminine voices stopped as Esther came into the room. For a moment the air seemed heavy with more than wet heat as the weight of all those eyes fell upon her, and she tensed. Then the girls turned back to their companions, and the soft sound of subdued laughter and whispered conversations filled the steamy room again.

"Come with me, my lady," Luara said briskly, leading her to one of the unoccupied wall baths. She turned on the two faucets that were set in the wall and, to Esther's amazement, hot water came out of one and cold out of the other. Muran had stayed behind to speak to a woman whom Luara called the Mistress of the Baths, and Esther felt comfortable asking the servant girl how they managed to get hot water to come out of a faucet.

"It's piped in, of course," the girl replied. "The furnace is under the floor."

The only time Esther ever got to bathe with hot water was when she took the trouble to heat it up on the outdoor stove. Most of the time she made do with cold. Now here she was, sinking up to her shoulders in a tub of water that was the perfect mix of hot and cold.

It felt strange, but she thought she liked it.

To her great relief she had been allowed to keep her robe on, but that did not stop Luara from reaching under it to scrub every inch of her body until it tingled.

Once the bath was over and Esther was standing with water streaming off of her, they went into the next room where Luara said she was to have her hair washed. Two very pretty girls told her to sit upon a stool, and then they poured a horrid yellow mixture on her head and began to rub it through her hair.

"What is that?" Esther asked, her eyes closed tightly so she wouldn't be blinded.

"It's only egg yolks," Luara replied. "Excellent for cleaning the hair without drying it out."

The two girls rubbed vigorously, working the egg yolk into every strand of her hair. Then, when they had finished, they rinsed it by pouring buckets of warm water over her head. Esther shook her head like a wet dog once they were done and watched with fascination as the water simply disappeared through the drainage holes in the brick floor. Thinking she was finished, she started to get up, but Luara's hand rested on her shoulder to prevent her.

They washed her hair again and then one of the girls rubbed in some kind of sweet-smelling oil. And they washed her hair again.

At this point, Muran and the Mistress of the Baths had wandered over to watch the proceedings.

"A good start," the bath mistress said encouragingly. "In a month it will shine like silk."

A month? She would be here for a whole month? And she didn't want her hair to look better. Not that the king would be likely to choose her anyway, she assured herself. But she had been hoping to see him sooner.

"Next we shall attend to the skin," Muran said, and she, Luara, and Esther moved to a third room where two more bath attendants were awaiting them.

First they rubbed her all over with pumice stone, an exceedingly uncomfortable process that was meant to smooth away any rough spots. Then they bleached her skin with egg whites—to try to make it less sallow, Esther thought. The worst part of the ordeal, however, came when they removed the hair from her legs and her underarms.

First one of the girls spread a paste on her skin, then after five excruciating minutes, when she was sure her skin was burning off her body, the women sluiced her with hot water. To Esther's astonishment, the hair washed off with the paste.

The final part of the treatment came when Esther lay upon a marble table while a slim girl with incredibly strong fingers rubbed oil into her skin. It was the first time all day that Esther actually relaxed, closing her eyes with pleasure as the clever hands rubbed away the tension in her muscles.

Finally Muran took her to a robing room where the Mistress of the Robes had set out new clothing.

"I can dress myself," Esther said when Luara bent to put a thin linen shift on under her now-dry bath robe. She was heartily sick of being handled as if she were a doll.

"I am sure that you can," Muran agreed. "But here you must learn to let others dress you."

Esther set her jaw as Luara slipped the shift on her. "If you will hold up your arms, my lady, I will remove the robe," the girl said.

Esther held up her arms and Muran regarded her critically as she stood in only the thin undergarment. "Your breasts could be a trifle larger, but they will do."

Esther had also had her fill of comments on her person. "Give me that tunic," she said to Luara, who handed her a long-sleeved, ivory-colored garment that Esther pulled quickly over her head.

The tunic fabric was beautiful. Esther could not stop herself from stroking the exquisite material.

"All our linen comes from Egypt," Muran informed her.

"It is very lovely," Esther admitted.

She stood for what seemed forever before the Mistress was satisfied that the folds of the tunic were falling evenly from her charge's narrow waist to her toes. Finally Luara took a long-sleeved, rose-colored wool robe and slipped it over Esther's head. The robe came only to her knees, so that the perfect folds of the tunic showed below.

By this time Esther's hair was only damp, and Luara combed it out and braided it with rose-colored ribbons.

"Now for the cosmetics," Muran said, turning to the girl who had come in with a tray covered with small turquoise and green glass bottles.

Esther's stomach rumbled audibly.

The cosmetic girl giggled and Muran glared at her.

"I have not eaten all day," Esther said, pleased that stomach noises would be another black mark against her.

"You shall eat as soon as we finish with your face," Muran promised.

After much consultation the women decided to merely outline Esther's eyes with kohl and dust a touch of rouge on her cheeks. When the cosmetic girl was finished, Muran led Esther to the big bronze mirror that took up almost one whole wall of the room and commanded her to look at herself. From the expression on the Mistress's face, she clearly expected Esther to be enchanted.

Esther looked into the mirror and saw a strange aristocratic Persian lady with huge, kohl-lined eyes. She felt a wild longing for her old scratchy wool clothes and naked face. *What would Abraham think if he could see me now?* she thought.

"Well," Muran demanded. "Aren't you pleased?"

Esther did her best. "I look very nice. Thank you."

Muran gave her a puzzled look. She was about to speak when Esther's stomach growled again. Unexpectedly, the enormous Mistress of the House laughed. It was a deep, surprisingly infectious sound and it made Esther smile.

Muran's small, bright eyes widened. "Ah. *Now* I see why Hegai accepted you," she said.

CHAPTER SIX

It was a week before Esther could eat any of the food that was served to the girls, and many more weeks before she could eat without feeling nauseated. It didn't help that the girls she was living with behaved completely opposite to how she was taught to be. They were not modest; they boasted of their beauty all the time. They were not kind; they fought malicious and foolish battles over trivial points of precedence and privilege. The girls who were members of the high aristocracy looked down on the girls who were less exalted. And everyone looked down on her, the girl with the mother who was a merchant's daughter and whose father was a mere lieutenant in the cavalry.

All this while, as Esther was suffering the continuous regimens of baths and hairwashes and skin preparations, more and more girls were having their interviews with the Great King and being rejected. According to Luara, the maid who had been assigned to her, the girls who were rejected were sent to another part of the harem to wait while their families were notified to come and pick them up.

"Only two girls are being held as possible choices, Mistress," Luara told Esther. "Ahasuerus will see them again if he doesn't find anyone more to his liking."

Esther snorted indignantly. "This king has absolutely no concern for the feelings of other people. One has only to look at the way he treated his first wife to see that. And now these poor girls, being kept on like this just because he cannot make up his mind. He should be ashamed."

Luara, who had been combing Esther's hair, stopped and looked at Esther's face as it was reflected in the bronze mirror in front of them. "Mistress, we are speaking of the Great King. I would say that he has more on his mind than the feelings of the women who wish to be his wife and share in his glory. None of them mind waiting if it may give them the chance of being chosen."

Esther met her maid's blue eyes. Luara was certainly as pretty as any of the girls who were candidates. Esther hesitated, then asked something she had long wondered about. "How did you come to be here, Luara?"

Luara smoothed a strand of Esther's hair with the comb. "When I was twelve my father sold me to the Satrap of Babylonia, and then the satrap presented me to Ahasuerus as a gift. He thought the king would like my coloring."

Her voice was matter-of-fact, but Esther saw pain in those beautiful eyes. *What a terrible story,* she thought. "How long have you been here?"

"I have been in the harem for five years, Mistress."

Pity stabbed through Esther's heart. What a terrible life this girl had led. But she felt instinctively that Luara was not the kind who would welcome pity, so she said, "Well, I think it is disgraceful for one man to have all of these women just waiting around for him to notice them! We are like a stable full of expensive horses, groomed and bathed and fed so we will be ready for when our rider decides to come and take us out. It's . . . it's disgusting."

Luara's hand came down on Esther's shoulder. "Do not say that to anyone else, Mistress! Never say anything that might be derogatory of the Great King. You yourself mentioned how easily he got rid of Vashti when she got in his way. Be very, very careful, I beg you."

Esther could see that the girl was truly concerned. She lifted her own hand and rested it on Luara's. "Do not worry, I will be good." She gave Luara a reassuring grin. "Besides, none of these aristocratic girls want to have anything to do with me, so I won't even have a chance to tell them my thoughts. I shall be safe."

The girl whom the harem staff thought had the best chance of any of the candidates was named Barsine. She was exquisitely beautiful, with the ivory skin, thin arched nose, and glossy black ringlets that Persians most admired. Luara explained to Esther that not only was Barsine beautiful, she was a direct descendant of Cyrus the Great, the founding king of the Achaemenid dynasty. This was what made her more special than most of the others.

Esther knew all about Cyrus because the Jews also revered him. He was the king who had freed them from the Babylonian exile imposed by King Nebuchadnezzar, and it was Cyrus who had allowed her people to rebuild the temple in Jerusalem. She thought now that to the Persians it must be as important to be of the line of Cyrus as it was to Jews to be of the line of David.

In fact, Barsine had so many advantages that even the other candidates thought that she would be chosen; everyone hoped to be summoned before her so they might have a chance. When finally Barsine received the call for her appointment, she surprised everyone by asking Esther to keep her company while she was being dressed. "I won't be so nervous if you are there. There is a serenity about you, Esther, that is very calm-ing," she said.

So Esther sat with Barsine while the girl was prepared for the meeting that might change her life—and that of the rest of the girls in the harem. While Muran and the attendants fussed over Barsine's hair and dress, Esther tried to think of things to say that might distract her. She mentioned a little brown bird that had flown into the harem garden the day before.

"It looked so odd among all the Birds of Paradise, but it was such a breath of real life," she said. "Imagine, this little brown bird, pecking away in the harem of the Great King of Persia. I thought it was wonderful."

Muran straightened up from her position on the floor beside Barsine and gave Esther a long look. "Are you thinking that perhaps *you* are that brown bird, Esther?"

Esther felt her eyes widen at this too-perceptive remark. She forced a laugh. "Compared with Barsine, I certainly am a brown bird, Mistress."

At that moment, Hathach, the eunuch who had been assigned to Esther and Barsine, looked in the door and said, "It is time, Mistress."

Barsine drew a long breath.

"Good fortune," Esther said sincerely.

"Thank you," Barsine whispered. Then she pulled her-self together, the unusual vulnerability vanished, and she said haughtily, "I am ready."

It was Hathach who brought Esther the news about Barsine. "The king has instructed that she be kept in the harem until he has seen the rest of the candidates. The two other girls who have been kept are to be dismissed."

While this was not the exact news Esther had hoped for, still it was positive. Clearly Ahasuerus had liked Barsine.

Then Hathach surprised her by saying, "I am to bring you to the Mistress of the House. If you will follow me?"

Muran's apartment was in a far more luxurious part of the harem than Esther's small room. The Mistress turned as Hathach announced Esther, then gestured to a large cushion placed upon the floor. "Sit, Esther," Muran said. The Mistress then lowered herself to a wide divan, lifting her legs so she could recline in comfort. Esther was amazed that so massive a woman could perform such a maneuver with what seemed to be relative ease.

"Hathach has told you about Barsine," Muran said as she settled her robe modestly around her legs.

"Yes. And I must say I am surprised, Mistress. If the king does not want Barsine, then what can he be looking for?" Esther's long legs were bent under her and the skirt of her orange-blossom robe spilled over the cushion.

A little silence fell as Muran's glittering dark eyes raked over Esther's figure. She sat quietly under the scrutiny, her spine straight, her hands folded quietly in her lap.

"Indeed," Muran finally answered. "That is a question Hegai and I have been discussing."

The door to the apartment opened and a young girl came in bearing a tea tray filled with sweet, sugary pastries and fruit. She put the tray down upon a low table, poured tea into pretty enameled copper cups, and brought a cup to both Esther and Muran. Next she proffered the tray to Muran, who helped herself to a large, sugar-coated, nut-filled pastry. Esther, not accustomed to the luxury of fruit in winter, chose an orange.

"That will be all, Gazel," Muran said, and the girl effaced herself quietly from the room. The Mistress bit into her pastry with obvious pleasure, but Esther held her orange. She didn't think she would be able to choke down anything just now.

When Muran had finished her pastry, she licked the sugar from her fingers delicately. Then she gestured for Esther to bring her the tray of delectables. This time she chose a ripe peach. "We all had hopes for Barsine," she said as she examined the peach.

"I know. Barsine is so beautiful. And she is a direct descendant of Cyrus. I thought that was important to the king."

"Apparently, it is not." Muran bit into the peach and a little juice squirted onto her chin.

"What can he be looking for?" Esther asked again.

Muran put the peach down, wiped her chin, and rested her jeweled hands on her stomach. "I will tell you something, Esther. This supposed competition has little to do with looks.

Quite simply, Ahasuerus wants a wife whose loyalty will be to him. Darius made him marry Vashti, whose loyalty was to her father, Mardonius. And everyone knows he hates Ahasuerus, despite his being Ahasuerus' uncle."

Esther remembered Abraham saying much the same thing when first they heard of the king's edict. She said now what she had thought then. "If that is so, would he not be wiser to choose a girl whose family he already knows is loyal?"

"The number of families whose loyalty was pledged to Ahasuerus over Xerxes can be counted on the fingers of one hand," Muran said.

"But surely that has changed," Esther protested. "Now that Ahasuerus has been named Great King, the loyalty of the nobles will be to him."

"Ahasuerus would count that as expedience, not as loyalty," Muran said.

Esther nodded slowly. "I suppose I can understand that. But he did not reject Barsine, Mistress. He merely wants to see more girls."

"If he had found Barsine acceptable, he would have taken her immediately. No, Esther, Hegai and I have come to the conclusion that Ahasuerus is looking for a different kind of girl for his wife."

Esther sat perfectly still, terrified of what might be coming next.

Muran crossed her still, dainty ankles. "To be frank, Esther,

Hegai agreed to see you only out of courtesy to the Deputy Treasurer, who made the request for one of his people. Technically, of course, you are an Achaemenid, but your father's family are lesser nobility, and your mother's family appear to be merchants."

"Yes," Esther agreed to the lie.

"Hegai was surprised by you," the Mistress went on. "He accepted you, but you must realize that you are different from the other girls who are candidates. If he had been looking for a woman for Xerxes, Hegai would never have taken you. But Ahasuerus is different. Both Hegai and I feel that there is a possibility that you will please him."

No! No! No! Esther thought in horror.

Muran went relentlessly on, "We want to take you in hand and make a special effort to prepare you. You have great potential, my dear, and we are prepared to invest our time in you."

Esther hesitated, then spoke in a rush. "I will be honest with you also, Mistress. I agreed to present myself to please my family, but I did not expect to be accepted by Hegai. I truly do not feel that I am qualified for such a high calling."

With a great heaving of flesh, Muran arose from her divan. She beckoned Esther to come to her, then she turned the girl around so that she faced the large bronze mirror that hung on one of the room's walls. The Mistress ran her finger up and down Esther's cheekbone. "There is a sweetness in your face that is pleasing, Esther. And you have the most beautiful eyes of any of the candidates. Most importantly, you are an out-sider. You have no political connections, no family who will be begging for favors, no grudges or feuds to settle. Hegai and I agree that Ahasuerus might think you will suit him very well."

Terror, tasting like bile, rose in Esther's throat. She had managed to survive in the harem with some equanimity because she had truly believed that her uncle had misinter-preted his dream, that she had no chance at all of being chosen by the king. Now, listening to Muran, the real possibility that she might indeed be asked to take up this burden struck her like an arrow to the heart.

How could she do this?

She said in a low voice, "I am afraid I will disappoint you."

"Nonsense," Muran replied briskly. "I will have you moved to a much larger chamber, and Hegai and I will begin training you intensively. I promise, by the time you meet the king, you will be ready."

Esther had been totally unprepared for such an offer. She had become used to considering herself the least likely of the candidates and now, to have Muran tell her this—she was more than frightened. She was terrified.

Could Uncle Mordecai possibly be right? Could I have been the savior he saw in his dream?

She still didn't believe it could be true. She was a woman, and she had seen with crystal clarity how little women counted in the Persian world. But . . . she was here in the harem and there was no way she could reject Muran's offer. That would be suspicious and she had to be careful not to involve Mordecai.

She drew in a long breath and said with as much composure as she could muster, "Thank you, Mistress. You are very kind."

Muran reached out to enfold Esther to her massive bosom. "There is nothing to fear, Esther. Hegai and I will always be there for you, to advise and to help."

She pressed her face into the rolls of fat between Muran's neck and shoulder and felt the Mistress patting her back. She shut her eyes.

What Muran says, what Muran wants to do . . . I'm here in the harem already. I suppose I have to agree to it. Besides, it is probably the only way to know if Uncle Mordecai was right. If the king chooses me, then I will know that I must follow the wishes of the Lord. But if he rejects me, then Uncle Mordecai will understand that he was wrong and then he will look for someone else to be our savior.

Her eyes still tightly closed, her face still buried in Muran's shoulder, Esther said, "All right, Mistress. I will do as you say."

CHAPTER SEVEN

Haman stood beside Ahasuerus on the large open-air platform that was situated at the southwestern corner of the palace. The king was riding out with a group of courtiers this morning. As usual, the men wore Median dress to ride in—jacket, trousers, and boots—and on their heads the cidaris, the high, flat-topped felt cap that denoted Persian nobility. They were all standing there because the king's brother, Xerxes, was late.

It was a day that promised spring would soon arrive; the air was warm and a light breeze blew. The members of the Royal

Kin, who were to accompany the king on his ride, stood at a respectful distance from Ahasuerus and Haman. They continued to wait for Xerxes.

Haman was worried, as he always was whenever the king was in the company of these men, most of whom were his enemies. His eyes went from face to face. All of them had at one time pledged their allegiance to Xerxes. Haman did not trust them, and he knew the king did not trust them either.

He urged the king, "Please be careful, my lord. Anything might happen when you are away from the palace and the people who care for you."

Ahasuerus gave the friend who had come with him from Babylon an amused look. "It is certainly true that Xerxes does not like me, but I hardly think he will try to murder me in front of the entire Royal Bodyguard, Haman."

Haman did not trust the Royal Bodyguard either, or at least its commander, who was a leftover from Darius' reign. But he held his tongue, and Ahasuerus' amusement increased. He said gently, "I am very well able to take care of myself, but I appreciate your concern."

"This court is filled with vipers, my lord." Haman lowered his voice to a whispery hiss. "There is danger everywhere."

"I realize that, Haman," Ahasuerus said a little impatiently. "But I have my loyal supporters too—like you, my friend."

For a brief moment the king laid his hand on Haman's arm and Haman's heart leaped with joy. He longed to be able to join the riding party and for a brief moment entertained a wild picture of warding off an army of Xerxes' followers to save Ahasuerus from assassination. But Haman was not an Achaemenid and did not ride well enough to join the band of Persian aristocrats.

Ahasuerus looked up at the clear sky and sighed. "Unfortunately, my ride today will be cut short. I have promised Hegai I will meet with another of the girls who wish to be queen. According to Hegai, the number is decreasing, for which I thank the gods. At least I have one decent possibility in case no one else is more acceptable." He frowned. "I did not realize how much of my time this search would take."

Haman, too, looked at the sky, gauging the hour. Xerxes was soon going to be unpardonably late. "Then why don't you take the one you approved and get it over with, my lord?"

"Perhaps that is what I will do. These interviews are not only time consuming, they are extremely tedious."

Haman noticed the men around them turning toward the large door that opened into the Court of the Royal Kin. Xerxes had finally arrived. He strode out onto the platform, a tall, assured young man with a handsome, dark, disdainful face, very different from his elder brother.

"Forgive me for being late, my lord," Xerxes said as he came to a halt in front of the king.

Ahasuerus made no move to extend the hand of kinship to him. There was a moment of uneasy silence, and Haman saw disbelief replace arrogance on Xerxes' face as he realized that his brother was actually going to make him perform the prostration. The silence stretched on, then Xerxes scowled and reluctantly began to go down on one knee. Just before he had committed himself fully to the prostration, Ahasuerus stretched out his hand and brought him forward instead for the kiss of kinship upon the cheek.

"Forgive me for being late," Xerxes repeated. "I'm afraid I lost count of the time."

Haman's lip curled with disbelief. Xerxes had deliberately delayed his entry to annoy Ahasuerus as well as to make a statement of his own importance to the rest of the Royal Kin.

Ahasuerus' face was unreadable. "Now that you are here, I will have the horses brought around."

While they waited, Haman stood on one side of the king and Xerxes stood on the other. The hatred between Haman and Xerxes was open and hot, but today Haman was quiet, listening to the brothers talk about the only topic they seemed to have in common: horses.

"Are you riding Soleil today?" Xerxes asked.

"Of course," Ahasuerus replied. "He needs exercise."

"Hmm." Xerxes snorted through his high-bridged nose. Haman knew it was a sore point with Xerxes that no one in Susa had been able to ride the magnificent Nisean stallion until Ahasuerus had done so. And he had done it with seeming ease. The feat had brought him respect from the members of

the Royal Kin, but resentment as well. They didn't like it that
the outsider from Babylon could do what they could not.

Haman listened in silence as the brothers spoke. Ahasuerus'
plan was to try to win over Xerxes, and Haman thought that
such an attempt was a mistake. The king would be wiser to
banish Xerxes from court, along with his mentor, Mardonius,
who had spent years trying to make Xerxes his adoring dis-
ciple. Mardonius, who had been Darius' right hand and the
father of Vashti, was even more dangerous than Xerxes because
Mardonius had no scruples at all. Haman did not doubt that
if Mardonius could find a way to have Ahasuerus assassinated,
he would take it.

But Ahasuerus believed he could turn his enemies into his
friends. True, he had done this in Babylon, but Persia was different. Persians cared nothing for reason and justice—Persian
nobles cared only for power.

The horses had come into the courtyard and the two
brothers moved toward the stairs. A young lieutenant moved
to assist the king to mount, but Ahasuerus waved him off and
mounted his huge Nisean stallion with easy grace.

After the king was in the saddle, everyone else mounted
up. Soleil did not like the noise, leaping in the air and kicking
out behind with his iron-shod feet. Ahasuerus laughed, patted
the sleek shoulder, and the stallion quieted. Haman, watching,
felt his heart cramp with worry.

The problem with you, my lord, is that you do not know how to hate.

But I will watch out for you. That is why I am here: to see to your welfare. I will always protect you. Always.

When Haman finally returned to the palace, he found the king's Grand Vizier waiting in Haman's office. The fact that Haman, who bore the ceremonial title of Ahasuerus' Bowbearer, even had an office had infuriated the Persians at court to no end. Grand Vizier Smerdis, who should be the second most powerful man in the empire, must be furious at being forced to present himself to someone he considered a Babylonian underling.

Ahasuerus had tried to placate his father's men when he came to the throne by letting them keep their old titles. But because he did not trust them, he listened to the men who had come with him from Babylon. Smerdis knew that Haman had the king's ear, and it irked him unbearably to be forced to come to this outsider. Haman, in his turn, disliked and distrusted the Persian office holders as much as they disliked and distrusted him.

Haman allowed himself a small, triumphant smile as he said with elaborate courtesy, "How may I help you, Grand Vizier?" and seated himself behind his desk.

Smerdis flushed a dark red and snapped out his words. "I am here about the work at Persepolis. The building of the new palace cannot go forward without the king's approval and the best building season is now approaching."

Ahasuerus had discussed this subject thoroughly with Haman, so he had his answer prepared. "I am afraid, Grand Vizier, that the Great King is not interested in spending money on yet another palace. He has told me that the palaces at Susa and Ecbatana are sufficient for his needs. What interests the king is land improvement. He feels that the country needs more irrigation projects so we can open up more land for growing. This means we must construct more underwater channels. That is where he wishes his money to go, not to the building of yet another palace."

"Darius was completely committed to building the palace at Persepolis," Smerdis said, his jaw clenched with anger. "It will be the greatest achievement of Persian architecture in the world. The palace here in Susa is built in the Babylonian style, and the palace in Ecbatana is Median. Persepolis will be purely Persian—a great monument for future generations to marvel over."

Haman smoothed a piece of paper on the desk in front of him. "May I point out to you, Grand Vizier, that Darius is no longer the king?"

Silence from Smerdis.

Haman said, "The king undertook many successful irrigation projects in Babylon, which I was happy to assist him with. I have asked the Chief Engineer for a report on the areas in Persia that will most benefit from such projects. If you are interested, you may join me at that meeting, Grand Vizier. I believe the king will be present as well."

"Watch your tone when you speak to me, you despicable Babylonian." Smerdis' face was almost as red as his robe.

Haman's head snapped up and he narrowed his eyes. "I am not a Babylonian, I am a Palestinian."

"A Palestinian," Smerdis repeated in the tone of voice in which he might have said *a rat*. "And no doubt one of the places you think will benefit most from an irrigation project is that desert you call home?"

Haman was so angry he was trembling. He stood, signifying the meeting was over. "I believe we have said enough to each other, Grand Vizier. I will tell the king about your recommendations in regard to Persepolis."

Smerdis leaned toward him, almost spitting his words. "I will tell him myself, you conceited Palestinian." And he stalked out of the room.

It took Haman awhile before he could collect himself. All his life he had faced this arrogant dismissal of his nation and his person. Only Ahasuerus had seen Haman the man for who he was and had chosen him to be a confidant. He was a friend of the king. He must remember that and not allow himself to be tormented by these lesser beings.

Haman smoothed out the report that was on his desk and began to read.

CHAPTER EIGHT

With the coming of spring, the harem women spent more of their time in the garden. The walled-in expanse of pools, flowers, trees, birds, and greenery was one of the loveliest spots in all of Susa. Darius had had rare trees and flowering shrubs brought from all over Asia to create it, and it provided the harem inhabitants with their only chance to be outdoors.

After their conversation, Muran had given Esther a large apartment and assigned Hathach to be her personal guard and Luara to be her personal maid. The remaining girls resented this preferential treatment, but since Esther had never been a favorite, she scarcely noticed any change in their attitudes.

She was walking in the garden with Luara one morning when they saw Hathach hurrying along the paths toward them. She and Luara stopped and waited.

"I have just come from Muran, and I bear important news, Mistress. You are to see the king this afternoon!"

Esther's hand went to her heart. "That can't be so, Hathach. The king is to see Alenda today, not me. Muran must have mixed us up."

"No, Mistress, there is no mix up. Alenda was sick all night and is in no condition to see the king. Muran has decided to send you in her place."

"Me?" Esther stared at the young man whom she had grown to depend upon. "I am not the next girl in line, Hathach." The order in which the girls were to be presented was based upon how long they had been in the harem. Esther was further down the list.

"I know, Mistress, but Muran wants you to go. You are to come directly to the robing room to be dressed and made ready."

Esther didn't reply, instead stood still, trying to take in what this news might mean for her. *Today*, she thought. Today this whole wretched masquerade would come to an end. The months of special tutelage by Muran and Hegai had made her more certain than ever that she was completely unsuitable for the position of queen. A few days from now . . . by then she might even be sleeping at home.

"Good," she said emphatically. "Let us go."

Esther and Hathach walked together down the unusually silent harem corridors. She had spent much time with Hathach these last few months and, aside from Luara, he was the only friend she had.

Until Esther had come to live in this place, she had known next to nothing about the eunuchs Persians used to guard the chastity of their women. Whenever she had heard them spoken about, which was rarely, it seemed as if there was something degenerate about them. Even Mordecai, who was usually so charitable, had not been able to hide his contempt for these abnormal creatures.

But these last few months Esther had learned that boys were made eunuchs just as girls were made slaves and concubines: Their parents sold them or gave them away to win favors from Persian officials. Both girls and boys were thrust into harems, and the boys were castrated so they would never be sexual threats to any of the women.

Most of the palace eunuchs were flabby around the waist and their voices were higher pitched than a man's. But Hathach was different. He fought his fate. His speech was slow and careful, so that he would not be betrayed into the high notes that he so obviously hated and feared. His diet was abstemious, and Luara had told Esther that he exercised fanatically.

Esther looked now at the tall, golden-skinned young man walking beside her and her heart filled with pain for him. She was going to leave this place, but Hathach was trapped for life, trapped not only by the harem but also by the mutilation that had been done to his body.

Hathach took her to eat a light meal of fruit and bread and then he brought her to the robing room where Muran, Luara, and a collection of girls awaited her. Esther sighed as she saw the eager expression on the Mistress's face. This ordeal was going to take many hours.

It was half an hour before the scheduled appointment when Muran pronounced herself satisfied with Esther's appearance. She stood, surveying her work, then turned Esther so she could look in the mirror. "You are perfect," Muran declared.

Esther obediently looked at the picture reflected back to her in the polished bronze. It had taken Luara three hours to weave pearls into many of the individual strands of her shining hair, which fell in a radiant glory to her waist. Her eyes were outlined in kohl and her eyebrows formed two perfect arches to frame them. Her immaculate nails were delicately tinted and her orange-blossom robe hung from her golden belt in perfect folds.

"You don't look like the same girl who came to me, that is for certain," Muran said with satisfaction.

"That is so, Mistress," Esther said politely.

For what seemed the hundredth time, Muran went over the procedure that Esther was to follow during the presentation. "The king will speak to you in the privacy of his own courtyard. You will be left alone with him, but Hegai will be nearby to escort you back to the harem whenever the king chooses to end the interview. It will last for half an hour. Ahasuerus has given all the girls that courtesy."

"Yes, Mistress," Esther said.

"He has dispensed with much of the court ceremony for these interviews, but, of course, you must make the prostration."

"Yes, Mistress."

"Wine will be served. You must pour it for him."

Esther had spent more hours than she believed possible learning the Persian way of pouring wine. "Yes, Mistress. I know how to pour the wine."

"And remember to smile, Esther. Your smile is your greatest beauty."

Esther would be sure to look as solemn as possible.

It was only when Hegai arrived to escort her to the rose garden where she would meet the king that Esther felt the first stab of nerves.

What if he should choose me?

This was a thought Esther had studiously avoided, but the

uncertainty was suddenly frightening. She had to be careful. She could not do anything that would disgust him or betray that she was anything but what she seemed: an Achaemenid girl from the lesser nobility who was hoping to be chosen as the Great King's wife. But she did not want to do anything that might make him like her either.

It will never happen. Never. He has seen scores of girls prettier than I. He will never choose me.

But her heart was thudding as she followed Hegai through the door that led from the harem into the palace and thence to a walled outdoor courtyard that opened off the royal apartments. There was a white marble fountain in the middle of the court, and rose vines grew all along the high brick walls. In a few weeks they would be in flower. Esther had a small rose bush in her own garden, and she prayed she would be home in time to see it bloom.

Hegai said, "The king rode out this morning and may be detained. We were told to await him here."

"I understand," Esther said.

Hegai chatted easily, obviously trying to distract her, but Esther did not hear a word he said. *I wonder if Uncle Mordecai knows I am meeting the king today*, she thought. *I hope they will tell him the results quickly so he can pick me up. How wonderful it will be to eat my own kind of food in my own house.*

She was entertaining herself with visions of what it would be like to be home again when the small door that separated the Rose Court from the royal apartments was pushed open and a page dressed in Median trousers and jacket entered. "The king is coming," the boy, who looked to be about eight years old, announced. "The Head Eunuch is to wait inside."

Hegai left and Esther stood as still as a stone beside the fountain. She felt dizzy and only then realized she had stopped breathing. She inhaled deeply a few times and felt steadier. Then the door into the Rose Court opened again and this time a man came in. He was bareheaded, with only a simple gold fillet confining the short fall of his hair, and he was dressed in a deep blue robe over a white tunic.

It was the king. Esther would have known that even if she had not been expecting him. There was something about the way he walked toward her, with the sun striking bronze sparks from his hair . . . anyone would have known he was the king, she thought.

He came to join her and stood for a moment, regarding her out of startlingly light eyes. "So," he said at last, "you are Esther."

I forgot the prostration! Esther thought in horror.

"My lord," she said a little breathlessly and began to sink down toward the ground.

He reached out and touched her arm to stop her. "It is not necessary," he said.

Esther was completely discomposed. She had been expecting a black-haired, hawk-nosed Achaemenid and instead to be confronted with *this!* She was so startled that she blurted out exactly what she was thinking.

"I have been practicing this prostration for months, my lord. The least you can do is let me perform it."

She froze as she heard her own words. She dropped her eyes and hoped her impertinence would not make him wonder about what kind of family she came from.

The king said with amusement, "By all means. I would not like to think of you wasting months of effort."

Without daring to look at him again, Esther sank down to the ground. *It must be done all in one movement*, Muran had told her time and time again. *It cannot be jerky. It must flow.* Esther touched her chin to the stone pavement and waited.

"You may rise," Ahasuerus said, and in one fluid motion, Esther regained her feet.

"Very nice," the king approved.

Esther looked up. His voice had been grave, but his eyes were smiling. "I think I flowed," she said.

"Is that what they tell you to do?" he asked. "Flow?"

"Yes, my lord. It is difficult. One must train the muscles."

Ahasuerus grinned. "I never thought of it quite that way."

That boyish smile utterly disarmed Esther, and instinctively she smiled back.

There was the faintest pause as he regarded her smiling face. "What else did they train you to do?" he asked.

"Well, I have learned how to serve you wine."

"Does that require muscles too?"

"No, my lord. That requires a steady hand."

He laughed.

They walked slowly about the court, the king asking questions, Esther answering. He was easy to talk to, and Esther quite forgot her resolution to be sober and off-putting, instead returning his comments with perfect naturalness.

"*Esther*," he said at one point. "That is a Babylonian name."

"Yes, my lord."

"I understand that your mother was Babylonian."

For the first time in their meeting, Esther felt a stab of fear. She did not want to lie to this man, so she said carefully, "My mother's family lived in Babylon before they moved to Susa."

He nodded. "But your father was Persian. A lieutenant in the cavalry, I heard."

This was safer ground. "Yes, my lord. He was killed in the raid the Greeks made upon Sardis."

"Ah." He stopped walking, and Esther halted beside him. He said, "You must be anxious to see Persia go to war with the Greeks to avenge him."

Esther replied quietly, "My mother lost her husband and I lost my father to a war, my lord. I am not anxious to have the same thing happen to other women. I think war should be the very last resort a country turns to."

"You sound as if you have thought about this." There was something in his voice that made Esther give him a quick, inquiring look. His face gave nothing away, however. He said only, "Perhaps we should go inside so that you may put your wine-serving skill to the test."

Ahasuerus did not take her to the main court of the royal apartments but into a lovely private room furnished with two divans, hanging lamps with shades of fretted gold, and a low wine table set with engraved gold goblets and plates.

A page brought in a wine pitcher and a golden bowl heaped with ripe fruit. He set them down upon the table and, after a nod from Ahasuerus, left.

"I am ready," Ahasuerus said to Esther.

"Are you laughing at me, my lord?" she asked reproachfully.

"I would not dream of doing such a thing."

Esther met his eyes and thought in sudden astonishment, *I cannot believe that I am talking this way to the Great King.*

"What are you thinking?" he asked softly.

"I am thinking how strange it is that I should feel so comfortable with you," she answered honestly.

"You thought I was an ogre?"

"I thought you were the Great King."

"I *am* the Great King," he said, his voice even softer than before.

Esther smiled at him. "I know. And now I am going to serve you your wine."

Esther said little as Hegai escorted her back to the harem. Her emotions were in such a turmoil she couldn't begin to sort them out.

She had liked him. She had liked the Great King of Persia. Ahasuerus. She had felt comfortable with him. Perhaps that wasn't so bad, but what she feared, now that she was away from his compelling presence, was that he had liked her too. That hadn't been her plan. How could she have been so foolish?

Hegai brought Esther directly to Muran's room, where they were met by a Mistress wreathed in smiles. "So?" she asked Hegai. "She was with him for over an hour. None of the others have lasted more than the set time."

Hegai rubbed his hands. "He took her into his private salon, Mistress. I think he has chosen." He turned to look at Esther. "I think he has chosen Esther."

"No!" Esther denied what she feared. "That can't be true. I am not aristocratic enough to be made a queen."

"He has never shown such a sign of favor to any of the other girls," Muran said. "The time he spent with you—the private salon—these are signs of approval, Esther." Muran seized Esther's cold hands and squeezed them. "How lucky we were that Alenda was sick and I had the opportunity to fit you in. I have always thought that you would suit Ahasuerus. You would not suit Xerxes or most of the other members of the Royal Kin, but Ahasuerus is different. I thought you might suit him and now it seems that I was right."

Muran was radiant.

"Nothing has been said," Esther protested. "All of this may not be important at all. He will want to see all of the girls before he chooses."

"No." Muran was positive. "He will choose you. I know it in my bones."

Esther didn't know if she wanted to scream or to faint. All she knew was she had to get away from Muran and Hegai, and when she pleaded fatigue they finally let her go.

Luara was waiting to help her out of her magnificent robes, and after Esther was more comfortable, she dismissed the girl and sat on a cushion, her back against the wall.

In her heart, Esther was terrified that Muran and Hegai were right. The king had shown more interest in her than in any of the other girls. What would she do if he chose her? What would it mean, having to marry the Great King of Persia and spend the rest of her life imprisoned in this palace?

She had liked him. She had liked him and had felt comfortable talking to him, but she would never know him. He was a foreigner, a stranger, the Great King who could never be a husband to her the way she had envisioned having a husband. She thought of Abraham and tears came to her eyes. If she had married Abraham, her life would be set out for her. She would keep his house and bear his children. She would be his confidant and his friend. She would be happy. All of a sudden she longed for Abraham with all her heart.

Ahasuerus was not a man of her people. He was a man who worshipped a strange god and had a harem filled with concubines. She would never, ever understand a man like that. How could God wish her to marry him?

Her thoughts were interrupted by a knock at the door. She stood up and called permission to enter. It was Hegai, his fleshy face wearing a triumphant smile. "I have come to tell you, my lady, that the Great King has chosen you to be his queen. Congratulations."

It was the first time Hegai had ever called her *my lady*.

Esther went perfectly still. *It's over*, she thought. *My life as I have known it is over. I will never see my family or my friends again.*

Hegai was saying, "You must be married in Susa, but the king wants to go to Ecbatana before the hot weather sets in, so we have only a month to arrange the wedding. And there is so much to be done!"

Esther's mouth was so dry she didn't think she would be able to speak. She nodded to Hegai that she understood what he was saying. When she finally got her voice back, she broke into his running commentary to say the one thing that was of importance to her. "I wish to see Mordecai, the man who recommended me to you."

Hegai scowled. "He is a Jew, my lady. You cannot meet with him. We will contact your father's family. They may visit you."

"I want to see Mordecai," Esther repeated. "I want to thank him. If it wasn't for his good offices, I would never have gotten this chance."

"You may see a man who is unrelated to you only if I am present," Hegai said.

"I understand. You may be present, but I must see Mordecai."

Hegai looked indecisive.

"I am not asking you, Hegai, I am telling you," Esther said evenly.

He looked startled, then his features smoothed out. "Very well, my lady. I will arrange it."

After the Head Eunuch had left, Esther slowly returned to her seat on the pillow. How could she bear this? How could God expect her to bear this? How could she live the rest of her life isolated from everyone of her faith? How could she endure such loneliness?

I don't know if Uncle Mordecai was right or wrong when he thought God had a mission for me. I don't understand it. I don't understand anything. All I know is one thing—I want to go home. Father in Heaven, I want to go home!

And the tears began to spill down her face.

CHAPTER NINE

Within two hours of the king's decision, Esther was moved into a large apartment that was close to the palace but still in the harem. Muran informed her that she would not take possession of the queen's palace apartment until after the wedding had taken place.

It was to the elegant, silk-hung reception room of this apartment that Hegai brought Mordecai the day after her acceptance by the king. Esther awaited her uncle with her emotions in a turmoil of contradictions. The room had several divans, but she stood squarely in the middle of the beautiful

Persian rug—which made the rug in her old home look like a rag—as Mordecai was escorted in.

Hegai touched his arm to stop him at the door, and Mordecai's eyes met Esther's across the space between them. She thought he looked older than she remembered.

"Hegai," she said crisply, already having rehearsed this statement, "you may stand outside in the corridor and leave the door open. That should satisfy the requirements, I think."

Hegai started to protest, but Esther was determined to speak to her uncle in private. "If you don't like it, complain to the king," she said, her voice even crisper than before. "But it is what I wish you to do."

There was a brief silence, then Hegai bowed his head and retreated. Esther realized she had won.

"Come in, Mordecai," she said clearly so Hegai could hear. "I have called you here today to thank you for your good offices in bringing me to the attention of the king. Come, sit down and let me pour you some wine."

She indicated the divan farthest from the doorway.

Mordecai advanced into the room and sat down, all the time staring at his niece as if he were seeing a stranger. "You look so different," he said when he was seated.

"Yes, I imagine I do," Esther replied. It was a struggle to keep her voice even. Part of her wanted to throw herself into her uncle's arms and beg him to take her away, and part of her wanted to blame him for doing this to her.

Mordecai lowered his voice so Hegai could not hear. "How are you, my dear?"

"How do you expect me to be? I am to marry the Great King of Persia. Surely I should be dancing with joy." Even to herself, her voice sounded cold.

Mordecai glanced at the door, then lowered his voice even more. "Chicken," he said, "I am so sorry."

At the use of her nickname, the tears came like a flood. He held out his arms and she threw herself into them, sobbing as if she would never stop. When finally her weeping began to subside, Mordecai said, "When I heard the announcement, I could scarcely believe it. I did not even know you were to see the king. Then Filius came running to tell me that the king had kept you with him for over an hour. And today the announcement was made official."

"It's what you wanted, isn't it?" Esther said into his tear-soaked shoulder.

"Yes, it was. But, in my heart, I don't think I believed it would really happen. Now that it has, I am stunned."

A flicker of hope flared in Esther's heart. "Is it too late to get out of it?"

He put her away from him and gazed into her face. "Listen to me, my dear. This is God's doing. There is no other reason for the king to have picked you out of all the well-connected Persian girls he has seen. It is the will of God. You must accept that, Esther, and do what you can to protect the Jews and our country from the dangers of that Edomite, Haman."

Esther's whole body stiffened. He was not going to help her. He wanted her to go through with it, to marry this man who did not care for her, would never care for her, would only want her body so she could bear him legitimate heirs. He had a whole harem full of concubines to occupy him when he got bored with her. This very apartment was situated next to the apartments of his two favorite concubines, concubines who had already borne him children. She did not doubt that he would continue to see these women after the marriage. The Persians saw nothing wrong in such things, but Esther did not know how she could bear it.

She did not say these things to her uncle, however. Nothing would change Mordecai's belief that she had been chosen to be the savior of the Jews. Like a bird in a cage at one of the markets she used to frequent, she was well and truly caught.

After Mordecai left, she went into her bedroom, laid down on the soft bed—no sleeping mats in this apartment—and fell into an exhausted sleep.

Esther had thought her time in the harem was stressful, but nothing equaled the pressure of the month leading up to her wedding. Hegai and Muran talked to her about royal protocol until her head was spinning and she was convinced she was certain to commit an error that Ahasuerus would find mortally offensive. Then Hegai told her that her father's father, the grandfather she had never seen, the grandfather who had rejected her and her mother after her father's death, was going to be the one to escort her to her bridegroom on her wedding day.

She couldn't protest. She knew it would be impossible for Mordecai to assume that task, that the only reason she had been accepted as a candidate was because of her father's family. So it was with a divided heart that she awaited the arrival of Arses, her grandfather, who was coming to see her in the very same room where she'd had her only meeting with her uncle.

As with Mordecai, it was Hegai who escorted the visitor to her apartment. He knocked discreetly and, when she called for him to come, he opened the door and intoned, "My Lady Esther, may I present to you Arses, Retired Captain of the Immortals."

A tall, gray-haired man walked into the room and halted when he was still a few feet away from her. "Granddaughter," he said in a harsh voice, "how do you wish me to greet you?"

Esther looked into the splendid, carved features of her father's father. She hesitated. Part of her wanted to punish him by making him bow to her, but her better self prevailed. "You may give me the kiss of kinship," she replied.

The tall, old man, with his proud, Persian face, came

forward to kiss her on the cheek. He stepped back and they regarded each other in silence.

"You were a pretty child," he said at last, "but you have grown into a beautiful woman."

Esther stiffened with shock at his words. "You have seen me before?"

His dark eyes were steady on her face. "I saw you when you were two years old. It was I who brought you and your mother from Sardis back to Susa after the Greek raid that killed my son."

Esther was stunned. "I did not know that."

The old man's imperious black brows, so like Esther's own, twitched, and he nodded imperceptibly toward the Head Eunuch, who was standing by the door.

Esther said immediately, "Thank you, Hegai. I would like to be alone with my grandfather."

The relationship was close enough for Hegai to leave, and grandfather and granddaughter stood in silence until the door had closed behind him.

"I am not surprised that you knew nothing of me," Arses said. "Mordecai made it perfectly clear that he did not want you to have any contact with your father's family. We have respected his wishes, but I am happy to be meeting you now."

A second shock, even more unsettling than the first, went through Esther. "I always thought it was you who did not want to have anything to do with me."

Arses shook his head. "After my son's death, I asked your mother to make her home with me, but she wanted to return to her own people and chose instead to live with her brother."

Esther's shock was turning into indignation. "Uncle Mordecai never told me this! He told me that it was you who did not want to see me."

"That was not the case," Arses said.

Esther was furious. All these years she could have known her father's family, and Mordecai had not even given her the choice. "He lied to me," she said. "He had no right to do that."

Arses gave her a long silent look, then said, "I do not like Mordecai, but I will not say that he was wrong in this, Granddaughter. Once your mother made her choice, it was best that you not grow up with a divided allegiance. You could be either Persian or Jew—you could not be both."

Esther's hands closed together in a tight grip and she said in an unsteady voice, "But I must be both now, Grandfather."

"You cannot be both," Arses repeated. He gave a short, harsh laugh. "Mordecai came to see me the day after you were accepted into the harem, to ask me to vouch for your birth. I confess, at first I did not believe that he had brought you here. He was so outraged when his sister married a Persian! I could not imagine him allowing you to wed any man who was not a Jew—not even the Great King himself." The deep-set dark eyes glinted with amused satisfaction. "He is the one who put you into this position, Esther, and now he must live with it.

Once you marry the Great King, you will no longer be a Jew. You will be a Persian."

He doesn't understand, Esther thought. *He doesn't understand that you cannot just stop being a Jew. It's impossible.* "Did Uncle Mordecai tell you why he wanted me to do this?"

Arses shrugged. "He told me some nonsense about a Jewish massacre and being afraid the Temple in Jerusalem would be destroyed again. It sounded absurd to me. Ahasuerus is a just man, an honorable king. He would never allow such a thing. And how Mordecai could think that *you* would be able to prevent it!" He shook his head. "I always thought he was a fanatic."

"He is not a fanatic!" Esther instinctively rushed to her uncle's defense. "He is simply a Jew who fears for the safety of his people and wants to protect them."

"By using a *woman*?"

Arses' contempt was scalding and, even though Esther had thought the same thing, her temper flared at the criticism of her uncle. She compressed her lips to keep from making an angry reply. *He is an old man and a Persian*, she told herself. *There is nothing to be gained by trying to change the way he thinks.*

So she looked at the low wine table set in front of the divan and asked in a determinedly pleasant voice, "Would you care for some wine, Grandfather?"

Arses smiled and accepted.

Esther served him wine and asked him questions. She learned that Arses had been a Captain of the Immortals, the famous ten-thousand-man cadre of Persian infantry, so called because their number never varied. "The men of our family fought with Cyrus in his campaigns against the Medes and the Babylonians," he told her with pride. "We were always infantrymen until your father came along. He was horse-mad from the time he could first sit on a pony. When he was a boy he used to gallop up and down the mountains until I was certain he would kill himself. It had to be the cavalry for him; he would hear of nothing else."

A shadow of sadness passed over the splendid old face at this memory of the son who had died too young. Esther felt tears sting behind her eyes and blinked to chase them away. She felt again the painful loss of never knowing her father.

Arses drained his second cup of wine. "Ahasuerus is a great horseman himself. When he was only a boy, just admitted to the cavalry, he won most of the great races at the Ecbatana racecourse. They had to stop him from entering after a while, because no one would bet against him."

Esther murmured, "I did not know that."

Arses shrugged, as if to say that nobody expected a woman to know such a thing.

"Let me give you some advice, Granddaughter," he said, putting down his wineglass and turning to her.

Esther sighed. "Why should you be different from anyone else?"

Arses ignored the comment and narrowed his eyes.

"Ahasuerus chose you for more than your beauty, my girl. He wants a wife from a family whose loyalty he can trust. He does not know that your mother was a Jew. He knows only that you are the daughter of a Persian house that has always been loyal to its king." His deep-set eyes commanded her. "It is your Persian blood that has gotten you where you are, Granddaughter. It would be well if you remembered that."

Esther lowered her lashes, shielding her eyes from that imperious stare. "I will try to, Grandfather," she said.

The old man nodded emphatically. "Your son will be the next Great King. That is what is important now."

Esther felt a shiver run all through her, but she kept her face serene and nodded that she understood.

Esther did not see Ahasuerus during the month that was given over to wedding preparations. Hegai told her that the king had left for Babylon to deal with some problem that had arisen there, and all they knew was that he would return before the day of the wedding.

Her bridegroom's absence had not made the wait easier for Esther. She had met him once, for an hour, and now she was going to marry him. She had no idea what it meant to be married to a king. If she had been marrying one of her own people, if she had been marrying Abraham, she would have understood what her position was, what her relationship to her husband would be, what duties she would be expected to perform. She would know what to occupy herself with during the day. What did a queen do?

She had no answer for that question, and when she was told on the day before the wedding that the king had returned to Susa and wished to have dinner with her, she thought she would faint she was so filled with panic.

She asked Hathach to escort her. He and Luara were the only two people in the enormous palace with whom she felt comfortable, so, even though it annoyed Hegai, she insisted that she wanted Hathach. He took her through the harem door into the king's apartments, down the bedroom corridor, and into a small dining room that opened off the King's Court.

Inside the room there was a table, exquisitely laid with cups and ewers and plates of purest gold. Two beautifully carved chairs were set on opposite sides of the table. The small page standing beside the table came forward and said to Hathach, "The Lady Esther is to be seated. The Great King will join her shortly."

Hathach pulled out one of the chairs for Esther and when she was seated, he said softly, "I will await you in the court." Both child and eunuch exited through the billowing curtains, leaving Esther to await her future husband.

She sat alone in the room, stiffly upright, her spine not touching the back of her chair. In an attempt to quell the terror she felt rising inside her like an incoming tide, she forced herself to count the number of green bricks in the wall mosaic directly opposite her. On the count of two hundred and three, the curtains parted and Ahasuerus walked in.

Esther began to rise, hoping her legs would not collapse under her. The king gestured for her to remain in her seat and came to drop a light kiss upon her brow. His lips were cool against her skin and he smelled faintly of spice. "I must apologize for my prolonged absence," he said in his soft, slightly drawling voice. "I did not mean to vanish for so long a time, but it could not be helped."

He really is this beautiful, Esther thought as she gazed up into his face. *I was beginning to think that I had imagined it.*

"It has been a difficult month," she replied, speaking the truth because she didn't know what else to say.

He took the seat across the table from her and said with facile sympathy, "I am sorry to hear that. What has been the problem?"

"Well . . . there is so much protocol to learn, my lord." She looked down at her plate, then back up again and confessed, "I am convinced I am bound to do something so dreadful that you will order my head chopped off."

His gray-green eyes glinted with amusement. "What could possibly merit such dire retribution?"

"I might step on your purple carpet," she said.

The curtains parted and several pages came in laden down

with platters of food. Persian meals were always served all at once rather than in separate courses, so the table was soon covered with everything from meats and vegetables to fruits and sweets.

As the pages were unloading their trays, Ahasuerus said, "You have my permission to walk upon my carpet, Esther. And after we are married, no one will dare to question you about the propriety of what you do. You will be the queen."

Far from reassuring her, his words only served to intensify her terror. Fighting back tears, Esther stared hard at a steaming dish of chicken and did not reply. Ahasuerus said to the pages, "You may leave. We will serve ourselves."

After the pages had gone, he sat for a moment in silence and Esther could feel him looking at her. Then he said quietly, "What is wrong?"

Esther drew a shaky breath but still did not look up from the chicken dish. "I am afraid," she said, and rubbed a nervous finger along the edge of her empty golden plate.

"Of stepping on my purple carpet?"

She shook her head and answered with all the desolation in her heart, "Of everything."

He leaned back in his chair, his hands resting lightly upon the carved arms. After a time, when he still did not speak, Esther dared to glance up. Their eyes met and held, and for some reason she did not understand, her heart began to hurry its beat.

"There is nothing to fear, Esther," he said. There was no amusement in his eyes now; they were perfectly grave. "I will take care of you. Trust me."

She looked back at him, her fingers plucking nervously at a napkin. He reached across the table and put his slim, strong, horseman's hand over her restless fingers.

"Will you do that?" he asked.

She took a deep breath. "I will try."

CHAPTER TEN

A Persian royal marriage was a state occasion in which the bride played a very small part. The wedding day began with the king riding in his gold-plated chariot through the streets of Susa, followed by an impressive cadre of Magi, the name given to Persian priests. The Royal Bodyguard marched in full regalia, and thousands turned out to cheer and to strew flowers under the wheels of the king's chariot.

The marriage feast itself took place in the Apanada, the huge open-air platform off the rear of the palace. For the king's wedding it had been transformed into a huge pavilion:

Silken curtains hung from golden rods between Darius' great cedar columns, and the floor was covered with carpets of purple, scarlet, and gold. A hundred silver-footed divans had been installed for the guests to take their ease upon.

In the center of the pavilion was the bridal tent itself, to which only the King's Magi, the Head Eunuch, and the immediate families of the bridal couple had been invited. Esther had insisted that Mordecai be included in this guest list, and eventually Hegai had agreed and sent him an invitation.

While the king was processing through Susa, Esther was in the Queen's Apartment being dressed by Muran and an assortment of maids. When she was finally ready, they had to wait until she was summoned by one of the king's pages. As the time for her entrance drew near, Esther felt a kind of numbness settle over her. Her emotions had been so overwrought for such a long time that she simply couldn't feel anything anymore.

Waiting in the room with her were Muran, Luara, her grandfather, and Hathach. Her grandfather spent the time amusing himself by throwing a set of decorated cubes on one of the wine tables. Hathach stood in a corner, looking stoic. Luara kept throwing her anxious looks, and Muran periodically fussed with a pleat on her already perfect white tunic.

At last a knock came upon the door and Hathach opened it to admit a page, who announced: "The king and his party have reached the bridal tent and are finishing drinking the healths. The Lady Esther is to make her entrance."

"I would like a little water." They were Esther's first words in a long time.

Muran filled a silver cup a quarter-full with water from an ewer. "Don't drink too much," she warned. "You can't leave to go to the lavatory."

Esther wet her mouth, took two swallows, and handed the cup back.

"The escort is here in the hallway, my lord Arses," the page said.

"Fix her veil," Arses said to Muran, who settled a golden coronet draped with gossamer silk on the crown of Esther's head. Her sight blurred and she narrowed her eyes, trying to see through the filmy material. Then her grandfather took her hand, placed it firmly upon his arm, and walked her to the door.

The trip to the Apanada seemed short to Esther; before she knew it, she was following the two rows of little boys into the silk-hung pavilion that had been created for the wedding day. The stares of the hundreds of male guests reclining on the divans hit her like a blow, and she clutched her grandfather's arm.

"Steady, Granddaughter," Arses whispered. "Almost there."

Next the pages formed up to make an aisle on either side of the scarlet runner that led to the open flap of the bridal tent. At a stately pace, Arses walked Esther between the solemn-faced little boys. The gathered guests were silent as they watched her progress; the only sound was the soft rustle of the blowing silk draperies.

How can this be happening to me? Esther felt her heart fluttering in her throat, and when they entered the bridal tent and were greeted by a musical salute from the king's flute players, she actually jumped.

Arses made a soothing sound, the sort of sound he probably used to quiet a nervous horse.

From behind her veil Esther searched the tent, seeking only one person. She found him finally, sitting beside Hegai. His grave, intelligent eyes were watching her, and he must have felt her eyes because he suddenly gave a reassuring smile.

Uncle Mordecai! Esther felt a rush of relief. Somehow it made it easier that he was here.

They were now approaching the focal point of the tent, the king's golden chair. She saw that Ahasuerus had risen and was coming to meet her. Esther felt her grandfather's hand on her head. He pulled her veil off and the men in the tent, all members of the Royal Kin, saw her face for the first time.

Esther looked at Ahasuerus. He was wearing his golden crown, which made him look taller and more forbidding. He bent his head and kissed her lightly on the mouth. Esther had not expected that, and she almost jumped again. Then the king allowed Arses to give him the greeting of kinship, a kiss upon the cheek. Finally he took her hand into his and led her to the smaller chair that had been placed beside his. They did not sit, however, but stood in front of the chairs facing the door. Esther clutched the hand holding hers, needing support, and Ahasuerus tightened his grip.

The flute players fell silent.

A tall, thin man wearing the distinctively patterned robe of the Magi approached the bridal couple. On a plain silver tray he bore a single loaf of bread. He knelt and Xerxes formally offered Ahasuerus his sword. With one swift slash of the razor edge, the king cut the bridal loaf. Xerxes received the sword back and Ahasuerus turned to Esther with a piece of the bread in his hands.

"I, Ahasuerus, pledge to you, Esther, the power of my sword and the strength of my body, to protect and provide for you and your children. From this moment on, I will be your husband and you will be my wife."

He extended the bread to Esther, who took it into her hands, which were only shaking a little. She raised it to her mouth and bit off a tiny piece. After she had chewed and swallowed, she made the reply she had memorized: "I, Esther, pledge to you, Ahasuerus, the faithfulness of my body and the honor of your name. From this moment on, you will be my husband and I will be your wife." Her voice was low, but clear enough to be heard around the tent.

The Royal Singers began to chant the wedding song. The guests applauded. The additional guests in the outer pavilion were informed that the vows had been completed and they applauded as well. Servants came in with platters of food and jugs of wine. The feasting began.

Esther could not swallow a morsel. She drank a cup of wine because her grandfather had told her it would give her courage, but all it did was make her feel dizzy and a little sick. It was hot and stuffy in the tent, and the noise of the music and the talking was giving her a headache. She was thoroughly miserable, but when Ahasuerus leaned over and said in her ear, "It is time for us to retire," she didn't want to leave.

She put her hand into the hand the king was holding out to her and felt his rings press into her fingers. This time she kept her return grip loose. She rose with him and glanced once more toward her uncle, whose face was looking grim.

Arses came forward and replaced the veil upon Esther's head. The Royal Singers lifted their voices and, led by twelve pages, Esther walked with Ahasuerus out of the bridal tent, along the scarlet runner, down the steps, and into the palace. The king said something to the pages and the little boys all prostrated themselves, then all but two of them scattered.

"Your women are waiting for you in the Queen's Apartment," Ahasuerus said to Esther.

"Yes, my lord," she replied, and together they walked through the almost deserted King's Court, up the shallow stairs, and into the corridor of the Royal Apartments. Muran was standing in the open doorway of Esther's rooms and she prostrated herself when she saw the king.

"You have an hour to make the queen ready," he said to her when she regained her feet.

"Yes, my lord," the Mistress replied. Esther remained standing before the door of her room as Ahasuerus turned to the door on the opposite side of the corridor. One of the pages opened it for him. The king went in and the door closed behind him. Still Esther did not move. She felt physically weighed down by the burden of this moment. *It's too much*, she thought. *It's too much, Uncle Mordecai. You should never have done this to me.*

"Come in!" Muran said urgently.

Very slowly, Esther obeyed. Muran led her through the reception room and into the bedroom, which Esther had not seen before. The room was huge and airy. The bed was low and wide, with four golden posts and a canopy of gold-plated lattice work with jewels scattered through it. Esther stared at the bed, her heart beating heavily in her chest.

"I hope you're not going to be silly about this, Esther," Muran said sternly. "I have explained to you what is going to happen and there is nothing to fear. The king is a man of great experience. He will know how to do it right. He will be gentle. Now come along into the bath so we can get you ready."

The queen's bath was another splendid room, divided into two halves. One half was decorated with a rug and a low divan piled with cushions, while the other half held a marble bath raised on a marble step. At each end of the tub was a seat with a high back and a single armrest. Luara held Esther's hair out of the way while Muran bathed her. The scent of jasmine filled Esther's nostrils, but this time the luxury of warm water did not relax her. She stood like a statue while they dressed her in a soft, sleeveless night robe and led her back to the huge bedroom. The bed was also enormous; enough for a whole family to sleep in, Esther thought with repressed hysteria. It was draped in golden silk and its canopy was studded with jewels.

Muran folded back the soft linen sheets and Esther got in, sitting up with her back against the cushions. Muran straightened the sheets while Luara arranged her hair so that it fell symmetrically over her shoulders.

Esther turned to look at the large window. The Queen's Apartment had windows in every room, and tonight the shutters were open to the warm evening. Accustomed as she had grown to the windowless harem, the window gave an illusion of freedom. The breeze felt lovely. If only she could just slip through that window and disappear.

Muran said to Luara, "The king will be coming shortly. We had better leave."

Luara came over to smooth the sheets one last time and say softly, "It will be all right, my lady."

Esther nodded and the women left. She had never felt so alone in her life.

Her modesty had been outraged many times in the harem, but what was to happen next would be the greatest outrage of all. Esther closed her eyes. *Dear Father in Heaven. Help me. If it is truly Your will that I should be here with this man, help me. Because I do not think I can bear this alone.*

Then the door opened and Ahasuerus came in. Her gaze lifted slowly to look at him. He was wearing a white long-sleeved night robe and there were sandals upon his feet. His damp hair was feathering at the ends as it dried. She registered all of these things as she sat motionless upon the soft mattress in the golden bed.

He approached the bed confidently, but when he reached it, he stopped and looked at her, his eyebrows lifted as if in surprise. "Esther. You look as frightened as a soldier going into battle for the first time."

"I think I might be," she whispered.

He came to sit on the side of the bed, saying with a trace of humor, "It will not be so terrible, I promise you."

Her gaze held his. She bit her lip, trying to think of what she might say. He was waiting for a reply. "You see . . . I don't know you," she got out.

He looked puzzled. "Women never know their husbands."

He was right. Certainly Persian women did not know their husbands. She thought fleetingly of Abraham, and of how much safer she would feel if it was he who was with her tonight.

She forced a smile. "I am sorry, my lord. Muran would say I was being silly."

"You are being honest. You must always be honest with me, Esther. And there is nothing for you to fear, I promise. Did I not tell you I would take care of you?" He reached out and picked up a lock of her hair, running it through his fingers. "You are very beautiful," he said deeply.

Esther said the first thing that came into her head. "So are you."

He grinned at her, a youthful boyish look that for some reason made her feel better. Then he leaned forward and kissed her mouth.

It was not like the brief kiss he had given her in the bridal tent. This was a long kiss, a kiss that began tenderly but one he soon deepened and made slightly more demanding. She was passive at first, hesitant to respond, but then, as he continued the kiss, asking patiently, she opened her lips. After a while, her hands came up to hold his shoulders. Carefully he laid her back on the bed, continuing to kiss her as his hands began to move, slowly and knowledgably, over her body. Esther closed her eyes.

CHAPTER ELEVEN

The packing for the court's move to the summer palace of Ecbatana began the day after the wedding. Esther watched in bemused amazement as all of the chamberlains rushed about from dawn to sunset, trying to make certain that nothing would be left behind. The Wardens of the Linen, of the Silverware, of the Furnishings, and of the Wardrobe flitted between the different palace courts like birds on the wing, appropriating items as they went.

The progress of the move could be charted by the slow filling of the oxcarts that were lined up in the stable yard.

When the carts were finally filled, the oxen would be hitched, the men would mount their horses, and the King's Household would begin its annual trip to the mountains.

Esther was to travel in her own covered cart accompanied by Hathach and Luara. Three other carts were devoted to her other maids, her furniture, her clothing, and her traveling bath. The king, who was riding, had four carts devoted to his needs. Then there were the carts for his harem women and their servants and eunuchs. These were much fewer than they had been in Darius' day. To Muran's disgust, the king had chosen to leave most of the harem in Susa, taking only his two favorites and their children.

The courtyard was a chaos of men, horses, and oxen on the morning the journey began. First on the road were the thousand men of the Royal Bodyguard and after them came five thousand members of the Royal Kin. Next came the Magi, carrying the sacred fire of the Persian god Ahuramazda in a specially made golden case. Last in the line of horsemen came the king, accompanied by the lords of the court. After the horses came the carts carrying the families and harems of the men who were riding. Then there were the supply carts, needed because it was impossible for such a large host to live off the land. They left the palace later than the king wanted and it was six o'clock before they stopped on the first day. They had made it to the foothills of the mountains.

"How long is it going to take to get the camp set up and the food cooked?" Luara wanted to know. "By the time we get to bed it will be time to get up again!"

Esther accepted Hathach's assistance from the cart and answered, "Tomorrow we will leave earlier so that we cover the king's goal of twenty miles by four o'clock." She had this information because Ahasuerus had told her on one of his regular nightly visits to her room.

"Just so, my lady," Hathach agreed. "If the king had let them stop earlier, we might be on the road forever instead of ten days."

"I for one cannot wait to get there," Luara declared, stretching her back. "I want to smell some real mountain air."

Esther looked at her maid, whose cheeks were flushed and eyes shining. Since her marriage she had managed to have Luara's status changed from harem concubine to Queen's Waiting Woman, and the girl's intelligence and tart tongue were a great comfort to her.

"Do you love the mountains so much, Luara?" she asked.

Luara's blue eyes blazed. "I was born in the mountains, my lady. Once they are in your blood, you cannot get them out."

Hathach, who had been born in the mountains as well, agreed. Then he said, "I will have them set up your tent right away, my lady."

Esther smiled. "Thank you, Hathach. I will be glad to refresh myself."

Darkness had fallen by the time the camp was set up. Esther was sitting down at the table in her fully furnished tent when a page appeared at the doorway and spoke to Hathach. The eunuch nodded, then crossed to Esther. "The king has invited you to take supper in his tent, my lady," he said.

Esther's heart leaped. She put down the piece of bread she had been about to eat and forced herself to say calmly, "Very well, Hathach. When does he expect me?"

"As soon as you are ready, my lady."

Esther looked at the untouched table and laughed. "I believe I am ready now. I am certainly hungry enough."

"Let me fix your hair, my lady," Luara said.

Esther made an impatient gesture. "You just fixed it an hour ago, Luara. I haven't mussed it. It is fine."

"Where is the queen's veil?" Hathach asked one of the other serving women.

Someone came running with it and Luara put it on over Esther's long, braided hair. "I won't be able to see in the dark with this covering my face," she complained.

Hathach said, "Hold on to my arm and I will lead you, my lady."

Esther took his proffered arm and together they walked out into the camp.

Already it was cooler than it had been in Susa. The tents for the families of the Lords of the Court were set up around Esther's, and she could hear children's voices coming from several of them. The world looked indistinct and shadowy through her veil and she held tightly to Hathach's arm.

It was not very far to the king's tent. Esther waited while Hathach spoke to the guard at the door. The guard stepped aside immediately, and she accompanied Hathach into the brightness within.

Through her veil she could see that the king was sitting at a carved wood dining table, which was completely set with a service of gold. The pungent aroma of spiced pork drifted from one of the food dishes. A man was standing by Ahasuerus' side, speaking to him in a low voice. The king was smiling, as though something humorous had been said. Two oil lamps provided the light, one hung from a roof support and the other was set on a low table nearby.

"You may remove your veil, Esther," Ahasuerus said. "I wish you to meet Haman, my Bowbearer."

Esther froze at the name and her heart began to hammer. This was the man whom Mordecai feared so much that he had wanted to place her in the palace to counteract his influence. She lifted her hands slowly and pulled off her veil. "My lord Haman," she said in a careful voice.

"My lady." The Edomite bowed low.

He had figured in Mordecai's talk as some kind of monster, so she was surprised by his relative youth and handsomeness. She watched as he turned back to Ahasuerus and said, "I will leave you now, my lord."

"Yes, seek out your own family and have your supper," Ahasuerus replied.

Esther was shocked when the Edomite did not prostrate himself, but instead bent and kissed the king on the cheek. Only members of the Royal Kin were allowed to do that. The king must hold Haman in extremely high regard to allow him this privilege.

After Haman left, Esther walked toward the table where the king still sat. "I have heard Haman's name before." She hoped she sounded merely curious. "He is a Babylonian?"

"He lived in Babylon but his family is from Palestine," Ahasuerus replied. "Sit down, Esther, and tell me how you survived the day's journey. I am sorry it was so long."

"It *was* a long day," she admitted, taking the chair that was being held for her by a page. "It is so hot and airless inside that cart."

Ahasuerus indicated a platter of seasoned pork and one of the pages hastened to serve it to him. "It will get better now that we are in the mountains. At night, in fact, you may even feel cold."

The page looked questioningly at her and she nodded that she, too, would have the pork. Over the last months she had become so accustomed to eating unclean food that she rarely thought about it anymore. "Cold in June? Surely that is impossible."

"Not at all," he replied. He finished chewing his pork,

swallowed, and looked at her from under half-lowered lids. "Don't worry, though. I will keep you warm."

Esther knew that look, that tone of voice. Her body reacted to him instantly, and the reaction frightened her. She had never dreamed she would feel this kind of attraction for Ahasuerus. Living in the strict world of her Jewish culture, she hadn't even known this kind of attraction existed.

Ahasuerus, of course, knew all about it. He knew exactly what to do to make her desire him. He had probably made love to hundreds of women. What they did together, which seemed so wondrous to Esther, was something he did with many other women. He had brought his two favorite concubines, Ilis and Mardene, with him on this trip to Ecbatana. He had children with them. She could not, must not, mistake his skill for something more than what it was. She must not make the mistake of falling in love with him.

She made no reply to his suggestive comment, but glanced with embarrassment at the little boys who stood behind the king's chair, waiting to serve them. Then she looked at Ahasuerus, whose face was perfectly serene. As Esther watched his slim, strong hand use his knife to spear a chunk of pork, she realized that he had spoken as if they were alone because, to his mind, they were alone. Ahasuerus had lived in his high station for so long that he truly did not notice the human presence of those who served him.

Esther, however, was all too conscious of the listening

boys, and she sought to introduce a less personal topic. "Will there be horse racing in Ecbatana? I understand there is a race track."

Ahasuerus smiled. "There's a splendid race track in Ecbatana. The best in all Persia, I would say. The footing is superb and it's wide enough for ten horses to go abreast."

Esther speared a piece of pork for herself. "Isn't it difficult for horses to run in the thin mountain air?"

"Not for our Niseans," he replied proudly. "Nisean horses are mountain-bred, Esther. The Royal Stud is located not far from Ecbatana. Mountain-bred horses have bigger hearts and lungs than horses that are bred in the plain."

Happy to have found a topic of conversation that so engaged him, Esther asked, "Was there a race track in Babylon, my lord?"

"No." He had finished the pork on his plate and now he pointed to a dish of stewed apricots. As the page put some on a new plate, Ahasuerus said, "The two things I missed most while I was in Babylon were the mountains and the horse racing."

She smiled at him. "Will you ride in some races yourself this summer?"

Most of the pleasure left his face. "I don't know."

Esther put down her knife. "But why not, my lord? Is it not an appropriate thing for the king to do?"

"It's not that." He shrugged with seeming unconcern. "Try

some of these apricots." He gestured to the page to serve some fruit to Esther.

But she was not willing to let the subject drop. "My grandfather told me you used to win all the races when you were a boy."

He stabbed at an apricot. "I rode in a few races last summer, but I had the distinct feeling that no one was trying to beat me." He gave her a rueful look. "It took all the fun out of it."

Esther regarded him thoughtfully. "Your opponents did not think it would be politic to beat the Great King?"

"Exactly." His tone was dry.

"Then you must convince them that you want a real race."

"I tried that." He pushed the plate of apricots away. "They all assured me that they were trying to win, but I didn't believe them. So I gave it up."

Silence fell. Ahasuerus took a long swallow of his wine. Esther ate an apricot and thought. "What if you offered a special prize to the winner?"

"I tried that." He made an impatient gesture. "Really, Esther, there is no need to concern yourself because I am not going to race my horses!"

For some reason, she *was* concerned. It didn't seem fair to her that he should have to give up his favorite sport. "What kind of prize did you offer? Gold?"

He leaned back in his chair and said, "Yes."

She shook her head. "A money prize wouldn't work. You

need to offer a prize that will show you honor the man who can best you."

He rested his hands on the arms of his chair. "Like what?"

"Well . . . what if you let the winner take a victory lap around the racetrack in your state chariot? Drawn by your own horses?"

Silence. It went on for so long that Esther was afraid her suggestion had offended him. She opened her mouth to apologize, but before she could get the words out he began to smile. "They will kill themselves to win such an honor," he said with satisfaction.

"So long as they don't kill you trying to do it," she retorted.

His teeth were very white in the lamplight. "Soleil and I will be too far out in front of them for them to do anything."

She loved it when he looked happy. "I must confess I don't quite understand, my lord. If you know you can win, why are you so upset when you do?"

He picked up his knife and gestured for another serving of apricots. "It's no fun winning unless you know the others are trying to beat you." He threw her a quick look. "Surely you can see that?"

She shook her head. "I think it must be a male characteristic, my lord. A woman's world isn't about winning and losing."

"What is it about, then?"

She thought for a moment, then answered, "Surviving, I suppose."

She picked up her knife and they ate for a while in silence. Finally he put his knife down and said, "I do not like to think that you see your life as simply a matter of survival. You are my wife. My queen. What is it you want that you cannot have?"

She answered quickly, before she could change her mind. "Freedom."

His eyebrows drew together. "I do not understand you."

She, too, put down her knife and regarded him gravely. "I was not brought up in a family that keeps its women in harems, my lord."

"Ah." He gestured for the page to give him some of the sweet. "The freedom of Babylonian women came as quite a surprise to me when first I went there."

Esther thought of all the elaborate precautions taken to secure the isolation of Persian women. "I can imagine that it did, my lord."

"Did you know that Babylonian women are allowed to maintain control of their own dowries?" he asked in amazement.

"Yes, my lord, I did know that."

His amazement increased. "They even have women scribes!"

Esther said, "I can read. I was taught when I was young."

He did not look impressed. It was not considered either necessary or desirable for a Persian noble to learn to read; that was what they had scribes for. So he said with a mixture of amusement and condescension, "Were you indeed?"

Esther, who was enormously proud of her reading skill, did

not appreciate either the amusement or the condescension. She gestured for the page to refill her cup with the clear water from the Choaspes River that had traveled in one of the ox carts from Susa. She sipped the water in silence.

"I did not mean to insult you," Ahasuerus said, still with that infuriating intonation in his voice.

"I am glad your offense sprang from ignorance and not intent," Esther said coldly.

Catastrophic silence. Esther stared at her cup. *I should apologize*, she thought. *He is the Great King. No one talks to him like that.*

But he had belittled her ability to read, something she could do and he could not. He might have some kind of magical power over her, but she could read and he could not, and the apology would not come.

"Clear the table," Ahasuerus said to the oldest page.

Husband and wife sat in silence while the little boys piled the platters of food onto trays. "Tell the guard at the door that I do not wish to be disturbed," Ahasuerus said.

"Yes, my lord." The pages prostrated themselves, lifted their trays, and fled.

During all this time Esther had sat staring at her hands and growing more and more afraid. As the last page left the room she dared to look up. "I am sorry."

His face was serious, not angry. He said, "I do not want you to feel like a prisoner who must simply survive."

The oil lamp that hung from the support at the top of the tent swung a little, as if the tension in the room had made it tremble. "Sometimes I forget who you are," she whispered, "and I say things I should not say."

"Esther." There was a note of devastating tenderness in his voice when he said her name. "The only thing you must remember when we are alone together is that I am your husband."

She looked at him uncertainly.

He held out his arms and said softly, "Come here."

Esther lay awake in the big bed, her body pressed into the soft mattress by the weight of his arm. She stared up at the slightly swaying lamp. Outside she could hear the deep voices of men as the guard at the tent door changed. Somewhere a baby was crying. She turned her head slightly and looked at Ahasuerus.

He was sleeping on his stomach, his face toward her, one arm flung over his head, the other one across her waist. His light brown hair was spilled across the pillow and his long lashes lay against his flawless cheekbone.

The tent still smelled faintly from the spiced pork.

Esther looked back up at the lamp. When she was growing up she had once heard an adult mention something called *the temptation of the flesh*. This must be what she had meant, the way his slightest touch vibrated throughout her entire body, making her want to become part of his very being.

But the attraction she felt wasn't merely physical. She enjoyed being with him. She liked him. She had liked him when first they met, and she liked him more every time they were together. He was always courteous and witty and interesting, but there was a sense of carefully harnessed power in the man. She reminded herself never to forget what had happened to Vashti.

Her mind went to the task Mordecai had given her. How could her uncle ever have thought that she could influence the king in any political matter? Here in this bed, with Ahasuerus' bare arm across her waist, it seemed mad to her that her uncle could have conceived such an idea. The business of the Persian court was not the business of women, and that was that.

Yet Mordecai believed that it was the will of God that had made her Persia's queen. In the deepest part of her own soul, Esther wondered if her uncle was indeed right. There was no other way she could find to account for the incredible events that had befallen her. She sent up the words that had become her most constant prayer: *Father in Heaven, now that I am here, what do You want me to do?*

So far she had received no answer.

CHAPTER TWELVE

Haman was a creature of the city and found little to admire in the stark landscape of the Zagros Mountains. As he rode beside the king on the seventh day of the journey, he watched Ahasuerus inhale the cold clear air as if it were an intoxicating beverage. Haman shook his head in bewilderment.

"Isn't this marvelous?" Ahasuerus turned to him with enthusiasm.

"I don't know if I agree, my lord. All we have seen for days are mountain goats scrambling around the bare rocks and sometimes an occasional shepherd."

"But that is what is so wonderful," the king replied. "These clean open spaces without the constant mass of people pressing in on you. And look at those flowers. How can you say that they're not beautiful." He gestured toward the rough ground on either side of the road where pink and purple and yellow wildflowers made a riotous display of color.

It seemed extraordinary to Haman that anyone who was accustomed to the exquisite beauty of the palace in Susa could be excited by these small hillside flowers.

He was starting to reply to the king when a horse pushed up between him and Ahasuerus, forcing him off the path. Annoyed, Haman looked to see who it was, and his annoyance turned to anger when he recognized the king's uncle, Mardonius. Mardonius hated Haman and Haman returned the sentiment. Under Darius, Mardonius had been a man of consequence and, though Ahasuerus had not taken away his title, it was Haman who was part of the king's inner circle, not his uncle, and Mardonius resented this bitterly.

As Haman tried to find room for his horse on the path, Ahasuerus asked in a cool voice, "Is there something wrong with your eyesight, Uncle?"

Mardonius scowled. "Of course not. Why do you ask?" He paused, adding grudgingly, "My lord."

"You almost ran down my Bowbearer."

Mardonius' hot red-brown eyes briefly flicked over Haman's face. "Oh," he said. "The Palestinian."

Haman clenched his teeth.

"He is waiting for your apology," Ahasuerus said.

Mardonius stared at the king as if he could not be serious. Haman was peripherally conscious of the *plop, plop, plop* of their horses' footfalls and the creaking of harness and cartwheel from behind. He struggled to keep his own gaze level as he returned Mardonius' glare.

The silence went on for almost too long before Mardonius turned to Haman and said in a careless tone, "My apology. I didn't see you."

Haman, who did not trust himself to reply, nodded.

Xerxes had ridden up to take a place on the king's other side and now he said in a conciliatory manner, "We wished to speak to you, Brother. May we ride with you for a while?"

"Certainly." Ahasuerus' eyes met Haman's briefly and Haman let his horse drop back. The wind was blowing in his direction, however, and their conversation was perfectly audible to him.

Mardonius went right to the point. "Do you realize that they are laughing at us in the streets of Athens?"

The king appeared undisturbed by this news. "Your Athenian friends in Susa were forcibly exiled from their own country and now they are looking for a Persian army to give them back the power they have lost." Ahasuerus smoothed his horse's long mane. "I am not inclined to go to war just to please your friends, Uncle."

Xerxes said passionately, "How can you not understand that Persian honor demands that we wipe out the stain of Marathon? Remember how, after the defeat at Marathon, Darius had his page say to him every day before dinner, *Master, remember the Athenians.* It is hard for me, for us"—he gestured to include Mardonius—"to understand your reluctance to undertake this war!"

Haman stepped his horse a little closer, to make certain he could hear the king's reply.

"I have been considering the Greek situation for some time now, my brother," Ahasuerus said.

Mardonius' head whipped around like a wolf that has scented prey. "You have?"

Xerxes' face had also brightened. "You were successful in Egypt, my lord. Everyone agrees you handled that campaign brilliantly. Why should you not be successful against the Athenians as well?"

Mardonius scowled. Haman knew he couldn't stand hearing Ahasuerus called brilliant, even if such flattery might work to his own advantage. "You were lucky in Egypt," Mardonius snapped.

They are like flies buzzing around a purebred stallion, Haman thought. *Why does he tolerate them? Why does he not just swish his tail and flick them away? Or better still, stamp them out with his hooves?*

"Luck is always welcome, but it is not wise to trust to luck alone," Ahasuerus replied. "If you do that, you are liable to lose your ships, or your army, or both."

Mardonius went rigid. "Is that an attack on me?"

"You were the Grand Marshal in the last war against Athens and you lost three hundred ships off Athos."

Haman allowed himself a small smile. He was about to see Mardonius get what he deserved.

Mardonius protested, "We lost the ships in a storm! It was bad luck!"

"It is well known that along that coast the wind from the Hellespont can become a gale, and that the Athos peninsula takes the full force of the wind. You cannot have lacked advisers with local knowledge, Uncle, yet you let your fleet be caught off a rocky shore in shark-infested waters."

"No one told me about the blasted wind!" Mardonius shouted.

"Also, you did not take proper measures to safeguard your land camp," Ahasuerus continued remorselessly. "The local tribes attacked and killed many more of your men. That was not bad luck, Uncle. That was bad leadership."

"I don't have to stay here and listen to this slander," Mardonius said through his teeth, and his horse exploded forward, sending up a spray of gravel into the faces of Ahasuerus' and Xerxes' mounts.

A tense silence fell.

"He is very proud," Xerxes said, trying to excuse the inexcusable. "You wounded his pride, Brother. And Mardonius was not at Marathon. It truly was bad luck, not bad judgment, that lost us that battle."

"Where was the cavalry at Marathon, my brother?"

Haman could see Xerxes' body stiffen. "It had been sent round by sea to try to reach Athens, my lord," he said steadily.

"Leaving the infantry horseless on the beach at Marathon?"

It obviously killed Xerxes to say it. "Yes, my lord."

"A mistake."

Xerxes looked grim.

"And these are the same leaders who wish to lead a new advance against the Greeks."

"As you have said, my lord, we have learned from our mistakes."

"If I ask men to go to war for Persia, then it is my responsibility to ensure that they are properly led. I was not impressed with the leadership in the last war against Athens and I tell you now, Xerxes, that I will not entrust Persian troops to incompetent leaders."

"You cannot think to appoint Babylonians to lead Persians!" Xerxes cried.

"I had Persian leaders in my Egyptian campaign, and I was well satisfied with how they performed."

"But . . . none of *us* went to Egypt with you," Xerxes blurted.

"No," Ahasuerus agreed pleasantly. "You did not."

Haman watched Xerxes' incredulous face as he stared at his brother. "You cannot replace all of the leaders who fought against Athens!" Xerxes said. "You will have a revolt on your hands if you do that, Brother."

"You are probably right," the king agreed. "But I am responsible for my people, and I will not allow poor leadership to make any more widows and orphans than those we already have."

"So you will court a revolt?"

"So I will not go to war against Athens," said Ahasuerus.

"Did you mean what you said about not taking up the Greek war?" Haman asked. He had resumed his place by the king's side after Xerxes had ridden off after Mardonius.

They were crossing the last of the undulating ground of the plateau; ahead of them the road narrowed as it once more began its relentless climb into the mountains. They were still three days away from Ecbatana.

"Yes, I mean it," Ahasuerus replied. "For the present, at any rate. Too many of the incompetent leaders in the last war were my cousins. Xerxes is right when he says there would be a revolt if I tried to replace them all. Nor am I convinced that now is the time to spread the empire wider. The Egyptian revolt is quelled, but there is unrest in the north among the Scythians. I do not want to commit a large army to the Greeks only to find myself threatened on another front."

"There is unrest in Palestine also, my lord," Haman said, happy to have found a chance to broach this subject. "Just before we left Susa I received word from my family that a priest in Jerusalem is inciting the Jews to go to war against the Edomites."

A faint line appeared between Ahasuerus' brows. "Are the Egyptians involved in this?"

"No, my lord," Haman reluctantly acknowledged. He knew if he could prove Egyptian involvement, the king would act. Unfortunately, Haman had no such proof to offer.

He said, "This quarrel is about the land in south Judea that the Jews deserted. My people have pastured their flocks there for over a hundred years, and now this priest has decided that the Jews should take the land back. But it is not their land any longer, my lord. It is ours."

"Did this 'desertion' occur due to the Jews' displacement under Nebuchadnezzar?"

Haman knew that it did. When Nebuchadnezzar had forced half the Jewish population to march to Babylon, the stretch of south Judah he was talking about had been emptied.

"Partly," Haman agreed grudgingly.

"Who is this priest?"

"His name is Obadiah."

"I will make inquiries of the satrap," Ahasuerus said. "I do not want a war in Palestine. Palestine is the gateway to Egypt."

"It is not the Edomites who want war, my lord," Haman said quickly.

"I understand, Haman. I will make inquiries."

And with that Haman was forced to be content.

Chapter Thirteen

Ecbatana at last. After days of traveling through increasingly precipitous mountain passes, where Esther giddily peered down sheer clefts of rock inhabited only by mountain goats, she had begun to think Ecbatana must be an illusion. Surely no one could build a city in the midst of such terrain! But for centuries Ecbatana had been the capital of Media and one of the chief stops on a main trade route from Mesopotamia to the east. Now the summer resort of Persian kings, it was situated upon a wide and fertile plain that lay six thousand feet above the level of the sea.

The sky was crystal clear on the afternoon the king's caravan finally arrived in the outskirts of Ecbatana. Esther and Luara sat in the front of their traveling cart and looked curiously at the streets of the town as they passed slowly by. The houses were built from wood and sun-dried brick, as they were in Susa, with open porticos supported by wooden columns. As they progressed, however, Esther noticed that the houses became much larger and more widely spread apart. They were set, in fact, in what appeared to be a vast park filled with various kinds of evergreen trees and brilliantly colored mountain flowers.

"These are the houses of the lords of the court," Hathach said into Esther's ear from his place behind her. "The palace is too small to accommodate more than the royal family and its attendants."

And indeed Esther could see that many of the horsemen in front were leaving the caravan and dispersing through the park, presumably to their own homes. "Where is the palace?" Esther asked, peering ahead.

"You will see it shortly," Hathach replied.

They continued along the graveled road until finally Esther thought she saw the outline of a tall building in the distance.

"Is that the palace ahead of us now, Hathach?"

"Yes."

"But where is the wall?"

"The Medes felt no need of a wall, my lady. The mountains are protection enough."

The cart drew closer and Luara cried out in delight, "But it's lovely!"

They cleared the last of the obscuring trees and Esther had her first full view of the palace. It was indeed much smaller than the palace at Susa, and its brick and wood exterior was painted all in white. Instead of windows, most of the rooms on the second floor had arched doorways, which opened onto white-railed wooden balconies.

Hathach said, "I was here only once, with Darius, but I have heard from those who were here last summer with King Ahasuerus that the court is much more relaxed at Ecbatana than it is at Susa."

Esther thought of the stifling protocols of Susa and said fervently, "That sounds wonderful."

Ahasuerus had always loved Ecbatana. Ever since he had first come here as a child he associated its clear, crisp climate and open-air balconies with freedom. His mother had usually accompanied Darius to Ecbatana, while Atossa, Xerxes' mother, had chosen to remain in Susa. Ecbatana had been the one place from all his childhood that had not been shadowed by Atossa's jealous and dominating personality. All of his memories of Ecbatana were happy ones.

As soon as he reached his apartment he dismissed his

attendants, pushed open the balcony doors, and went outside. Flinging back his head, he inhaled deeply. He could almost feel youth and vigor flowing into him with the fresh mountain air. In a few days, he thought, he would ride out to view the Royal Stud. He had bred Soleil to several of the best mares late last spring. The foals should be about a month old now, and he was eager to see them.

He looked up. The sky was a deep cobalt blue, a color one never saw in either Babylon or Susa. *A perfect day for racing,* he thought. These last few days of the long, slow journey had seemed interminable, and now that he was here he felt full of pent-up energy. He wanted to do something, but everyone was busy unpacking and settling in. He bounced a little on his toes, too full of energy to remain still.

The courtyard below was filled with servants unloading the carts that had carried the household goods. Voices shouted in Aramaic as chairs and tables were wrestled off the carts and piled on men's backs to be brought into the palace. The scent of male sweat drifted to the king's nostrils.

They all knew he was on the balcony, of course, but they were following protocol and not looking at him. He bounced on his toes once again. He felt like whistling.

Above the noise from the courtyard, he heard the sound of a door opening. Ahasuerus turned his head and saw that his wife had come out onto the balcony next to his. In the Ecbatana palace the king's room was on the same side of the building as the queen's room, separated only by his bath. As Ahasuerus watched, Esther reached her arms over her head, rose up on her toes, and stretched upward toward the clear blue sky.

She should not be out here without her veil, he thought. But no one was looking and he understood her delight in the fresh air. "Getting the stiffness out?" he said.

Her heels came back to earth and her head whipped around. "My lord! I did not see you there. You startled me."

He rested his hands upon the railing closest to her. "So, do you like Ecbatana, Esther?"

She moved to the railing directly opposite his. "Everything is wonderful. I have never seen such a sky!"

His lungs expanded as he drew in more of the crisp, clear air. He felt a little drunk, although he had only water with his midday meal.

Esther said, "It is so beautiful that it makes me dizzy."

He looked at the face that was some fifteen feet away from his. Seen in the merciless light of the afternoon sun, her skin looked even more warmly colored than usual, and the rosy tint of her cheeks had definitely spread to the bridge of her nose. He said, "Is that sunburn I see on your nose?"

She looked like a child caught with her hand in the honey pot. "I have been sitting in the front of the cart, my lord. It was too suffocating to stay inside all the time."

Persians did not find sunburn beautiful, and he was a

quintessential Persian. But on Esther, he found that the sunburn was charming. The adrenaline of finally being at Ecbatana was pumping through his blood. He gazed at his wife and his exuberance suddenly found a focus point.

"I'm coming to see you," he said.

He went down the corridor to his wife's room and pushed open the door. The only other people in the room were her eunuch and serving girl. Esther was standing on the balcony, looking at him through the open door. He said to the servants, "You may go."

The two turned, prostrated themselves, then backed slowly out of the room.

He joined his wife on the balcony, lifting a hand to trace his forefinger along her sunburned nose. But Esther was looking at the door that had closed behind her servants. Her eyes lifted to his and she said a little indignantly, "What are you doing, my lord? What on earth will Hathach and Luara think?"

He bent to say softly in her ear, "They will think that I am going to make love to my wife."

Her lips parted and she gazed at him, not speaking.

He put his hand on her hip and gave her a gentle push. "Inside," he said.

She went before him into the bedroom. He opened the balcony doors wider so that the room would be filled with the clean mountain air. When he turned again it was to find her standing by the bed, watching him. Her eyes were huge and black.

He crossed the room to stand before her. He put his hands on her shoulders. "Say my name," he commanded.

"Ahasuerus," she whispered.

He smiled.

When Luara was allowed back into Esther's room, she acted as if nothing unusual had happened. She quietly went about remaking the bed, and when she had finished she said to Esther, "Would you like me to do your hair for you, my lady?"

Esther flushed. Ahasuerus had insisted that she unbraid her hair and Esther had only had time to tie it back after she had dressed herself.

"Yes, that would be helpful," she replied in a low voice.

Luara picked up a comb and went to work. After a while she said, "You know, my lady, you and the king *are* married."

Esther turned and looked up into her maid's shrewd blue eyes. Her own face relaxed into a smile. "Muran would say I am being silly. It is just . . . everyone knew what we were doing."

"My lady. The king comes to your room almost every night. Do you think we believe he comes to talk to you?"

Actually, Esther thought, *we do talk*. After. She found the talking almost as nice as the other thing.

"It will be good for him to be here for the summer," she said. "He carries many burdens."

Luara agreed. "Yes, he does. You must be one of the few people around him who doesn't want something from him. You are good for him, my lady. And"—her lips twitched in a small smile—"I think he is good for you."

Esther thought again about that conversation with Luara later in the evening, as she lay in her solitary bed. There was a drinking party tonight to celebrate their arrival in Ecbatana, and she knew it would run very late and Ahasuerus would not be coming to her room.

Say my name, he had commanded her. She wondered how many people there were in this world who could call him by his name. Not too many, she suspected.

When she was with him, she was happy. The spell of his physical presence chased away all the worry and fear and doubt and uncertainty and guilt that besieged her at other times— that were besieging her now. What was she doing here? She knew that Haman was close to Ahasuerus, but she never saw or spoke to Haman. Ahasuerus never mentioned the situation in Palestine to her, and she didn't see how she could bring it up in any way that would seem remotely natural.

Be our voice to the king. That is what Mordecai and the Jewish elders had commanded her. According to her uncle, that was what God had commanded her.

It was unfortunate that no one had ever told her exactly how she was to accomplish this desirable goal.

CHAPTER FOURTEEN

The king had a fever.

"Anyone who gets soaking wet looking at horses, then doesn't have the sense to change his clothes before he rides in a race is asking to be sick," Esther told him.

Ahasuerus lay in bed propped up against two dark-blue silk cushions. Esther was standing beside him, looking exasperated and trying not to show how worried she was. The king's face was flushed with fever and his eyes were too bright. Haman, the other person in the room, had closed the doors to the balcony.

"Keep those balcony doors open," Ahasuerus ordered, his normal voice a little raspy from a sore throat. "I want to look at the sky."

"You have a fever, my lord," Haman protested. "Cold air is not good for you."

The fever flush in the king's cheeks seemed to deepen. "I said to open the doors."

"My lord." Haman's slurred Babylonian accent was gentle. "Please be sensible."

Ahasuerus scowled.

Esther understood how much fresh air meant to Ahasuerus and said to Haman, "Perhaps we could open one of the doors. If the king remains under the blankets he will be warm enough."

Haman shot her an annoyed look.

There came a knock upon the door.

Haman said, "That will be my wife's Egyptian physician, my lord." He came back to Ahasuerus, leaving the doors firmly shut behind him. "He has a remedy for fevers that never fails."

Ahasuerus was starting to get angry. "I don't want any foul-tasting medicines, Haman. I want you to open the doors and leave me alone."

Esther gazed down into the haggard, fretful face of her husband. Even ill, he was still beautiful. "I will open the doors, my lord, if you will see the doctor," Esther said gently.

Ahasuerus clenched his fist and pounded it once into the mattress. Esther thought that his helplessness was angering him more than the idea of seeing a doctor. She put her hand on his forehead and smoothed back his tumbled hair. "Your hand feels so cool," Ahasuerus said.

"And your head feels so hot," she returned. "Please, my lord, won't you see the doctor?"

There was the sound of voices at the door and both Haman and Esther waited. "Oh, all right," Ahasuerus grumbled.

Haman went to the door and came back with a small, dark man who was carefully carrying a goblet of chased silver. "If you will drink this, my lord King, you will feel very much better," the doctor said.

Ahasuerus started to push himself up in the bed. Haman went to help him and the king motioned him away. The doctor put the goblet into the king's reluctant hand.

Esther started as loud voices sounded in the hallway, then the door flew open and a man almost tumbled in. "Ahasuerus!" he shouted. "Don't drink that potion!"

It was Xerxes.

Esther's blood froze in her veins.

"Why not?" the king said. He sounded merely curious.

"Someone told me this doctor might have been bribed to poison you." Xerxes was breathing quickly, Esther saw, as if he had been running hard.

Ahasuerus' face went perfectly still. The little doctor was white with terror. "Who is supposed to have bribed him?" the king asked.

Xerxes pointed to Haman. "This treacherous Palestinian."

Esther reached out to grab the goblet from Ahasuerus' hands, but he was too quick for her. Horrified, she watched as he tilted the goblet back and drained it.

"I knew it would taste terrible," he said.

Esther's hand was still on the king's forearm, and he let her take the empty cup from him. She could hardly hold it, her hand was shaking so badly.

Xerxes was staring at his brother, his nostrils pinched tight beneath the haughty arch of his nose. "Are you mad? I told you the drink might be poisoned!"

Ahasuerus' eyes glittered fever bright as he said to Xerxes, "The most important judgments a man makes in his life are his judgments about whom he can trust. Think about your so-called friends, Xerxes. Are they followers of the Truth? Or of the Lie?" There was a tense pause while the two brothers stared at each other. "There was nothing wrong with the drink," Ahasuerus said. "Who told you it was poisoned?"

There was a white line around Xerxes' mouth. He looked furious. "It doesn't matter," he said, turned on his heel, and stalked out of the room.

Esther looked at the doctor. "Is it really all right?"

The doctor was still as white as bleached linen. "Yes, my lady," he croaked. "It is good medicine. It will help the king."

Ahasuerus' early temper seemed to have abated with the drink. He took Esther's shaking hand into a reassuring grip and said humorously to Haman, "The lengths some people will go to just to get me to take some medicine."

The Edomite's golden brown eyes were bright with tears as he regarded the king. He said huskily, "Thank you, my lord. Please try to get some sleep. You will feel better when you awaken."

"I will go to sleep after you open the doors."

"Yes, my lord." Haman did as he was asked and came back to the bed.

Esther pulled the covers up over Ahasuerus' shoulders and tucked them in so he would be warm. He closed his eyes. She looked over at Haman and caught him gazing at the king, his expression unguarded.

He truly cares for Ahasuerus! she thought in astonishment.

Then she remembered the fearless way the king had swallowed the supposedly poisoned medicine. *And Ahasuerus knows it.* She looked down at her husband's fever-flushed face. "The most important judgments a man makes in his life are his judgments about whom he can trust," he had said.

"You may leave us, Haman," she said quietly. "I will watch over the king."

After the Edomite had closed the door behind him, Ahasuerus opened his eyes and looked at her. "That was a little too exciting. Are you all right?"

Esther wasn't all right. Everything about what had just happened upset her. She asked the first of the questions that was on her mind. "Who could have told Xerxes that the medicine was poisoned? And why would someone do such a thing?"

His expression was somber. "If I had given the medicine to Xerxes, he would have taken it away to be tested on a slave or an animal. By the time it was tested, someone would have made sure that it was indeed poisoned."

Esther felt a shiver of fear run all through her. "Was this Xerxes' doing, my lord?"

He said wearily, "I don't think so. Xerxes would be delighted if I was killed in battle, but he is too honorable to have anything to do with poison. Someone who wanted to destroy Haman was behind this."

"Why would someone want to do that?"

"Because Haman is my friend, and they don't want me to have friends." Ahasuerus' eyes were heavy. "That potion is making me sleepy."

"Then go to sleep," she said softly. "I'll stay with you for a while."

His eyes closed all the way and in a short while he was asleep. Esther stayed by the bed, as if her very presence could keep him safe.

She was deeply afraid. There had been no poison this time, but perhaps at another time there would be. All of his father's old courtiers hated him. Hathach, who was Esther's eyes on the world, had told her the specifics of the various court factions that were aligned against the king, and she knew that

Ahasuerus did not have many people he could trust. He had left two of his closest boyhood friends in Egypt to keep the peace in that country. He had made his other boyhood friend, Coes, his Lancebearer, and Haman was his Bowbearer. Coes and Haman were the only two men he could fully trust among the throng of Royal Kin who filled the court, most of whom only wanted him for what they could get out of him. She had begun to suspect that, under all the magnificence and power that were his, Ahasuerus was a lonely man,

Esther's thoughts turned to her own situation. What would have happened to her if the drink had actually been poisoned and Ahasuerus had died?

I would have been free to go home. I am not with child, so there is no question of an heir other than Xerxes. I would be free to go back to my old life, as I have longed to do ever since I first came here.

If Ahasuerus died.

But she did not want Ahasuerus to die.

That was perhaps the scariest thought of all. She had told herself over and over that she must not fall in love with this king, that she must not confuse loving embraces with love of the heart.

You must not be foolish, Esther. The king does not come to you night after night because he loves you. He comes because he needs an heir. And once you do have a son, you will be trapped here forever. The best thing that could happen to you would be for Ahasuerus to die. Then your grandfather could take you away and, after a while, you could go back to Mordecai and no one would notice or care. Perhaps Abraham might even still want to marry you.

She heard Ahasuerus stir and she reached out to put her hand over his, to reassure him that she was there.

Ahasuerus was better the next day, and the Ecbatana summer progressed with one beautiful day following the other. Esther had her own covered carriage in which she could take long drives all over the plateau. Everywhere she went that summer the wheat was as tall as the horses and mixed in with it were wild hollyhocks, bluebells, and giant purple thistles. Poppies grew in the thousands, making a bright patchwork of red and pink and orange in the grass. Esther felt herself relaxing as the clean, clear air of the mountains blew away her worries. For a few wonderful weeks she almost succeeded in being happy.

The one person she did worry about during that otherwise peaceful time was Hathach. As lovely day passed into lovely day, he seemed to become more and more silent and withdrawn.

She observed him closely one clear, bright morning as the sun was shining into her apartment through the open balcony doors. He was standing by those doors watching the men in the courtyard mounting up for a day at the racetrack. The sound of deep male voices and the noise of shod hooves on gravel floated clearly upward through the thin mountain air.

The young eunuch's face was a mask of misery.

Esther looked down into the courtyard from behind Hathach's shoulder. Ahasuerus had come out of the palace and was leaping lightly onto the back of a muscled bay stallion. The sun shone on his scarlet riding jacket and winked off the gold hoops in his ears. He picked up his reins in one hand and turned to the man whose horse stood beside his. It was Coes, his childhood friend, who was laughing at something the king had said.

The scent of horses drifted to Esther's nostrils. Then Ahasuerus began to trot his stallion forward. Esther watched the easy roll of his slim hips as they followed the motion of his horse. In two minutes the courtyard was empty. Hathach turned slowly back into the room.

"Is it so bad?" Esther asked gently.

His face froze. For a long, silent moment they looked at each other, both of them standing in the sunshine from the open doorway. Esther waited, but still he said nothing.

"Do you ride, Hathach?" she asked.

He nodded. In the sunlight his hair shone as black and shiny as a crow's wing. "I am of the Sargartian tribe, my lady. We pasture our herds in the mountains to the north of here. I have ridden since I was a small child."

"Then I will ask the king to give you a horse," Esther said.

His frozen face did not change. "My people do not have horses such as these, my lady. We ride shaggy hill ponies. I do not ride like the king."

Esther saw again the supple hips and soft back of Ahasuerus as he rode out of the courtyard. "You can learn to ride horses such as these, Hathach. Perhaps you will not ride quite as well as the king." She lifted her eyebrows humorously. "But then no one else does either."

The tension that was drawing his lips into a straight line relaxed slightly. "That is true. He is magic on a horse, my lady. Did you know that he rode one of Xerxes' horses in the race yesterday and he won? On a horse that had never won before!"

This was news to Esther and not altogether welcome. She frowned. "I'm not sure that was wise, Hathach. Xerxes already resents him too much."

"He had to, my lady. Xerxes challenged him. And he won! Xerxes was furious."

"I did not know you went to the racetrack," Esther said.

All of the brightness died from his face. "Occasionally I do, my lady. When I have no duties to perform for you."

Esther looked at her eunuch, at the high cheekbones, the thin black brows, the proud nose. Hathach was eighteen, of an age to be one of the young men riding out with the king. But he would never have the opportunity to do the things men do, and Esther's heart bled for him.

"You are young and strong and I see no reason why you cannot ride a big horse." Her voice was deliberately matter-of-fact. "Furthermore, you are my chief spokesman—my Grand

Vizier, as it were." She smiled warmly. "When we return to Susa it will be useful to me if you have an available horse."

At these words his look of pinched misery lifted. "You had better not let Hegai hear you calling me your Grand Vizier, my lady," he warned. "He thinks that is his job."

"You are more than my Grand Vizier, Hathach," Esther said. "You are my friend."

"Give your eunuch a horse?" Ahasuerus asked over dinner that evening. "Certainly he can have a horse if you want him to. But what is the point?"

The two of them were eating in the small dining room that was part of the royal apartments. Ahasuerus ate there with Esther three evenings a week. The other nights he dined in the main dining room with the men of the court.

"He will also need someone to instruct him," Esther continued. "He tells me that he rode when he was a child, but only on hill ponies."

"There is a big difference between a hill pony and a Nisean, Esther." Ahasuerus was dressed in a blue jacket and black trousers and wore only a simple gold fillet around his forehead. He had affected the Median style of dress since they came to Ecbatana.

Now he sliced a chunk of chicken in half and the rings on

his fingers flashed as he wielded his knife. "We'll find him a nice quiet nag. Though I still don't see the point."

"He needs a Nisean," Esther insisted. "A big one. One that prances and snorts. That kind of horse."

He put down his knife and looked at her. "Why?"

"Because he is a eunuch, my lord, and he hates it. Having a horse like that will help to restore his pride."

He continued to look at her and did not reply.

She sustained his gaze fearlessly. "Perhaps he could learn to ride in races. Hathach would like that."

"You appear to have expended a great deal of thought on this eunuch," Ahasuerus said.

"He is not 'this eunuch.' He is Hathach."

One eyebrow lifted. Ahasuerus ate a piece of chicken.

Esther tried to explain in a way he could understand. "Hathach is of the Sargartian tribe, my lord, and when he was eleven years old your father passed through their summer pastures. Hathach's father was the chief of the tribe and he invited Darius to dine in his tent. Darius accepted. After dinner he complimented Hathach's father on his son's beauty. Hathach's father had him castrated and sent to Susa as a gift to the Great King."

Ahasuerus' brow furrowed faintly. He swallowed the chicken and said, "My father was not a man for boys."

Esther felt like hitting him. "That is not the point!"

He picked up his wine cup and drank. A page stepped

forward to refill it. "Furthermore," he said, "Hathach should never have told you that story. It is not at all suitable for a woman's ears."

Sudden anger surged through Esther. She laid her hands flat on the table before her and glared at him. "Don't you have any heart?" she demanded. "Is it so impossible for you to imagine the sufferings of this boy? There you sit, not just a king, but a man! You have a beard on your face. Under your belt you are whole and unblemished. How would you feel if that was taken from you, my lord?"

He was staring at her in astonishment.

"How would you feel if you knew you could never lie with a woman again?" she demanded.

Silence.

Then, "Devastated," he said quietly.

The quietness extinguished her fury as anger would not have. She put her hands into her lap and clasped them together, out of his sight. "I am sorry, my lord. I don't know why I'm shouting at you. None of this was your fault."

He drank from his refilled cup. "So you think that having a man's horse will help Hathach feel less . . . mutilated."

Esther sighed. "It sounds stupid when you put it that way."

He shook his head. "It isn't stupid, Esther. You are probably right. It probably will help." He sipped again and regarded her over the rim of the cup. "I will tell Coes to find him a fire-eater and teach him to ride it."

Esther's smile was radiant. "Thank you, my lord. You are very good."

All she could see of his face were his eyes, and their expression was enigmatic. "It is you who are the good one," he said. "It constantly amazes me how aware you are of people; even the servants who wait upon you. You see them, and you see their needs, and you care enough to do something about them." He shook his head. "It amazes me."

He lowered the goblet and she could see that he was smiling.

She said, "What is this I hear about you winning a race on one of Xerxes' horses yesterday?"

He sighed. "I tried to get out of it, but he was insistent. He has a new horse, you see, and thought he could beat me if Soleil didn't run."

"It didn't occur to you that perhaps it would have been wiser to *let* Xerxes win?"

His eyes glinted. "It occurred to me."

Esther cast her eyes upward. "Men!" she said.

He chuckled.

She became serious again. "Xerxes resents you, my lord. I am very much afraid that one day he will try to do you an injury."

"He has every reason to resent me," Ahasuerus replied. "All his life my father encouraged him to believe that he would be the next Great King. It was a severe blow to him when I was named instead."

"Is that why you are so patient with him? He slights you whenever he has the chance, yet you continue to tolerate him."

Ahasuerus nodded. "He would not do anything to hurt me, Esther. You saw how he warned me when he thought my medicine was poisoned. For all his faults, he was brought up to honor the code of Ahuramazda: tell the Truth and hate the Lie."

"He is not that much younger than you, is he?"

He shook his head. "Six months, that is all."

"He *seems* younger."

"He has been indulged all his life."

Their conversation was so easy, so family-like, that Esther felt emboldened to ask, "Why did Darius favor Xerxes over you for all those years only to reject him in the end?"

"I think he saw that Xerxes was too easily led," Ahasuerus replied.

"And he knew that in Babylon they called you the 'second Cyrus.'"

He shrugged. "Perhaps."

Esther leaned a little forward. "Will you please try to be careful around him, my lord? He is hot tempered and could easily do something he might later regret."

He smiled at her. "I will do my best, Esther. I promise."

CHAPTER FIFTEEN

As day after lovely day slid by, Esther found herself falling deeper and deeper under Ahasuerus' spell. She felt as if she were almost changing into another person, and only occasionally did this bother her. The king slept in her bed and three times a week he dined with her privately. What more proof could she ask that he cared about her?

So she thought until one afternoon in mid-August she saw him ride into the palace courtyard with a little boy of about eight on the saddlecloth in front of him. They were in the forefront of a party of the Royal Bodyguard, and the sight of the child's hair, the exact same pale brown as the king's, pierced Esther to the heart.

When she had lived in the harem in Susa she had occasionally heard the sounds of children, but they had their own apartments and their own nursemaids and their lives rarely touched the lives of the harem women. Only once had she seen the king's two favorites, Mardene and Ilis, the mothers of his children.

Now she watched as Ahasuerus sprang from his horse, then raised his arms to lift down his son. The little boy clung to his father's hand as they began to walk across the courtyard and Ahasuerus bent his head to say something to the child. Esther watched until they disappeared under the arched doorway that led to the stable yard, then turned slowly back into her room.

"Is something the matter, my lady?" It was Luara, who had been putting away some of Esther's newly laundered clothes.

Esther shook her head and did not reply.

Luara stood before the polished cedar cupboard, her arms piled with linen shifts. "You look upset."

Esther stared at her blankly.

Luara balanced the laundry on one arm and came to feel Esther's hand. "You are freezing," she said worriedly. "Do you want me to light the brazier?"

Esther shook her head. "Leave me for a little while, Luara. I would like to be alone."

"All right," the girl replied reluctantly. She went to the door, looked around as if she wanted to say something more, then refrained. The door closed softly behind her.

Alone, Esther stood in the middle of the room, her hands clenched together in front of her.

How often does he see those women?

Her hands clenched tighter. There was a pain in her chest that was making it difficult to breathe. *Is that where he goes when he is not with me?*

She struggled to calm herself, to rise above the searing jealousy that was raging in her heart.

Stop this! she admonished herself sternly. *He has slept in your bed almost every night since you came to Ecbatana. You have no cause for complaint.*

But this morning she had started to bleed; there would be no child this month. She didn't know if she was happy or sad about this. A child would chain her more securely than any physical bond could ever do. A son would be Ahasuerus' heir, the next Great King. He needed a legitimate heir.

But would he still come to her bed if she became pregnant? Or would he feel that he had done his duty to his country and go back to his favored concubines?

I will not be able to bear it if he goes to the harem, she thought. *I will not be able to bear it.*

Her heart twisted with anguish. How had it come to this? She had tried so hard not to love him. How could you love someone you didn't fully trust? She didn't understand it, but it seemed that she did love him.

She stared out at the courtyard, which now held only servants. *God has abandoned me,* she thought. *Everyone has abandoned me. My heart is breaking and no one cares.*

Esther was saved from the torture of imagining Ahasuerus in another woman's arms when she heard that he was taking a large party of men on a hunting trip to the mountains that lay to the north of Ecbatana. He told her this when he stopped by to speak to her before he went to have supper with the men of the court in the palace dining room. They would be gone for several weeks, he said.

Esther struggled not to betray her joy at this news. "What will you hunt?" she asked.

"Lions," he said. "And there are tigers in the mountains to the north. I have never gotten a tiger."

"Lions and tigers?" she said faintly. All of a sudden the hunting trip did not look quite so wonderful.

"And bear and leopard." He was looking absolutely delighted.

"You have done this before?"

He grinned. "Yes."

"Well." She swallowed. "You will be careful?"

His eyes glinted wickedly. "Careful is no fun, Esther."

She glared at him and he laughed and kissed her cheek. "I had better get to the dining room or dinner will go on all night and I have to be up early in the morning."

At this news, Esther smiled radiantly.

Hathach moved to open the door for the king, and Ahasuerus stopped and looked at the young eunuch. "I understand from Coes that you are a very decent horseman, Hathach."

Hathach could not hide his surprise or his pleasure. "It is kind of you to say so, my lord."

"Can you use a spear?" Ahasuerus inquired.

"Yes, my lord."

"Would you like to come with me on this hunting trip?"

Hathach went so pale that Esther was afraid he was going to faint.

"You can ride with Coes and his comrades," Ahasuerus went on, making clear that Hathach would be one of the hunters and not one of the servants.

Color flooded back into the young eunuch's face. "I would like very much to go hunting, my lord."

Ahasuerus nodded. "Better see someone in the Guard about getting weapons."

"Yes, my lord!"

The king gestured that Hathach could now open the door. He went out and Hathach turned to Esther. "Is it all right?" he asked anxiously. "You will not need me, my lady?"

"It is all right," she said.

He glanced at the door. "Perhaps I ought to go to the barracks now."

"Yes. Go and arrange for your weapons, Hathach."

After he had gone, Luara spoke from the corner of the room. "That was very kind of the king, my lady."

Esther's gaze was on the door, which she could not see clearly due to the tears that were filling her eyes. "Yes," she said unsteadily. "It was."

"He didn't do it for Hathach, though," Luara continued.

Esther opened her eyes wide, then closed them. When she was certain she had forced back the tears, she turned to Luara. "What do you mean? Of course he did it for Hathach."

"No, my lady," Luara replied softly. "He did it for you."

When the hunting party returned to Ecbatana, it was as if they brought the end of summer with them. The snow that had tipped the northern mountains in June was creeping downward over the lower slopes, and it was too cold at night to leave the balcony doors open. It was time to return to Susa.

Esther hated the thought of leaving Ecbatana. The summer had been like a hiatus in time for her. Susa was grim reality. Ahasuerus would be pulled back into the rigid rituals of his royal position, and she would be confined again to the stifling existence of a Persian wife. There would be no more riding around the beautiful, sunny fields of the plateau in her wagon. No more picnics with Luara and Hathach in the niches of the mountainside. No more cozy dinners with Ahasuerus in the small dining room of the Ecbatana palace. She was going back to Susa.

Susa and Uncle Mordecai and all the conflicts she had so successfully ignored during the magic Ecbatana summer.

Esther had not spoken to her uncle since her marriage, and once back in Susa she found herself making excuses to herself for not sending for him. Then one day Hathach brought her a request from Mordecai himself, and she could delay no longer.

She decided to meet with her uncle in the Rose Court and, as she sat on the bench by the white marble fountain, she tried to think of what she could say to him. Finally the door opened and Hathach appeared. "Mordecai is here for his appointment, my lady."

"Send him in," Esther replied and jumped to her feet to greet her uncle.

He looked just the same, she thought, and sudden gladness filled her heart. It was so good to see him!

She kissed his cheek and said, "Come and sit beside me."

She took his hand and led him back to the bench, where they sat side by side. She smiled at him.

"You look well, Esther." He sounded a little surprised.

"I *am* well, Uncle Mordecai. It was lovely in Ecbatana. Susa feels so hot and stuffy in comparison."

"The heat now is nothing to what it was a month ago."

"I know. I remember well how sizzling Susa is in the summer."

Mordecai frowned. "I did not come here to talk to you about the weather," he was beginning to say when the door opened again and Ahasuerus walked in.

Mordecai moved from the bench to his knees, to prostrate himself on the brick floor. "My lord king," he said reverently.

"You may rise," Ahasuerus said in his drawling Aramaic. He had come to stand next to his wife.

"My lord," Esther said when her uncle was once more on his feet, "this is Mordecai, the friend of my family who introduced me to the palace. He is one of your Treasury officials."

"I am delighted to meet you, Mordecai," Ahasuerus said. "If you are the one responsible for bringing Esther to the palace, then I owe you a great debt."

"It was an honor, my lord," Mordecai murmured.

Ahasuerus turned to Esther. "I know I said I would have dinner with you, but some messengers from Egypt have arrived unexpectedly and I must dine with them."

"I perfectly understand, my lord. It was not necessary to tell me yourself, you could have sent a messenger."

Ahasuerus shrugged. "I was passing and I saw Hathach outside the door."

She smiled. "I'm afraid I appropriated your rose garden; it is so much cooler out here. I hope you were not planning to use it?"

He smiled back. "Not at all. You are welcome to it any time."

She loved it when Ahasuerus smiled. She wished he would do it more often. "I hope the messengers do not bring troubling news."

"I hope so too," he returned drily. He nodded once more to Mordecai and went back out the door.

When Esther turned again to her uncle she found him regarding her in astonishment. "You and the king sound— married!" he blurted.

She could feel herself tense. "We *are* married, Uncle Mordecai. That was your plan, remember?"

As soon as the words were out, she regretted them. She had given him an opening and he took it immediately. "Yes, that was my plan. And I am glad that you are on such good terms with the king. It sounds as if he speaks his mind to you. What have you been able to find out about his strategy for Palestine?"

The tension was making Esther's neck hurt. This was exactly the kind of interrogation she had feared, exactly the question she did not wish to answer. She said carefully, "He does not have any particular strategy that I am aware of. His only concern is that Palestine remain peaceful. As you know, it provides the only land access to Egypt, and Egypt is the jewel in the crown of the Persian Empire. Ahasuerus will only act if fighting breaks out in Palestine and he feels he must do something in order to safeguard Egypt."

There was a long silence as Mordecai regarded his niece. Esther looked back, trying to appear helpful.

"Esther. We knew all of this before we sent you to the palace. What we want to know, need to know, is if Haman has persuaded the king to intervene on the side of the Edomites should war indeed break out."

"He has never said such a thing to me."

"Have you asked him?"

"No. The occasion for such a question has never arisen."

Mordecai kept looking at her, saying nothing. All of a sudden Esther was flooded with an emotion she could not immediately identify. It was so strong that she began to tremble. She said, "You can trust Ahasuerus to act honorably, Uncle Mordecai. He is a good man."

Mordecai slowly shook his head, as if he could not believe what he was hearing. "Good man or not, he is a Persian, not a Jew. As you said yourself, he will do only what he perceives to be in the best interest of the empire, and that perception could well be influenced by Haman. You must find out if Ahasuerus will favor the Edomites, and if that is the case, you must get him to change his mind."

Esther finally realized what she was feeling. She was angry.

Very, very angry. She spun around, walked a few steps away, then spun back to confront her uncle. "Do you know what Ahasuerus prays before each meal?" she demanded.

"No." Mordecai was clearly impatient with this change in subject.

Esther took one step closer. "This is his prayer: 'May Ahuramazda protect this country from invaders, famine, and the Lie.'"

Mordecai shrugged. "We all know the Persian code, Esther. 'Ride well, shoot straight, and tell the truth.' It is not exactly complicated."

Esther's anger was growing hotter. "No, it is not complicated, but neither are the commandments that God gave to Moses complicated, Uncle Mordecai."

He was growing angry now himself. "I do not understand what you are trying to say with such blasphemous talk. There can be no comparison between the prayers of a Persian and the prayers of a Jew!"

"What I am saying is that *I* am a Lie, Uncle Mordecai. My whole marriage is based upon a Lie. You had no right to ask me to do this. You have no right to ask me to do anything more. I will *not* spy on my husband for you!"

They looked at each other, at odds for one of the few times in their lives.

Mordecai said sternly, "You cannot hide from who you are, Esther."

"I am Ahasuerus' wife and that is what must concern me now."

"You are a Jew!"

"Yes, I am a Jew. In my heart I will always be a Jew. I say our great prayer every day, Uncle. 'Hear O Israel, the Lord our God is One.' I know that. I believe that. I will never follow the religion of the Persians.

"But I don't live like a Jew. I don't eat like a Jew. I don't observe any of our traditions or our feasts. And I never will again, as long as I am married to Ahasuerus—the marriage you pushed me into!"

Mordecai was pale. "Listen to me, Esther. It may be true that you are living like a Persian, but you must never forget that God has chosen you for a sacred mission. You cannot, dare not, turn your back upon that."

She was so angry that she thought her eyes must be shooting flames. "Did He really choose me, Uncle? Are you very sure of that? Have you ever thought that your precious dream might have meant something else entirely? Or that it might have meant nothing at all?"

Mordecai took a step toward her. "Listen to me, chicken. When God gives a great gift, He expects the receiver to use it for His good. God gave you great beauty, my child. Because of that beauty, the king chose you to be his wife. I can understand that you may have fallen under Ahasuerus' sway—he is a man who knows how to please women . . ."

At these words Esther turned her back on him. His voice continued, "But you are not one of his light-minded harem women, Esther. You are a Jew. You belong to a people chosen by God. Do not ever let the pleasurable embraces of a man cause you to forget that."

"Hathach!" Esther called loudly.

The door opened and Hathach came in. "You may escort Mordecai back to his post."

"Yes, my lady."

"Think about what I have said," were Mordecai's last words as, grim-faced, he followed Hathach out the door.

After Mordecai had gone, Esther remained for a long while staring into the rippling water of the fountain. The words she had spoken to Mordecai, words that had boiled out of her like fire from a volcano, were words that she had been bottling up for a very long time. Words she had never consciously allowed herself to think.

But they were true. She was a Lie. She had deceived her husband by not telling him she was a Jew, and now she was entangled in the net of a falsehood she could not escape.

How could she tell Ahasuerus who she was? He, who worshipped the Truth and hated the Lie, how could she tell him that she, whom he thought to be untouched by any political motives, had married him because of her uncle's scheme to get his ear?

Dear Father in Heaven, Esther prayed in despair. *I came here because I thought that was what You wanted of me. Send me a sign. Please, I beg of You, tell me what I am to do!*

Chapter Sixteen

The south wall of the palace enclave consisted of four towers of brick, sixty feet high, which were connected by a curtain wall. Against the inner face of this wall were the barracks of the Royal Bodyguard.

Life in the barracks was not luxurious. The men of the guard slept on mattresses that were laid upon dirt floors and their magnificent armor hung from pegs hammered into plain wooden walls. The food was good, though, and the drink plentiful. Their officers lived in the palace or in their own homes in the city, but most of the ordinary guardsmen had little complaint about their lives. It was better than what they had come from.

This is what one of those ordinary guardsmen, Milis by name, was thinking as he sat in front of his barrack one Monday afternoon polishing his bronze helmet. He had ridden out with the king earlier in the day, but the afternoon looked to be a lazy one. He could hear shouting in the stable yard as a fight broke out and the men around him rushed to watch, but Milis was content to sit in the sun and relax.

His head snapped up when he saw the Commander of the Royal Bodyguard himself appear between the tall arches that separated the barracks from the palace courtyard. Teresh did not usually visit the barracks. Milis was even more startled when he realized that Teresh was coming directly toward him. He jumped to his feet, his helmet still clutched in his hands. He was almost the only man in the yard at the moment; everyone else had run to see the fight.

"Milis," the Commander said. "Just the man I wanted to see."

"My lord." Milis saluted. He was astonished that Teresh even knew his name.

"Step inside for a moment," Teresh said.

Milis' heart was pounding as he ducked into the shed that was his home. It was a mess. No one had rolled up their mattresses that morning, and bridles and clothing were strewn all over the floor. "I . . . I am sorry for the disorder, my lord," Milis began.

Teresh made a gesture of dismissal. "I am not here on an inspection, Milis. Although I suggest that is what you tell your comrades if they ask what I wanted with you."

Milis tried not to look as mystified as he felt. "Yes, my lord."

"I am here because your immediate lieutenant tells me that you are a good man. Loyal to the Guards. Obedient. Ambitious."

"Yes, my lord," Milis replied, more mystified than ever.

"I have a job for you," Teresh said. And proceeded to explain what it was he wanted done.

Milis did not eat a bite of his dinner Monday afternoon. He drank quite a lot of beer, however, and by Monday night his head was aching. His problem, unfortunately, was still with him.

On Tuesday morning the king did not ride out, so Milis asked his closest friend in the guard, Artanes, to accompany him on a visit to town. Once the two young men were walking through the dusty back streets of Susa, Milis dragged his friend into a deserted wine shop and huddled with him over a stained wooden table in the corner.

After the plump proprietor had brought them a jug of wine and two cups, Milis said, "Teresh came to see me yesterday and he gave me a special assignment."

"You?" Artanes was surprised. "Why you?"

"Because he thinks I am loyal to him."

"So, what is this assignment then?"

"He wants me to kill the king."

"What?"

"Quiet," Milis hissed, and looked around the empty shop.

"What are you talking about?" Artanes whispered.

"He wants me to hold a pillow over his face when I am on guard duty. He wants it done Friday, on the day of the Mithra Festival, when the king and all the lords of the court get drunk on the gods' potent brew. He wants me to pick a companion so there will be two of us to overpower him."

Artanes shook his head, as if trying to clear it. "It's a joke. You're trying to trick me."

Milis' bony face was grim. His deep-set eyes burned. "It is no joke, Artanes. This is not something I would joke about."

"No," Artanes said in a subdued voice. "I suppose you wouldn't."

"What are we going to do?"

"We?"

"You are not going to refuse to help me?"

"I will not help you kill the king!"

"Shhh." Milis gave a quick, hunted look toward the proprietor, who was setting out more cups on his serving table. He lowered his voice till Artanes had to lean across the table to hear him. "Of course I am not going to kill the king."

"Did he say *why* he wanted Ahasuerus dead?"

"He said that Ahasuerus was refusing to go to war against the Greeks. That Persia was humiliated in the eyes of the world. That if Xerxes were king he would avenge the defeat of Marathon."

"If Ahasuerus had commanded at Marathon we would not have lost," Artanes said.

Deep lines creased Milis' narrow forehead. "I don't think Teresh knows that I transferred to the Guard from the Immortals. Or that I was in Egypt with Ahasuerus. He got my name from the lieutenant, who recommended me because I was loyal and obedient." He swirled his untouched wine and some of it sloshed over the rim of the cup. "And ambitious. He promised me a lieutenancy, Artanes. A nice bribe for an ambitious man."

The two guardsmen drank some of the warm red wine.

"You realize that if we don't do the job, the Commander will find someone who will," Artanes said.

Milis rubbed his forehead as if it still ached from last night's beer. "I like Ahasuerus. He came among us during the Egyptian campaign. He even spoke to me once."

"We must warn him," Artanes said.

"How? What chance do you and I have to approach the Great King?"

"Sometimes we are assigned to ride out with him."

"Yes, and do you want to push right up to him, with Teresh looking on, and blurt out our news?"

Artanes scowled. "No. I suppose not."

Milis swatted at a fly that was buzzing around the puddle of wine he had spilled on the table. "If we don't have access to the king we must talk to someone who has."

"And who is that?" Artanes inquired.

"I think Smerdis is our best choice. He is the Grand Vizier. He will be able to warn Ahasuerus."

"And how are we to get to Smerdis?"

"He meets with the palace administrative staff on Thursdays in the Household Court. We can see him then."

"Another glass of wine?" the shopkeeper called from the serving table.

"No, thank you." Milis stood up and Artanes followed slowly.

"I wish we weren't involved in this. I have a bad feeling about what is going to happen."

"I will go to see Smerdis on my own, if that is what you want." Milis' bony face was resolute.

"No, I will go with you." Artanes squared his shoulders. "I like Ahasuerus too," he said.

Now that Esther was back in Susa, she suddenly found herself popular with members of the Royal Kin. At first, when the requests for an appointment with her began to come in, Esther acquiesced out of politeness. But she soon realized what was happening. Ahasuerus' numerous relatives thought she might exercise some power with him, and they were trying to influence her to get something out of the king that they wanted.

Esther was disgusted when she realized this and told Hathach to deny any more appointments. They were like parasites, this swarm of smiling relatives who lived off the largess of the king and did nothing to earn it.

She was also feeling the heat of Susa, and on one particular afternoon she decided to spend an hour or so in the Rose Court, which was the coolest place in the palace. There were two pages in front of the Rose Court's closed door when she arrived with Hathach. Esther smiled at the little boys and said, "I did not realize the king was in the garden."

The boys smiled back. All of Ahasuerus' pages loved Esther. "He is with Lord Sargon, my lady."

Sargon was one of the king's many brothers who had tried to visit Esther. She hesitated, heard a loud voice that was not Ahasuerus' coming from the courtyard, and decided to take a nap instead. When they had returned to her room, Hathach said, "Will you be needing me, my lady?"

"Not for a while, I'm going to sleep. Do you want to go to the stables?"

"I thought I would exercise Shirez."

"Go right ahead, Hathach. Luara is here if I need anything."

As soon as the door had closed behind Hathach, Luara said

in an amused voice, "Ever since he got those scars in the lion hunt he has been like a different person."

"I know." Esther walked slowly toward the bed. "He also got blood poisoning and almost died. But apparently that doesn't matter." She sat down on the edge of the bed. "Men."

The white silk drapes were partially drawn across the open windows to keep out the sun, and the air in the bedroom was warm and still. Luara said in a strained voice, "You know, Hathach *is* a man, my lady. They didn't cut him completely when they did it."

Esther became instantly attentive. "I don't think I understand what you mean."

Luara came to kneel in front of her. "I mean they didn't take everything." The girl was looking anxiously into Esther's eyes. "He cannot father children, but he is still . . . capable, my lady."

"Capable," Esther repeated. Then, suddenly, she comprehended what Luara was saying. "Do you mean he can still . . ."

"Yes, my lady."

"Have you . . ."

Luara held her gaze bravely. "Once, my lady. Yes."

Esther had never dreamed of this possibility. She blinked, trying to take it in.

Luara's blue eyes were anxious. "Are you angry with us?"

At that, Esther's heart swelled with compassion. She held out her hands and took Luara's into a strong grip. "Of course I am not angry. How could you think I would begrudge either of you whatever happiness you might find in this prisoner's life you lead?"

"It is not a prisoner's life," Luara said, tears trickling down her face. "Not since you took us to serve you. One never feels like a prisoner if one can be with the people one loves."

Unbidden, Esther's eyes moved toward the corridor and the king's door that stood opposite hers. "That is true."

"My lady." Luara, still on her knees before Esther, turned her hand so it was she who was holding the queen's in her own sturdy fingers. "He has not been to the harem. He only went in Ecbatana to see the children, and he has not been since you returned to Susa. I asked a few of the girls who would know, and that is what they told me. They say Mardene and Ilis are furious."

It was as if the sun had come out after a long and dreadful spell of grayness and fog. He hadn't gone to the harem. He had been faithful to her. She smiled radiantly. "Thank you, Luara. Thank you for telling me."

"Let me make you comfortable, my lady. You look tired; you should rest." She bent down to remove Esther's shoes.

"Yes, I am tired. I don't know what is the matter with me lately. The heat never used to affect me this way."

Luara held back the silk sheet so that Esther could get into bed. She said gently, "Perhaps it is not just the heat, my lady."

Esther's eyes met the wise blue eyes of her maid. "What do you think it is?"

"I think you may be with child."

After Luara had left her, Esther lay on her back and contemplated the many colored jewels tucked into the lattice work of the canopy. Luara's words had not been a surprise. Esther's bleeding was four weeks overdue, and she was never late.

I should be so happy, she thought. *My first child. I should be bursting to share the news with my husband, who I know will be very pleased to hear it.* She put her arm over her eyes, blocking out the sight of the jewels.

If I were married to Abraham, it would be so different. We would both be excited; all our families would be excited. We would have a baby, like every other couple has a baby, and we would make a family of our own. It would have been so simple.

But nothing was simple any more. If her child was a son, he would be the next Great King of Persia. The web that entwined her would grow even denser; the prospect of escape more impossible.

If Ahasuerus found out that his son's mother was a Jew and not a Persian aristocrat, what would he do? Would he put her away as he had Vashti? Separate her forever from her child?

That could not happen. She could not allow that to happen.

She could never, ever, under any circumstances, do anything that might take her child away from her.

She knew how a bird must feel when it is caught in a cage. No matter which way she flew, she was trapped. There was no way out.

Where was her Father in Heaven now? Was He watching? Did He really have some plan for her? If He did, she couldn't see it. All she could see ahead of herself was lies and heartbreak.

The room was warm and the bed was comfortable and finally she dozed off. Her last thought before she slept was: *But I never loved Abraham the way I love Ahasuerus.*

When she opened her eyes again, the king was approaching her bed.

"Are you feeling all right, Esther? Your girl told me you were napping. You never nap."

"I am fine, my lord." She pushed herself up, lifting her hair off her hot neck. "I was just tired. I have not yet become accustomed to the heat."

"You liked it in Ecbatana, didn't you?"

"I loved it."

He sat on the edge of the bed. "I love it there too. There are fewer people and fewer . . . complications." He sighed. "But one can't turn one's back on the world forever. Unfortunately."

He looked a little tired too, she thought. "I was going to sit in the Rose Court earlier but you were before me."

He said grimly, "One of my father's too-many sons has

been getting into trouble again, and I had to deal with it. As usual."

There had been a note of deep disgust in his voice when he said the words "too-many sons." She perfectly understood his feelings. "How many brothers do you actually have, my lord?"

Ahasuerus sighed with exasperation. "My father had twelve sons with his wives and thirty sons with his concubines. All of these ... 'princes' have royal blood in their veins and feel they are entitled to a position of power in the empire. They cannot all be made satraps and governors, however. There must be some places kept for other, capable Persian nobles. So those who remain in Susa spend their time bickering and spending money and in general creating more trouble than they are worth."

Esther did a quick calculation in her head. "That is forty-two sons!"

"Forty too many," Ahasuerus said bitterly.

Esther said tentatively, "A few of them have come to see me. They wanted me to influence you."

He stared at her, his gray eyes suddenly cold. "You never told me that."

His voice had a distinct chill. Esther said quickly, "Once I realized what was happening, I had Hathach deny any more appointments. The Royal Kin are none of my business."

He held her gaze for a moment more, then his eyes softened

and he smiled. "Good girl." He let out a long, frustrated sigh. "Cyrus had only one wife, and he was on campaign too much to have the time to father a pack of royal drones on his concubines. I wish my father had followed his excellent example."

Esther's words tumbled out before she could stop them. "Is that why you had only two concubines for all those years?"

He did not seem offended by the question. "Yes. The fewer illegitimate children the king has, the better it is for the country."

He glanced at the window as if judging the time of day by the light and then he kicked off his soft leather shoes, stood, and began to take off his robe.

Esther said, "It's hot. I was going to have a bath before dinner."

"You will have time," he replied imperturbably.

Esther watched him, watched the hard male body that emerged from beneath the Great King's finery: the strong shoulders, the flat stomach and narrow hips, the long, muscled horseman's legs. She loved him so much; but right now she was feeling cross and a little hostile.

He slipped under the sheet beside her and she stiffened.

He felt it. "Is something the matter?"

She said, "I think you already have too many illegitimate children, Ahasuerus. I don't think you should have any more."

He sat up. He looked down at her. He had taken off his gold fillet with his clothes and his unconfined hair spilled forward over his forehead. He pushed it back. Their eyes met and held.

"Esther." His smile flashed: warm, intimate, delighted. "You are jealous!"

"I would like to take those two women and throw them off the South Wall," she answered fiercely.

He flung himself on his back beside her and laughed. It was her turn to raise herself so she could look down at him. "It isn't funny."

His face was flushed. "I think it's wonderful." He reached up and cupped her face between his hands. "I think you are right, my love," he said. "I think that from now on I will concentrate on making legitimate children."

My love. He had called her *my love.* As her hair tumbled around them, she thought hazily that perhaps this was not the moment to tell him he may have already succeeded.

CHAPTER SEVENTEEN

Later that Thursday afternoon Haman stood by the window in the reception room of the royal courtyard, staring out at the orange trees that formed a privacy screen between the wing that held the royal apartments and the south platform. Ahasuerus was late for their appointment, but the servants had told Haman that the king was with the queen and could not be disturbed.

Haman shifted the roll of parchment he was carrying from one hand to the other and stared blindly at the trees. The day's light was fading and soon it would be time for dinner.

Ahasuerus had gone into his apartment over an hour ago and he had not yet come out. They had said he was with the queen. He was supposed to be with Haman.

Finally there came the sound of voices from the corridor that led to the king's apartment.

He's left her at last, Haman thought bitterly. *Perhaps now he'll have time for me.*

He moved away from the window to stand under the golden disk, symbol of Ahuramazda, that hung on the wall directly opposite the arched doorway into the corridor. On the disk, in bas-relief, was a winged globe with the head and shoulders of the god rising out of it. This particular symbol appeared in all the king's private rooms. Its significance was that Ahuramazda, who reigned in the sky, watched over and protected the king, who was his viceroy on earth.

Finally, well past the time of their scheduled appointment, the king came into the reception room.

"Haman," he said pleasantly, "I'm sorry that I was detained."

As always, Ahasuerus was immaculately groomed. His hair, still damp from the bath, was perfectly ordered. The folds of his robe fell with mathematical precision. But the faintly languid look in his eyes would have told the sharp-eyed Haman what he had been doing earlier, even if Haman had not already known.

During the years since first he had laid eyes upon Ahasuerus, jealousy had become Haman's familiar demon. In

Babylon he had been fiercely jealous of the small, tight-knit circle of the king's boyhood friends. He had envied bitterly their ease with him, the beautiful ease of old friends who have known each other forever. But over time he had come to see that even Ahasuerus' old friends had never breached the shell of reserve that lay between the king and the rest of the world. For all their undoubted comradeship, their obvious love of Ahasuerus, his essential self remained beyond their reach. It was this perception that stoked Haman's burning desire to be the person who truly got close to the king.

Never before had he been jealous of a woman. Never before had he begrudged Ahasuerus his sexual pleasure. But never before had he seen Ahasuerus so bewitched. Haman was beginning to suspect that Esther might prove to be more of a rival than he had ever thought a woman could be.

He went now to kiss the king's cheek in greeting. He stepped back and said, "I have been waiting for over an hour, my lord." He heard the querulous note in his own voice and winced.

Ahasuerus heard the note also and his eyebrows lifted. However, he merely repeated, "I am sorry."

Haman forced a smile. "I apologize if I sounded testy, my lord. It is just that I greatly desire to speak to you about this treasury audit I conducted."

Ahasuerus said, "I do not have time for that now, my friend. We will go over your audit on another day."

"Certainly, my lord." Haman's voice was expressionless. He tucked his fingers into his belt, then took them out again.

Ahasuerus said, "I have some good news for you, however. A messenger arrived in Susa earlier in the day from the Satrap of Palestine. He writes that there *is* a so-called prophet who is trying to incite the Jews to take up arms against the Edomites in South Judea. You were right about that. However, this prophet has not been able to rouse the people. The satrap writes that there is no sign of a Jewish army being raised. The people of Jerusalem are going about their business as usual. So you see, my friend, there is no cause for alarm. Your people are safe."

Haman lowered his gaze to conceal his bitter disappointment. He had been so sure that the satrap would find evidence of a Jewish rising! He said with forced good humor, "That is excellent news indeed, my lord."

"I thought you would find it so." Ahasuerus smiled. "It is good news for me as well. I most emphatically do not want to send Persian troops to quell a border dispute in Palestine."

"I understand, my lord."

Ahasuerus said, in his unhurried way, "I have invited the officers of the Royal Bodyguard to dine with me this evening."

Haman took the gentle hint. "Then I will be going, my lord. Perhaps we can go over this audit tomorrow?"

Ahasuerus shook his head. "Not tomorrow. But later in the week, certainly."

Haman turned at the door to make a courtesy bow.

Ahasuerus was standing in front of the open window and the glow from the setting sun lit his golden hair like a halo. Haman bowed stiffly and left.

It was nearly suppertime on Thursday evening when Milis and Artanes met together in a secluded corner of the barracks courtyard. No one was near them, but even so they kept their voices to a low murmur.

Milis said to his friend, "We told Smerdis about the plot this morning, and nothing seems to be happening. I don't think Smerdis has warned the king."

"I don't think so either." Artanes face was white and pinched-looking. "What if he *isn't* going to say anything? What if he is part of the plot?"

This was Milis' greatest fear. If Smerdis had told the king, Teresh would have been arrested by now.

Three guardsmen walked across the far side of the barracks courtyard, talking and laughing. Milis could feel the sweat pouring down his chest. He said, "If the two of them are in it together, our lives aren't worth a single golden archer."

Artanes looked around wildly. The courtyard was almost empty as most of the guards had gone to supper. Breathing fast, he said, "The only way we can save our lives now is to warn the king ourselves."

"But how?" Milis shut his eyes for a moment, trying to think. "How can *we* get access to Ahasuerus?"

"There must be *someone* who can help us!"

Silence fell. A faint memory flitted across Milis' mind and he gasped.

"Have you thought of someone?" Artanes sounded desperate.

"Possibly. One of the men who came through the Household Court this morning while we were waiting for our audience with the Grand Vizier? I recognized him because I was on duty in the harem courtyard the day he brought in a candidate for the king's hand."

"So?"

"So the candidate was Esther! Perhaps this man would be able to get to the queen for us."

"Who was he?"

"His name is Mordecai and he works in the Treasury."

"Let's go to the palace and see if we can catch him before he leaves for the day."

Milis nodded and the two young guards began to run.

Mordecai was already in the main courtyard by the great statue of Darius when Milis and Artanes accosted him. The three stood huddled together in the shade of the statue and, while a crowd of men hurried by on their way from their jobs in the palace to their homes in the city, Milis told Mordecai of the plot against Ahasuerus and of their failure with Smerdis.

When he had finished, Mordecai said grimly, "Come with me. We will go to the queen."

The three men threaded their way against the traffic in the courtyard back to the palace. They entered through the Service Court, passed under the huge enameled-brick mosaic of the Immortals, and went through the Treasury Offices and into the Household Court, where the guards had had their abortive audience with Smerdis that morning. From the Household Court, Mordecai turned north, passing through a series of offices and reception rooms until they had reached a portico where two tall, blue-robed eunuchs stood guard before the great double door that separated the king's private apartments from the public rooms of the palace.

"Find Hathach and tell him that Mordecai must speak with him immediately," Mordecai said to one of the eunuchs. "It is a matter of the greatest urgency."

The two sentries stared at Mordecai with impassive faces and made no reply.

Mordecai's voice sharpened. "Did you hear me? If you value your lives at all, one of you will go instantly and bring Hathach to me."

After another strained moment, one of the eunuchs turned, pushed open one of the massive doors, and disappeared.

The two guards and Mordecai waited in tense silence

under the eye of the remaining eunuch until the first one returned. He was followed by Hathach.

"Thank you, Lord," Milis heard the Jew say under his breath.

The smooth-faced young man looked from the guards to Mordecai. His expression was unreadable. "You sent for me, Master?"

Mordecai said, "Hathach, I must see Esther."

"*The queen* is resting at the moment. May I make an appointment for you?" Milis realized that Hathach had been offended by Mordecai's familiarity and he hoped the Jew had not made a critical mistake.

Mordecai said, "I must see her immediately. It involves the king and is a matter of life and death."

"A matter of life and death?"

"That is what I said. It cannot wait, Hathach, believe me."

Hathach once more scanned Mordecai's face. "Very well. If you will wait here, Master, I will ask the queen to see you."

The wait was only fifteen minutes, but to Milis it seemed an eternity. Finally Hathach reappeared with good news. "The queen will receive you, Mordecai. These guards must wait here."

Mordecai looked at Milis and said, "I will explain matters to the queen and then we shall send for you."

Hathach and Mordecai disappeared through the door, and Milis and Artanes stood in the portico with the two impassive eunuchs and waited. Milis thought of all the hours he had spent standing and waiting while on sentry duty. None of those long boring hours had dragged the way the minutes were dragging now. He stared through the open space between the wooden columns of the portico to the expanse of the Apanada that lay beyond. He began to count the columns in the Apanada.

Time passed slowly.

At last the door opened again and Hathach reappeared. He said in a clipped voice, "Come with me."

Milis and Artanes trailed Hathach's long, elegant back through the great double door into an anteroom and then into what was most certainly the king's private dining room. Opening off this room was the large, columned courtyard that was the private venue of the royal family.

Milis discreetly cast curious glances around as he followed Hathach's silent progress through the deserted courtyard. On the nights they did sentry duty at the king's door, the guards entered the bedroom wing directly from the Rose Court. Milis had never seen this part of the palace before.

They went up a few shallow steps and he recognized they had moved into the corridor of the bedroom wing. When Hathach opened a door on the left, not the right, Milis realized they were entering the Queen's Apartment.

The first person Milis saw when he stepped inside was the king.

"My lord." He dropped like a stone and felt Artanes drop beside him.

"You may rise," said Ahasuerus.

They got to their feet.

"Which of you is Milis?" the king demanded.

"I am, my lord." Milis took a half step forward. Out of the corners of his eyes he ascertained that Mordecai and an unveiled woman were sitting on one of the divans. *The queen,* he thought.

The king said, "Tell me what Teresh said to you."

Milis drew a deep, steadying breath and proceeded to recount the entire conversation.

"Now tell me exactly what you said to Smerdis this morning."

Once again, Milis replied.

Silence fell.

Milis saw the queen make a motion, which she quickly stilled. Her eyes were fixed on her husband.

"So," Ahasuerus said. His voice was calm, his face was composed, but his eyes were like twin chips of ice.

Mordecai spoke quietly. "Smerdis would have warned you if he was not part of the plot, my lord."

"Yes, he would have," Ahasuerus agreed.

"They wanted to smother you while you slept," the queen breathed, her voice filled with horror.

The king had made up his mind. "Hathach, bring Coes to me."

The eunuch went out again and the five people left in the room waited in silence. The king went to the window and stood looking out, his back to the rest of them. Mordecai sat on the blue-cushioned divan and stared at the tips of his shoes as they protruded from beneath his clean but worn-looking robe.

Milis peeked at the queen and saw she was looking at her husband's back. The king's very stillness was frightening.

Mordecai said, "Did I tell you, Esther, that Milis came to me because he was one of the guards on duty in the harem courtyard the day you and I first came here?"

She dragged her eyes away from her husband and turned to look directly at Milis. He dared to look back and found her smiling at him. He couldn't stop himself from smiling back. "It was clever of you, Milis, to remember Mordecai. You did well."

"Th . . . thank you, my lady," he said.

He watched her eyes return to the king, who had not moved.

They waited in silence. At last the door opened to admit the broad-shouldered young noble whom Milis knew to be one of the king's closest friends. Ahasuerus turned to face Coes and briefly, in a cold, controlled voice, he related the plot.

"I want you to take an escort of guards and bring Teresh to me," he ended.

Coes' faced was flushed with anger. "Yes, my lord."

Coes left and once again the room was silent. For the first time since he had come in, Milis saw Ahasuerus look toward his wife.

"Is this too much for you, Esther? Do you want to retire?"

She shook her head vehemently. "No. I want to stay."

"All right." And he went back to staring out the window.

She said, "These guards must be hungry, my lord. It is well past their suppertime. Perhaps Hathach could take them to the dining room for some food."

Ahasuerus nodded.

Milis was relieved to follow the eunuch out of the queen's room. He had no wish to be present when Ahasuerus confronted their commanding officer.

He could have been killed. Over and over the same thought repeated itself in Esther's brain.

He could have been killed. If Teresh had approached another man . . . if Milis had not thought of coming to Mordecai . . .

She shivered. The cold she felt had nothing to do with the temperature in the room.

But why? Why would Teresh want him dead?

It was only when both Ahasuerus and Mordecai turned to look at her that she realized she had spoken out loud.

"We shall find out soon enough." For some reason, Ahasuerus' icy fury was far more terrifying than boiling hot anger would have been.

Mordecai said, "Is there any chance that these guards

might be lying? Perhaps they saw this ploy as a way to win favor for themselves."

"We will know when I question Teresh."

He looked back out the window.

Esther longed to go to Ahasuerus, to put her arms around him, to comfort him with her love. But she knew that, even if they had been alone, it would not be the right thing to do. She could not comfort him. The leader of his own Bodyguard had just tried to have him murdered. Nothing she could say or do would change that.

When the door finally opened, all their heads turned, but Coes came in alone.

"Where is Teresh?" Ahasuerus demanded.

Coes replied somberly, "My lord, when he saw me coming with the guard, he killed himself."

CHAPTER EIGHTEEN

Esther, Ahasuerus, and Mordecai waited again while Coes next went to fetch Smerdis. Ahasuerus once more asked Esther if she wanted to go to bed, but she refused. She did not want to let him out of her sight. Mordecai also urged her to retire, but Ahasuerus looked at her face and said, "If you wish to stay, stay. But you can leave at any time."

"Thank you, my lord," she whispered.

Coes had better luck with Smerdis. The Grand Vizier was a sweaty puddle of fear and excuses as he came into the room to face his king. He swore that he was not a party to Teresh's plan. When the king called upon Milis and Artanes to confront him, he admitted that the guards had told him of the plot, but in his defense he pleaded that he had not believed it.

Ahasuerus had Smerdis arrested.

"You will have your chance to vindicate yourself before a judge," the king said, and Coes removed the protesting, petrified Grand Vizier from the room.

As the door closed behind the two, Esther felt an overwhelming tiredness sweep over her. She thought that if she stood up, she might faint, so she stayed where she was as Mordecai said, "He is guilty, my lord. I saw it in his face."

"Of course he is guilty." Ahasuerus' face was a mask, showing nothing. "I only wonder who else in the court may have been involved in this sordid plot."

Others? He thinks there might be others?

Esther's breath caught audibly. As Ahasuerus turned to her, she stared at him in terror. "Do you think there are others, my lord?"

A softer note crept into his voice. "No one else is going to try to kill me, Esther. Thanks to a loyal guardsman, the plot was discovered in time."

"This time it was. The next time you might not be so fortunate."

"I am going to make Coes the new Commander of the Royal Bodyguard, so there is no chance that this episode will be repeated." He walked to the divan and held out his hand to her. "You are exhausted. It's time for you to go to bed."

Esther let him pull her to her feet. "I don't think I will ever sleep again."

"Nonsense." He put an arm around her shoulders. "You have been through a bad time tonight, that is all. Once you are in bed, you will sleep well."

"I don't feel safe, Ahasuerus." She looked up at him. "I don't think I'll ever feel safe again."

"I'll have Milis and Artanes stand guard outside your door all night," the king promised.

"It's not myself I am afraid for."

Ahasuerus began to walk her toward the door. "Then I'll join you, and Milis and Artanes can guard us both."

"All right." At the door she turned her face into his shoulder, inhaling the scent of him. His arm tightened and he kissed the top of her head. Then he opened the door and said, "Hathach, take the queen to her bedroom and have Milis and Artanes stand guard outside her door."

Hathach took Esther's arm, and Ahasuerus stepped away from her. She turned her head and smiled uncertainly at her uncle. "Good night, Mordecai. And thank you."

Mordecai understood it was time for him to leave as well. Esther was not the only one who was tired; he was exhausted.

Mordecai said, "It is no secret that Teresh wanted you to go to war with Greece, my lord."

"I know." Ahasuerus walked to the divan and sat, gesturing Mordecai to join him. "Nor is it any secret that he was a friend of my Uncle Mardonius."

"Do you think Mardonius was involved with this plot?"

"I don't know, and since Teresh has killed himself, I will probably never know. It doesn't matter. I know I have to watch Mardonius. Teresh was only dangerous because I did not know about him."

"Treachery is an ugly thing, my lord," Mordecai said somberly.

"True. But loyalty is golden, and I am fortunate to have in my service many good and loyal men." For the first time that evening, Ahasuerus smiled. "Thank you, Mordecai, for acting so promptly. You probably saved my life."

It was the first time that Mordecai had felt the power of the king's extraordinary charm. You wanted to die for Ahasuerus when he smiled at you like that.

Mordecai answered gruffly, "I am happy I was able to serve you, my lord."

"I owe you two debts now."

"*Two* debts, my lord?"

"You brought me Esther."

Mordecai bowed his head in acknowledgment. He thought of how the king's voice had softened when he spoke to his wife.

He thought of the kiss Ahasuerus had dropped on Esther's hair. It looked as if he might care for her after all. Mordecai wasn't sure how he felt about that.

In the hours since he had first told the king about the plot to kill him, Mordecai had discovered that there was more to the man than that perfect face. He had been livid, but he had behaved with intelligence and control. He had not ordered the summary execution of Smerdis, as he was fully entitled to do under Persian law. "*He is a good man*," Esther had said. Apparently he was. But he was not a Jew.

Haman did not hear of the attempt on the king's life until the next day, which was the day of the Mithra Festival. No judges sat in session on that feast, so Smerdis was kept under house arrest in his home while the rest of the court went on with the usual celebration.

Ahuramazda was the chief god of the Persians and under Darius he had been worshipped as virtually the only god. Ahasuerus, however, had never neglected Mithra, the ancient horse god whom his people had worshipped long before they ever heard of Ahuramazda, the god of the sky. Ahasuerus had held the Mithra Festival in the autumn of each of the years he had ruled in Babylon, so Haman had seen the ceremony before, but this was the first time it was being held in Susa.

There were two traditional parts to the Festival. First the Royal Cavalry staged a splendid parade before the king. Ahasuerus reviewed it from the south platform of the palace, sitting in his golden lions-paw throne, shaded by a gold-embroidered canopy. A dazzling autumn sun poured down, shining off the riders' bronze helmets and sword sheaths. The horses' gleaming coats bore dark patches of sweat as they trotted by in perfect formation, each regiment led by its captain.

After the last of the magnificent red-coated riders had passed, the second part of the Festival took place: the Presentation of Horses, in which seven yearling colts were offered to the king by Armenian tribesmen as part of their country's tribute offering.

The Armenians, who had covered fourteen hundred miles of the Royal Road in forty days, filed across the courtyard, each of them leading a horse. The tribesmen walked proudly, not at all intimidated by either the throng of onlookers that packed the South Courtyard or by the prospect of meeting the Great King.

Haman stood behind and to the right of the throne, an honored position merited by his title of King's Bowbearer. Next to him, on the left side of the throne, stood Coes, the King's Lancebearer. Lined up behind Haman and Coes were a contingent of the Royal Bodyguard, without their Commander.

Haman's eyes were on the spectacle in front of him, but his mind was elsewhere. *Why didn't those guards come to me?* he thought as he watched the first Armenian mount the platform and prostrate himself before the king. The yearling he was presenting remained in the courtyard with a page holding its leather halter.

Ahasuerus said something to the man, who rose to his feet and looked with a mixture of gratification and wonder at his sovereign.

He is so perfect a king, Haman thought. *Even these primitive tribesmen are in awe of him.*

A few feet away from him, Coes shifted his weight from one foot to the other. Haman shot him a quick look. He was wracked by jealousy that Ahasuerus had called upon Coes and not upon him.

Coes is a soldier, Haman told himself. *That is why Ahasuerus sent for him.*

But it hurt. It hurt that the one who had seen Ahasuerus through this crisis had been Coes. Haman thought the king should have sent for him as well. It didn't help that the one to have alerted Ahasuerus had been the Jew from the Treasury. And the queen had been there as well. But not Haman.

The gold on Ahasuerus' crown gleamed as he leaned forward to say something to the second tribesman who was kneeling before him.

I am to sit beside him at the feast tonight, Haman told himself. *He will get drunk on Mithra's sacred haoma and he will laugh at my jokes and tell me funny stories and it will be like it was before.*

Before Ahasuerus had married that girl.

The Mithra feast was held in the main public room of the palace, the Service Court. The king and his chosen guests dined in the reception room while the rest of the guests were seated at tables that had been placed in the big, columned courtyard.

Haman did not keep his place beside Ahasuerus for long at the feast that evening. The king had been delighted with the Armenian horses, which were smaller and finer than the seventeen-hand-high Persian-bred Niseans. He was full of how he would experiment with breeding them to his own stock to see if he could add some of the Armenian fineness and speed to the Nisean size, and Xerxes soon took Haman's place so he could discuss this vital topic with his brother. Watching them, Haman thought with amazement that one would never know from the king's demeanor that he had just had a narrow escape from death.

The feast was not going the way Haman had planned. All during the dinner, which seemed interminable to Haman, he was forced to listen to the brothers discuss with clinical exactitude the various genetic points of every stallion and mare in the royal herd. It was the first time Haman had ever seen Xerxes at ease in his brother's company.

It was not until the food was finished, and Mithra's potent brew of fermented mare's milk was served, that it occurred to him that Ahasuerus might be testing Xerxes to see if he had been involved in the assassination plot. Haman looked at Xerxes' intent, unselfconscious face and knew that he had not been. Some men might have been capable of such dissimulation, but not Xerxes.

The absence of Smerdis and Teresh had been cause for a good deal of uneasy comment at the start of the feast, but the obvious light-heartedness of the king had soon changed all that. As the night wore on, and the mare's milk went around, the laughter grew louder and the voices more slurred. It was a moral obligation to get drunk at the Mithra Festival, and Haman looked out over the crowd of diners that were crammed into the Service Court and thought sourly that every Persian present was certainly doing his best to comply with tradition.

He felt someone touch his arm; he turned his head and saw Ahasuerus reaching across his brother. He said, "Come and sit beside me. Xerxes, exchange seats with Haman for a while."

At first Xerxes looked annoyed, then he shrugged and got up. He staggered and would have fallen to his knees if Haman had not caught him by the arm.

"I am fine," Xerxes announced haughtily, and fell into the

chair that Haman had drawn out for him. He put his face down on the table and promptly went to sleep.

Ahasuerus laughed. "Xerxes can't hold his haoma."

Haman said stiffly, "He appears to have consumed a great deal, my lord." He regarded the drunken scene in front of him. "As has everyone else in the room."

Ahasuerus leaned back in his golden chair. "It came at a good time, the Mithra Festival. I needed to get drunk tonight."

"Indeed, my lord," Haman answered with a disapproval he did not trouble to hide. "That is one way to deal with ugliness."

Ahasuerus looked amused. "You don't approve, do you? Don't Palestinians ever get drunk, Haman?"

"Sometimes, my lord."

"I don't think you do. I think you are upright and sober at all hours and under all circumstances. Is that true?"

Haman replied with dignity, "I know *this* is true, my lord. We are always loyal to our friends."

The king reached out and laid a hand upon Haman's forearm. Haman stopped breathing.

"I know you are, Haman. And that is why you are going to be my new Grand Vizier."

It was a moment before Haman understood. Then his mouth dropped open.

Ahasuerus saw his astonishment. He patted Haman's arm and returned his own hand to his cup. "I made a mistake when

I left my father's men in the important court offices. I am replacing them with men who are loyal to me."

"I don't know what to say, my lord." This was true. Haman was stunned.

Ahasuerus smiled and handed his new Grand Vizier a cup of haoma. "Drink to your new honor." It was a command.

Haman fought down his distaste and took a sip of the filthy liquid. He could not keep himself from shuddering.

Ahasuerus laughed, and when Haman had finally finished the cup, the king handed him another one, then another after that. By the time Haman finally got to bed, he was sure he was going to die.

CHAPTER NINETEEN

When Haman awoke the following morning, he wished that he *had* died. He had not believed it possible for a head to hurt as badly as his did. How did the Persians do it? How could they bear to put themselves through this agony? No amount of ephemeral good cheer was worth feeling like this.

He dragged himself out of bed, drank three cups of water, and refused anything to eat. His wife, who had never seen him in such a state, was sure that he was ill. "Stay home today, my lord," she implored. "You are not well. Surely the king can do without you for one day."

Haman peered at Zeresh's face through slitted eyes. "I am not sick. And I am not going to give those Persians reason to think that I cannot drink just as well as they can."

Zeresh's mouth dropped open. "Drink what?"

Haman groaned. "Don't talk so loudly. I will be back later."

Walking carefully, he went to the door. When he reached it he turned slowly and said, "By the way, the king has named me his new Grand Vizier." Grimly he walked out into the blinding sunlight.

Haman understood that this trial was not a necessity; as king, Ahasuerus was the Supreme Magistrate in the empire, and it was his right under law to judge those who were charged with crimes against the State or his own person. The king was allowing Smerdis a hearing by a judge because his conviction in open court would put to rest any rumors that the king had had him executed for political reasons. Haman agreed with the king's decision.

Royal Persian judges were known for their incorruptibility. They were chosen from among the Persian nobility and held office until their death. They could only be removed for miscarriage of justice, and this did not happen frequently. The Persian kings took the administration of justice seriously and dealt severely with judges who were dishonest. No one was likely to forget the fate of the judge whom Darius had found guilty of accepting a bribe. After the offending judge had been executed, he was flayed and his skin cut into strips, which were then used to cover the seat from which he once delivered justice. Darius had made his point, and there had been no cases of bribed judges since.

The Service Court today was filled with solemn-faced nobles, many of whom showed unmistakable signs of the previous evening's carouse. Haman remained on the fringe of the crowd so that he could make an unobtrusive exit if necessary. He had spent half the night heaving up his insides and his stomach still did not feel calm. He almost did get sick when he saw the tall, dark-haired man with a thin, intelligent face standing close to the judge's chair.

The Jew from the Treasury Office. Haman's eyes narrowed as he remembered all the times he had passed Mordecai and not known he was a Jew. He had only discovered Mordecai's background yesterday, when he had learned about the plot to kill the king. It was a bitter thought to Haman that it was a Jew who had saved Ahasuerus from the murderous plan.

There was a stir by the main door on the east wall of the Service Court, and Sisames, the judge who would be hearing Smerdis' case today, came in. His white hair showed his venerable years, and the distinctive scarlet stole of justice was draped around his stooped shoulders. He crossed to the high-backed judge's chair, then, with slow deliberation, turned to face the smaller door on the west wall. A narrow purple carpet ran from this door to the Great King's empty throne.

Everyone in the Service Court turned with the judge.

Minutes passed. Haman thought about his own miserable physical state and wondered if the king was indisposed.

Finally the door they were all watching so intently opened. A page stepped into the court and in a clear high treble announced the entrance of the Great King. A moment later Ahasuerus appeared, dressed in full court attire. His outer robe, dyed with costly Phoenician purple, was embroidered in gold with pictures of an eagle. His tunic was purple also, and the white trousers that showed beneath the robe were edged with purple as well. He wore a gold crown, gold earrings, gold bracelets, and about his waist a gold belt to support the short Persian sword that hung at his side. In his right hand he carried a slender golden scepter.

At the king's entrance the entire roomful of men prostrated themselves. They remained thus until he had crossed the carpet and taken his seat upon the high golden lion's throne that stood to the judge's right.

The men in the room rose to their feet. Sisames mounted his crimson footstool to sit in the judge's chair, where he called for the prisoner. Smerdis, wearing only a plain white tunic, was brought in by two guards to stand before Sisames. The charges against the Grand Vizier were read by a clerk, and Smerdis declared in a loud, defiant voice that they were untrue. Sisames then called Milis and Artanes to give their evidence.

Haman watched Ahasuerus as Milis related his interview with Teresh. No sign of any emotion except polite interest appeared on the king's face as he listened to the treacherous tale. Nor did the king betray any sign that he had been drinking the night before. Haman, who knew how much haoma Ahasuerus had consumed, was amazed.

Next Sisames called Mordecai, who related to the judge how the two guardsmen had approached him because they hoped he could get word of the plot to the queen.

Haman was horrified to hear that Esther had been introduced to the court by a Jew. He had heard that her mother's family was Babylonian. How did this Jew fit into her background?

The Jew was speaking Aramaic in the accent of Susa, not of Babylon. Many Babylonian Jews had emigrated to Susa, of course, and they had insinuated their way into the city's commerce, as they had done in Babylon.

They are like a pack of vultures, Haman thought bitterly. *Wherever they go, they make money by putting the local merchants out of business. They are never satisfied; they always want more. Look at how they want to take our land in Palestine away from us!*

Mordecai finally finished giving his testimony and next Sisames called Coes, who reported in an emotionless voice the suicide of Teresh. An audible shock ran around the room when the gathered courtiers heard this news.

After Coes had returned to his place, Sisames said to Smerdis, who had been standing in front of the judge the whole time, "How do you answer these charges, Grand Vizier?"

"My lord Sisames," Smerdis said, in the same loud defiant

voice he had used to declare his innocence. "It is true that these two guards approached me with their story about Teresh's plot, but it was so ridiculous that I did not believe them. That is the only reason I did not report what they said to the king, my lord. I simply did not think that such a mad plan, supposedly headed by the commander of the king's own Bodyguard, could be true!"

"Did you consider, Grand Vizier, what reason these men might have for concocting such a lie?" Sisames asked.

Smerdis turned his head toward Ahasuerus. "I thought they wanted to impress the king with their loyalty. Everyone knows how much the king reveres that virtue. I could not conceive that Teresh, a man I knew, would be plotting against the king's life. It did not sound possible."

Sisames coughed gently and Smerdis reluctantly returned his attention to the judge. Sisames said, "You did not think that the king's life was too valuable for you to take such a risk? You did not think that, even if there was only a very small chance that these men might be telling the truth, you should report their accusation and let the king investigate?"

Smerdis spread his thick hands. "My lord Sisames, I can assure you that I bear no animosity toward the king! I simply did not believe they were telling the truth!"

The lines in Sisames' old face deepened. "Then, if you thought these guards were lying, why did you not order their arrest?"

For the first time, Smerdis' voice dropped in volume. "My lord, I did not want to see Teresh's name blackened by this lie."

Sisames let a little silence fall. When he spoke again his voice sounded merely curious. "I see. You were willing to risk the king's life in order to safeguard the reputation of your friend?"

Smerdis cast a quick, hunted look at Ahasuerus, whose politely interested expression had never varied. "I did not think the king's life was in danger," he repeated once again.

"The guardsman called Milis will approach me," Sisames called.

Milis stepped forward once more, his booted footsteps clearly audible in the hushed silence of the room.

"You quite specifically told the Grand Vizier that the assassination was set for Friday night, the night of the Mithra Festival?"

"Yes, my lord." Milis' voice was firm.

"You told him this on Thursday morning?"

"Yes, my lord."

"And by Thursday night, when it became apparent that Smerdis had not gone to the king, what did you think?"

"I thought, my lord, that Smerdis might be involved in the plot with Teresh. I thought that my own life, and that of my friend, were probably in danger along with the king's."

"And that was when you went to Mordecai, whom you knew to be a friend of the queen's?"

"Yes, my lord."

Total silence reigned in the Service Court.

Sisames rose and turned to Ahasuerus. "Do you have anything to add to this testimony, my Lord King?"

"No," Ahasuerus said.

Sisames turned back to the accused and made his judgment. "Smerdis, son of Artaphernes, I find you guilty of treason against the person of the Great King and I sentence you to execution by beheading, this sentence to be carried out before noon today."

Smerdis went pasty white. He licked his lips, opened them as if to speak, then closed them again.

"Take him away," Sisames said to the guards.

As a half-fainting Smerdis was led away, the king rose and gestured for Sisames to approach him. "I thank you, my Lord Judge, for your wisdom and your resolution." His soft voice was effortlessly audible to the entire room.

Sisames replied, "He was clearly guilty, my lord. I wonder you didn't sentence him yourself."

"I was not as impartial as a judge should be," Ahasuerus said.

"You are an example of justice to us all, my lord," Sisames answered.

Ahasuerus' eyes swept around the Service Court, searching the faces of the men who were assembled there. His gaze stopped when it lit on Haman, who was standing by one of the columns at the edge of the crowd. "Haman, come here."

Haman was unprepared for the summons, but he managed to walk steadily across the floor, taking care not to let his feet touch the king's purple carpet. In private he was allowed to kiss Ahasuerus upon the cheek, but public protocol called for the prostration. He performed this now, praying he wouldn't be sick all over the ceramic tiled floor.

Ahasuerus told him to rise, then came down from the dais, and resting his hands lightly upon the Palestinian's shoulders, turned him around to face the court. "Behold my new Grand Vizier."

Haman was certain he could hear a shocked intake of breath run around the room. The timbre of the king's voice never changed. "I am Ahasuerus, the Great King, son of Darius, the Great King, an Achaemenid, a Persian, the son of a Persian." He paused. "Thus do I punish my enemies, and thus do I reward my friends."

As Haman felt the royal hands lift from his shoulders, he turned and prostrated himself once more. Ahasuerus stepped upon the purple carpet to make his exit and every man in the room dropped to the floor and almost ceased to breathe until he was gone.

CHAPTER TWENTY

E sther and Luara were sitting in the queen's reception room, looking at a display of rings. Esther did not want or need any new rings, but Ahasuerus had told her that it was her duty, as queen, to patronize the Susa jewelry merchants. Unfortunately, this did not mean that she should go to the shops; it meant that the merchants should bring their wares to her. For a moment a vision of the Jewish marketplace where she used to shop flashed into her mind. How Rachel and she had pitied the poor Persian women who were not able to go out to market. Never had she dreamt that one day she herself would be one of those poor creatures for whom she had felt such easy compassion.

She handed Luara a ring and said, "Try this one on and let's see how it looks."

Luara did so with alacrity, admiring the glittering jewel on her finger.

Esther's mind was not on the rings. Mordecai had asked for an appointment to see her and she knew she could not put her uncle off. She also knew what he was going to say and she did not want to hear it. Mordecai would be agonizing over Haman's appointment as Grand Vizier and he would want Esther to do something. He simply would not or could not understand that there was nothing she *could* so. It was not possible for her to question Ahasuerus about this appointment. For one thing, he had married her because she had no political interests, and for another, he would surely wonder why she was taking an interest in Haman's appointment when she had never shown an interest in any other appointments he had made. She could not do anything that might cause Ahasuerus to take a closer look into her background.

Esther hated being at odds with her beloved uncle. In fact, she had been very glad that he was with her during that long terrifying night when they discovered the plot against Ahasuerus. But Mordecai did not understand her position.

She could assure him that Palestine was quiet. The prophet Obadiah, whom Mordecai had feared would stir the Jews to rebellion, was preaching to deaf ears. Ahasuerus wanted peace; he would not be provoked to send troops unless there was an uprising. But no uprising seemed likely.

These were all things that Mordecai probably already knew, and she suspected he would not be satisfied with such a general response. But it was the best she could do.

She stood up restlessly and said to Luara, "You pick one of these rings, Luara. I probably will never wear it anyway. I'm out of sorts and I'm going to the Rose Court to recover my good temper."

"Certainly, my lady." Luara was enjoying looking at the rings far more than Esther had.

Hathach was waiting at the door, and Esther followed him as he went through the hallway crying, "Make way for the queen."

Esther told Hathach she did not wish to be disturbed and slipped into the Rose Court. It was autumn, her favorite time of year, that brief season between the heat of summer and the cold rains of winter. She inhaled the scent of the late roses, so richly colored and fragrant this time of year, and went to sit on the bench by the fountain. The sun was delightfully warm and she tilted her face toward it like a flower drinking in light.

Muran would tell her she was ruining her skin. If the Mistress ever learned about those wagon trips with Luara and Hathach around the plateau in Ecbatana, she would have been horrified. But Ahasuerus hadn't cared then if her nose got sun-burned, and he wouldn't care now.

At the thought of her husband, tears filled her eyes. It seemed as if she cried at everything these days. It was because of the baby, Luara said.

She had to tell Ahasuerus about the baby. She wanted to tell him. It was just . . . she felt as if she were being torn in two, and that telling him about the baby would rend her completely. Telling him would force her to make a final choice: she could be a Jew and tell him who she really was and why she had been sent to him; or she could be a Persian and continue to lie to him for the rest of her life.

Her great fear was that if she told him the truth, she would lose both Ahasuerus and their child. But if she lied . . . how could she live out her life knowing she was a fraud? Fearing that one day her husband might find out?

How did this happen to me? My Father in Heaven, I am only a woman. How can You ask me to choose between my husband and child and my duty to You? It isn't fair.

The sound of the door opening made her start and a flash of anger shot through her. She had distinctly said she did not wish to be disturbed.

Hathach said, "My lady, the king," and Ahasuerus walked in. For the briefest of moments, Esther remembered the day when she had first seen him in this very same place, the day he had chosen her.

He said, "Your girl told me you were here," and came over to join her at the bench.

It usually irritated Esther when Ahasuerus referred to Luara as *her girl*. She had reminded him several times that Luara had a name, but he never seemed to remember. There was a faint line between his brows, however, so she did not mention his omission but moved a little so he could sit beside her.

"Is something wrong?" she asked.

"I have had an interview with Hegai. He complains that you are slighting him."

Esther was astonished. "I? How can I have slighted him, my lord? I hardly ever see him."

"I know, Esther. That is the problem." A single rose petal lay on the ground next to the bench. He picked it up and smoothed it between his fingers as he spoke. "You see, Esther, the official role of the Chief Eunuch is to be the messenger between the queen and the rest of the world. You have given that job to Hathach, and Hegai is upset. Understandably upset, I might add."

Esther was surprised. "I never meant to hurt Hegai's feelings, my lord."

He smiled wryly. "It is not just his feelings you have hurt, Esther. You have stripped him of his power."

She didn't know what he could be talking about. "What power can there be in running errands for *me*?"

"A queen can have a great deal of power, Esther." He

turned to look into her eyes. "Particularly a queen who has her husband's ear. As you have mine."

At these particular words, she felt guilty color flush into her cheeks. His *ear*. That was the exact word that Uncle Mordecai always used. She lowered her eyes and asked, "Power to do what?"

"To influence me on policy," he said. "To win a favor for someone."

She did not reply, could not reply. She felt miserably, horribly guilty.

He said, "I know that you have no desire to do that. However, Hegai still feels that his job has been usurped by Hathach."

She still couldn't look at him. "I like Hathach. Hegai makes me nervous."

He frowned. "Has he done anything to upset you?"

She shook her head.

He waited.

"I suppose that I have never really forgiven him for that examination," she said at last.

"What examination?"

The question made her so indignant that she was able to look him in the eye again. "The examination they gave me when I first came to the harem. Do you *know* what they do to the girls who are brought to your harem, my lord?"

Of course he knew, she thought. However, he was prudent

enough to remain silent and she went on, "I have never been so humiliated in my life. It was awful."

He sighed. "I am sorry you were humiliated, Esther, but Hegai feels he has been humiliated also. And I think he has cause."

She put up her chin. "I will not abandon Hathach."

"I am not asking you to abandon Hathach. I am asking you to make Hegai your chief officer. Hathach can still run your errands."

She was bewildered. "But if Hathach is to run my errands, what will be left for Hegai to do?"

"He can act as a messenger between you and the other members of the court."

"I don't communicate with other members of the court, my lord. All they ever wanted was to ask me to ask you for favors, so I stopped seeing them. I told you that."

He frowned. "There must be *something* he can do for you, Esther!"

She looked at him for a moment in silence. "What did Hegai do for your mother?"

A white line appeared around Ahasuerus' mouth. "He did nothing for my mother. Xerxes' mother, Atossa, was the real queen, not my mother. Atossa was the one whom Darius listened to. Hegai acted as a messenger between her and the rest of the court. But he was also the chief messenger between her and my father."

Esther had, of course, heard gossip about Darius' first two wives. Artabama, Ahasuerus' mother, had been beautiful. In fact, people always said he resembled her. But Atossa, the second wife, had been a direct descendant of Cyrus and, once he married her, Darius had neglected Artabama and let Atossa bully her mercilessly. Muran had once told Esther that one of the reasons Darius and Ahasuerus fell out was that Ahasuerus always tried to stand up for his mother.

She thought now about what he had said. "Well, I don't see members of the court, so I don't need Hegai for that. And I see you all the time, my lord, so why would I need Hegai to be my messenger between us?"

There was a long silence. Finally Ahasuerus turned on the bench and looked down into her face. "That is true," he said, a strange note in his voice.

Several birds had perched on top of the high wall of the garden and were calling loudly to one another. The soft rush of water came from the fountain behind them. Esther said softly, "Is something wrong, Ahasuerus?"

He shook his head, as if he had just woken up. "No. Nothing is wrong. It's just . . . I don't think I had realized before quite how closely you have grown into my life."

He was quiet again and Esther waited. Then he said, "Unfortunately, the Hegai situation is only part of the dilemma I am facing. There is the question of the whole harem to consider." There was a flat note in his voice, a tone she had never heard from him before. He was looking down at the rose petal in his hands, which he was now tearing into small pieces.

"Is the harem a problem?" she asked tentatively.

"It can be a huge problem. Discontent in the harem can easily spill over into state politics. I am not the most popular of kings, as Teresh's recent plot demonstrated all too clearly."

His voice as he spoke that last sentence was too careful, and Esther's heart ached for him. She put a comforting hand over his restless fingers.

"You are not popular with the clique that supports a Greek war, but everyone else loves you."

His smile was a little crooked. "You exaggerate, Esther."

"No, Ahasuerus, I don't."

His fingers were warm under hers and they sat there together in the sun, thinking.

She said, "If you think the harem might be trouble, why not send all those girls home?"

He gave her a look that mixed amusement and exasperation. "I don't think it would be quite as easy as that."

Esther pictured the harem in her mind; the huge number of rooms and baths and gardens. "However did you manage to accumulate so many concubines?" she asked with true amazement.

He sighed. "Gifts. When I was in Babylon, every tribal chief within reach of the Royal Road sent me a beautiful girl as a gift. I couldn't say I didn't want them, so into the harem they went. And when I became Great King, the satraps scoured the slave markets to send me girls."

The flat note was back in his voice.

"Well," Esther said after a while, "I will take Hegai into my service and try to find something for him to do. And I will talk to Muran about the harem girls—perhaps she will have some ideas about how we can at least reduce their number."

His voice was slightly more buoyant as he said, "You know, Esther, you might have Hegai put it about that you will be extremely displeased with anyone who sends me new concubines."

"I don't know how much weight my wishes will carry, my lord, but I will be delighted to try."

"You would be surprised to learn how much weight your word will carry," he said, and slipped his arm around her shoulders to draw her close.

She rested against him, feeling the pleasant warmth of the sun on her skin. "It would be so nice if you weren't the king, if we were just two ordinary married people. Perhaps we would have a horse farm near Ecbatana. You would like that."

She felt his mouth touch her hair. "You must be the only woman in the empire who does not want to be married to the Great King."

"I don't want to be married to the Great King. I want to be married to you."

She closed her eyes and listened to the beat of his heart

under her cheek. Suddenly, from out of nowhere, she had an idea that might solve one of her problems.

She would recommend to Mordecai that he have the Jewish Community of Susa write a letter to the king assuring him that the Jews only desired peace in Palestine. Mordecai could deliver such a letter in person and make even further reassurances. She need not be involved in the matter at all.

Ahasuerus put his mouth against her ear and whispered, "Would you really marry me if I were only a horse farmer in Ecbatana?"

"Yes," Esther whispered back. "I would."

CHAPTER TWENTY-ONE

Haman was furious when once more Ahasuerus canceled their appointment to discuss the Treasury report. He had told Haman that he needed to speak to the queen on some issue pertaining to Hegai. Haman was scowling as he returned the Treasury scrolls to his office and he decided to take a walk through the public courtyards of the palace. The homage of the minor palace officials would put him back in temper, he thought.

Haman was not entitled to any form of deference from the Royal Kin, but ordinary men were constrained to bow to the

Grand Vizier as he passed by. To Haman, whose Palestinian origins had marked him an outsider in both Babylon and Susa, this reverence was particularly sweet.

As he walked with pretended purposefulness through the Household Court, he affected not to notice as man after man bowed from the waist. He passed into the Treasury rooms, and the officials there immediately bowed as well. Haman was concentrating on looking as if he were attending to some important business, when, out of the corner of his eye, he noticed that someone was not bowing. He glanced over, surprised to find one of the Royal Kin in so work-a-day an area, and saw that the upright man was not a member of the Royal Kin at all, but the Jew, Mordecai.

Haman stopped.

There were five men in the office. Four of them were bowing. Mordecai stood upright and looked him in the eye.

"It is correct protocol to bow to the Grand Vizier," Haman said icily.

"I do not bow to an Edomite," Mordecai replied through his teeth.

And with those simple words, Haman and Mordecai regressed to the primitive hatred of enemy tribesman, the animosity between them burning as hot and fierce as their desert homeland.

"You will bow to me, Jew," Haman hissed, his eyes mere slits of gold in his furious face.

Mordecai did not reply, but his look of amused arrogance was carefully calculated to infuriate. His back remained straight as a lance.

The tension in the room was almost tangible. Haman felt it, felt the eyes of everyone on him, on his humiliation by this swine of a Jew. He would get Mordecai, he promised himself. The only person in the empire with more power than himself was the king. Mordecai was going to be sorry he had scorned Haman.

Haman was still in a vicious temper when he reached home that evening. His wife, Zeresh, saw him come in through the courtyard gate and went into the front room to greet him. She read his face immediately. "What happened?"

He told her about Mordecai. Zeresh, who had lived in Edom until she married Haman, was not surprised. "All Jews are unbearably arrogant. My father says they have become even worse since they rebuilt the Temple."

Haman grunted.

She patted his arm. "Dinner is almost ready."

"I will wash," Haman said.

After the meal was over and Zeresh had gone to see to the children, Haman took a jug of wine and went to sit in the small side room that belonged to him alone. The evening was cooling down rapidly, and he had a servant put some charcoal into the brazier and light it. Then he leaned back in his cushioned chair, propped his feet upon a footrest, and closed his eyes. He sat in the same position for a long time, the wine untouched on a table beside him, his thoughts on the past.

He remembered the first time he had seen Ahasuerus. At the time, Haman had held a minor position as scribe in the Satrap of Babylon's household. The surprising news that Darius had named his eldest son to be King of Babylon had not dismayed the satrap, who had perfect confidence that he would continue to be the real power while Darius' son play-acted a royal role.

Haman had not bothered to watch Ahasuerus' royal entrance into the capital of his new kingdom. Babylon, that great walled city of terraces and opulent gardens, of massive brickwork and glazed tiles, had seen the traditional pageant often enough, and when Ahasuerus drove his golden chariot up the Processional Avenue from the Ishtar Gate, he had received a polite if unenthusiastic welcome from the local populace. Most of the officials, like Haman, had stayed home.

The young king was to reside in the palace Darius had built on the southern citadel, west of the palace of Nebuchadnezzar and just before the massive, moated wall of Imgut-Bel. It was not until the day of the king's entry that Haman learned of his appointment as Chief Scribe in the new king's household.

This was an honor he had never expected; it was an honor his minor position did not merit. He was stunned.

In all the Persian Empire, the position of Chief Scribe was peculiar to Babylon. Nowhere in the world was writing more commonly employed in the everyday affairs of life than in Babylon, where every important commercial transaction had to be sealed by a written contract. The Chief Scribe was in charge of all public scribes and all public declarations and inscriptions. It was an extremely responsible job, with a high degree of visibility, and it did not take Haman long to figure out why it had been given to a low-ranking Palestinian. The satrap had wanted to insult Ahasuerus. Everyone connected to the court realized the appointment was an insult. It remained to be seen if the new king would realize this as well.

Haman vividly remembered his trepidation when Ahasuerus had interviewed the men whom the satrap had appointed to the royal household. The new Chief Scribe had joined the crush of officials in the main courtyard and waited for his name to be called so he could go into the throne room, where Ahasuerus sat in state. When finally it was Haman's turn, he had pushed the curtain aside and stepped into the room, bowing so low that his nose touched his knees.

"You may approach," the king had said and Haman had looked up.

The sight of the eighteen-year-old Ahasuerus had struck him like a blow, the young king's beauty was so blindingly pure.

Haman had walked forward on unsteady legs until he was within the circle of that unexpected radiance.

Ahasuerus had regarded him gravely. "Tell me about your duties, Haman," he had said.

The audience had not lasted more than three minutes, but when Haman walked out of the room he had vowed to do everything he could to protect Ahasuerus from the pack of Babylonians he knew would try to pull the young king down.

This protective feeling had only grown stronger over the years, and now Ahasuerus had appointed him Grand Vizier, the most powerful post in all the empire. *Why then*, he asked himself, *am I so dissatisfied?*

The shadows deepened and the room turned dark. He sat on, undisturbed by his wife or his servants, who knew enough to leave him alone when he closed the door of his private room.

The face of Ahasuerus as he was today presented itself in the frame of Haman's mind. At twenty-seven, the king had lost that morning-of-the-world look that had so amazed Haman at their first meeting, and he had certainly shown himself competent to rule. But still Haman felt the familiar need to look after him.

He is too trusting. He sees only the good in people; he never sees the evil. Look at Smerdis and Teresh—he might have been killed. And now he will be grateful to that Jew for warning him.

Haman had labored for years to protect Ahasuerus from

untrustworthy friends. During that time he had never once found it strange that the only friend he ever thought Ahasuerus could trust was himself.

The following morning Ahasuerus summoned Haman to the small reception room off the Court of the Royal Kin that he used as an office. He was ready to hear the Treasury report.

When Haman finished detailing his discovery of the Head Treasurer's thefts from the Tribute payments, Ahasuerus' mouth was set in a hard line. He was dressed for riding. The window shutters were open, and from beyond the line of trees that gave the king privacy, Haman could hear the sound of horses being led into the south courtyard. Ahasuerus slapped a pair of gloves against his leather breeches and frowned. His hands were ringless, as they always were when he rode. He walked to the window and looked out. Over his shoulder he asked, "How did you discover the fraud?"

"It was simple, my lord. I compared the records with the amount of gold that was actually in the Treasury. They did not match."

Ahasuerus turned around. "That must have taken you a long time."

"It did. But it is one of the surest ways to uncover corruption, my lord."

"How can you be certain that it is Otanes and not one of the under-officials who has taken the missing gold?" Ahasuerus asked.

"If it had been one of the under-officials, he would have changed the records to match the amount of gold, my lord. Otanes could not do that as he cannot write. Also, the Head Treasurer is the only person to have unlimited access to the Treasury." Haman shrugged. "I am sure he thought he was perfectly safe, my lord. There is a tremendous amount of gold in the Treasury, and the chance of anyone bothering to reconcile the gold with the records was very slim."

"Do you think he was robbing my father as well?"

"I am certain of it, my lord."

Ahasuerus slapped his gloves against his breeches again but harder this time. He was angry. "The senior court officials are certainly keeping my judges busy these days," he said grimly.

"I am truly sorry to grieve you with this news, my lord."

"You are certain that the corruption does not spread beyond Otanes?"

Haman had spent an hour the previous evening trying to find a way to implicate Mordecai in this charge. To his disgust, he had been unsuccessful. "I am certain, my lord," he said regretfully.

"Very well. Send a guard to tell Otanes what he stands accused of. And inform the Chief Judge as well."

"Yes, my lord."

Ahasuerus' taut face relaxed into a smile. "As ever, I must thank you for your faithful service, my friend. I have chosen the right man to be my Grand Vizier."

A compliment from Ahasuerus could always send Haman's spirits soaring. "Thank you, my lord."

Ahasuerus pulled on his gloves and walked to the door. He tapped once and the page boy on the other side opened it immediately. The king went out to greet his horse.

A few days later Mordecai had an appointment with Ahasuerus to present a letter from the Susa Jews. Ahasuerus listened gravely as Mordecai read the carefully crafted words aloud. When Mordecai had finished, he said, "I am happy that the Jews of Susa desire peace in Palestine. The important issue, however, is what the Jews of Palestine desire."

"They desire peace also, my lord. It is true that there is a prophet in Jerusalem who is preaching war against Edom, but I have it on the best authority that the people of Jerusalem have paid him no heed."

"The satrap has told me the same thing." Ahasuerus laced his slender, ringed fingers together. "What I am wondering," he said softly, "is why the Susa Jews felt it necessary to approach me on this matter."

Mordecai looked into Ahasuerus' eyes. *There is a great deal of intelligence in that light-gray gaze*, he thought, and on the spur of the moment he decided to be honest.

"I will tell you what we fear, my lord. Edom has long desired a seaport. She took advantage of the years of the Jewish Exile to move settlers into Jewish land in southern Judah. She would dearly love to move even further west, across our entire country, to the sea. This is something we cannot allow."

Ahasuerus said, "Do you have any reason to believe that Edom will attempt such a movement?"

"Not at the moment, my lord."

"And in the future?"

"My lord, I would not be honest with you if I did not say that the Jews of Susa are greatly concerned about the fact that you have appointed an Edomite to be your Grand Vizier. We fear that if, for some reason, trouble should arise in Judah, you will hear only one viewpoint on the subject."

Ahasuerus unclasped his hands and the light glistened off a ruby in one of his rings. He said, "What if I told you that there is also a Jewish voice close to my ear?"

Mordecai's heart leaped. *Esther has told him who she is!* It was the only explanation Mordecai could conceive of that would account for the king's extraordinary statement. He saw that Ahasuerus was waiting for his reply and managed to say hoarsely, "I would ask who that voice might belong to, my lord."

"It belongs to you, Mordecai," the king said gently. "I am

appointing you to take Otanes' place as Head Treasurer of the empire."

Haman could not believe it when he heard the news. He was too stunned even to feel outraged.

I devoted months to proving that Otanes was embezzling gold from the Treasury and this is my reward. Otanes' position is to be given to a Jew.

There was nothing he could do about it. Haman knew better than to think he could question the king's judgment in regard to this appointment. However gracious Ahasuerus might be, he kept a space around himself that no one dared to step into. The greatest desire of Haman's life was to be the person who was allowed to enter that space.

He had never done so, but until now he had had the consolation of knowing that no one else was closer to Ahasuerus than he was.

In Mordecai, Haman scented a dangerous rival.

Mordecai was a friend of the queen's, and Ahasuerus seemed bewitched by his new wife. While Haman could not consider a woman a serious adversary, he feared the Jew.

Because of his connection to the queen, Mordecai would have access to the royal apartments.

Mordecai had been the man responsible for bringing to light Teresh's plot against the king's life.

Worst of all, Ahasuerus liked him. He would never have made him Head Treasurer otherwise.

For nine long years, admiration and jealousy had lived in uneasy coexistence within Haman's heart. With the appointment of Mordecai, the delicate balance of those emotions began to tip in the wrong direction.

CHAPTER TWENTY-TWO

Esther was stunned when Ahasuerus told her about Mordecai's appointment. Her uncle was to be Head Treasurer! This was almost as incredible as her becoming queen.

"You look surprised," Ahasuerus said.

"I am. I did not know you had such an admiration for Mordecai. You don't know him very well, after all."

"I know what is important; I know he is loyal. And I interviewed a few of the other men in the Treasury. They all spoke highly of his ability. I'm sick of appointments going to members of the Royal Kin who are incompetent as well as disloyal. Mordecai is the sort of man I need right now."

They were in Esther's bed, in Esther's bedroom, which was where, to the amazement of his court, Ahasuerus still regularly slept. They were retiring early because he had to be up before dawn. Tomorrow was one of Ahuramazda's holy days, so he would be riding out to the mountains with the Magi to the god's shrine.

Ahasuerus went to sleep quickly, as he always did, but Esther lay awake, her mind busy with this new development. She was happy for her uncle, of course. He deserved to be recognized for his honesty and his ability. But what would this appointment mean for her? With Mordecai now in a position close to Ahasuerus, what was her role supposed to be? If it truly had been God's plan for her to become queen, was it so that Mordecai could achieve this high position? Certainly he was now in a better place than she to know all of the political news, to be able to set the Jewish side of Palestinian issues before the king. So where did that leave her?

Ahasuerus lay next to her, his back toward her, his breathing deep and slow and regular. Uncle Mordecai had snored so loudly that sometimes Esther had had trouble getting to sleep. But Ahasuerus slept quietly, his breath only audible if she listened closely. She put out her hand and laid it lightly on his warm back. She could feel the horseman's muscles beneath the thin linen of his night robe.

She loved him so much. She hated having to lie to him. He, who hated lying more than anything in the world, had given his precious love to a woman who was a Lie.

For she thought that he did love her. She felt it in him. With her he could relax his guard, be simply Ahasuerus the person, not Ahasuerus the Great King. If he found out that she had been lying to him all this time . . . she shivered. It would hurt him unbearably. He did not give his love or his trust easily, and he had given both to her. And she was a Lie.

If she told him who she was right now, perhaps she could make him understand. She thought about this for a while, imagining the scene, trying out the different words she might use, but she always ended up back in the same dead end. How could she tell him the truth without involving her uncle? Ahasuerus knew that Mordecai had presented her to Hegai. Their connection could not be clearer.

The tears began to roll slowly down Esther's face as she recognized she was as trapped as she had ever been. Trapped by the necessity to maintain her uncle's credibility and trapped even more tightly by her love for Ahasuerus.

The thing she feared the most was for Ahasuerus to learn her identity from someone else. If Haman, for example, should look into Mordecai's background and find he had a niece named Esther who had disappeared . . .

Esther closed her eyes tightly and prayed: *My Father in Heaven. Please, please do not let that happen. If the truth has to come out, let it come from me. It would devastate Ahasuerus to hear it from anyone else. Please, Father. Take pity on Your daughter. I have tried to do Your will. I was obedient to my uncle, who sent me here to do Your work. Do not desert me, I beg You. Do not let Ahasuerus find out who I am.*

Worn out by emotion, Esther finally fell asleep and when she awoke, Ahasuerus was gone. She was still in bed picking at her breakfast when Luara came back in. "Take this tray away, Luara," she said fretfully. "It makes me sick to look at it."

Luara picked up the tray and said in the calm way that Esther so valued, "Do you feel well enough to see Hegai? He has been requesting an audience with you."

True to her promise to Ahasuerus, Esther had been trying to involve the Head Eunuch more actively in her affairs. Hathach had been understanding when Esther explained her plight to him. There was a great difference in Hathach these days. Simply, the young man was happy, far too happy to begrudge Hegai his place in the sun.

Esther told Luara to admit the Head Eunuch, who came in with his stately tread. When he reached the bed, he bowed.

"Good morning, Hegai," Esther said.

"Good morning, my lady. I hope you are well." His eyes flicked shrewdly over her pale face, and Esther had little doubt that he had guessed the reason for her pallor.

"Very well, thank you," she answered.

"I bring a request from the Head Treasurer, my lady. He would like to see you today."

After a long, restless night, Esther was not in the mood to confront her uncle. "Not today, Hegai. Put him off for me, would you?"

"Certainly, my lady." Hegai gave her that shrewd look once again. "I will tell him you are indisposed."

"Thank you."

"I have no other messages for you, my lady," Hegai said disapprovingly.

Esther sighed. "I know I am a sad disappointment to you, Hegai, but the truth is I am perfectly content to leave the business of the empire to the king. He is more than competent, you know."

Hegai's keen gray eyes moved from Esther to the unoccupied other half of the big bed. There was still a dent in the pillow where Ahasuerus' head had rested. Hegai looked back to Esther, noted the unbound hair that streamed around her shoulders, and said frankly, "I admitted you to the harem, my lady, because I thought you might suit the king. If I had known how well you would suit him, I would have sent you home."

Esther's lips curled in a smile of rueful acknowledgment.

In the sudden quiet the muted sound of boys' laughter could be heard drifting in through the shutter that Luara had opened to catch the morning sun. "The pages," Esther said with a smile. "They have a day off today."

Hegai grunted.

Esther straightened her back. "Since we are being honest with each other this morning, Hegai, let me bring to your attention a problem that the king does not quite know how to handle." She drew a deep breath. "The harem."

Hegai compressed his full lips.

She said, "The problem is that the king wants nothing to do with it."

Hegai stiffened. "The harem exists solely for the pleasure of the king, my lady. It has no purpose at all if he never visits it."

Esther pushed a long strand of hair behind her ear and said passionately, "I could weep when I think of all those mutilated boys, all those girls sold into slavery, to satisfy the desires of one man."

Hegai looked stunned. "Is this the reason the king is staying away?"

"No. That is my own observation, Hegai. The king's reason is more statesmanlike. He does not wish to burden the empire with dozens of illegitimate princes. *Royal parasites*, I believe he called them."

"I win!" The voice was close to Esther's window.

Hegai scowled. "Those boys should not be playing outside your bedroom."

"They are not bothering me. In fact, I enjoy hearing them.

Now, Hegai, I need you to think about this problem. What can we do to give the harem occupants a purpose in life?"

"They have no purpose in life if the king never visits. As you yourself pointed out, my lady, all of their access to another life has been taken away from them."

"The girls will not be so difficult," Esther mused, as if he had not spoken. "If we offer a high enough bride price, I'm sure we can manage to find husbands for the younger ones. The older women have less chance of marriage, but then, the older women are more content with the places they have won in the harem structure."

Hegai stared at her in horror. "Are you thinking of dismantling the harem?"

"No," Esther said with regret. "I would like to, of course, but the king would object to so drastic a move."

"I am relieved to hear that," he retorted with heavy irony.

"If we were going to disband the harem, I would not be asking you to help me think of ways to give it a sense of purpose, Hegai."

He sniffed. "You are doing well enough without my advice, my lady. You have disposed of the women. Now what of the eunuchs?"

Esther's eyes were on her index finger, watching it draw concentric circles on the silk coverlet that was pulled to her waist. She said, "I was thinking that perhaps the eunuchs could form a special guard unit—you know, like the Royal

Bodyguard, but one that would be composed solely of eunuchs."

The silence in the room was absolute. Then, "Are you serious?" Hegai asked.

"Well." Esther glanced up at him and then looked back to her finger. "Yes."

"The king does not need another guard unit."

"No, but this could be the Queen's Guard, Hegai. The eunuchs could have their own special uniforms and do their own special drills. They could march in all the processions, have their own weapons, their own horses . . ."

More silence. Esther laid her hand flat on the coverlet and looked at him. "What do you think?"

"I don't know," Hegai said slowly.

"It would give them something to do, you see, something they could take pride in."

"Has the king agreed to this idea?"

"I have not told him about it yet. I thought I would first ask you if you thought it was a good idea."

Hegai looked flattered.

"*Do* you think it's a good idea?"

"It might be," Hegai said.

"Do you think I should approach the king about it?"

"Yes," Hegai said decisively. "I do."

After Hegai had left, Luara came back in to dress Esther for the day.

CHAPTER TWENTY-THREE

I t was the morning of Ahasuerus' monthly Public Audience. This session was meant to be a time when the citizens of the empire had a chance to speak directly to the Great King. The tradition had begun with Cyrus, but under Darius it had evolved into more of a ritual than an actual forum. Only a few petitioners were allowed to approach Darius; the rest were shunted off to a judge or another court official. Darius had never sat for more than an hour at his Public Audience.

Ahasuerus, whose Public Audiences in Babylon had been crowded, was always surprised by the small number of people

who came in Susa. At first he thought it might be because
Darius had made so many improvements in the lives of the
common people that they had few complaints. Ahasuerus had
not liked his father, but he always recognized the value of his
accomplishments.

After a while, however, Ahasuerus began to feel that there
must be something else to account for the paucity of petitioners. No large group of people could be this content.

On this particular morning, Ahasuerus waited for the petitioners in the Great Reception Room of the palace. As usual
he sat upon the Imperial Throne, which was golden with four
lions' feet and had a canopy that was inlaid with jewels and
supported by golden pillars. Behind the throne at these audiences stood a servant holding the royal fly whisk made of the
tail of a wild bull. Another servant to the right of the throne
held a napkin and vase. In front of the servants, to the right
and left of the throne, stood the King's Bowbearer and King's
Lancebearer. In front of the throne two incense bearers were
positioned, indicating by their presence the point to which a
petitioner was allowed to approach.

Ahasuerus himself was dressed as he always was for these
audiences. He wore the king's robes of costly, imperial purple.
Gold bracelets and a gold collar added to the effect, while a
golden girdle supported his sword and in his right hand he
grasped a golden scepter.

Ahasuerus had been brought up with this protocol and had

seen no reason to make any changes. So now he looked out at the handful of people waiting to see him, heads bowed, hands displayed to show there was no threat of assassination, and was puzzled that there were so few.

Haman announced the first petitioner: "My lord, Akis the Merchant begs to approach you."

Ahasuerus nodded his approval.

A tall, gaunt man with a narrow face and severe features approached the throne. He prostrated himself as soon as he reached the incense bearers.

"You may rise," Ahasuerus said.

"My lord." The man rose, glanced quickly at the king, and fell abruptly silent.

"Do you have something you wish to say to me?" Ahasuerus asked in what he hoped was an encouraging voice.

"Yes, my lord." Akis visibly pulled himself together. He cleared his throat. "I have come as a representative of the Susa merchants to ask you to do something about the brigands who inhabit the road between Susa and Persepolis. For years we have been paying them tribute for free passage, but they have become bolder of late, robbing our caravans even though we have paid them not to."

This was not something Ahasuerus was aware of. He frowned. "You are speaking of the Royal Road between Susa and Persepolis?"

"Yes, my lord. These brigands have taken over the heights

of the Persian Gates and no one can get past them. I had two men killed there a month ago, my lord. That is why I have come to the Great King to beg for help."

Two men killed? Ahasuerus' frown deepened. "For how long has this been going on?"

"It is only in the last few months that they have begun to raid the caravans."

"Yes, but for how long have you paid them tribute?"

"Forever, my lord. They are Mardians, and you know how Mardians are, my lord. They care for nothing but their own greed."

"Was Darius aware of this problem?"

The reply was prompt. "My lord, Darius himself paid tribute for passage through the Persian Gates."

Ahasuerus found this astonishing. "I did not know that."

"You were gone in Babylon for many years, my lord. I would not have troubled you, my lord, but the Susa merchants will not be able to send their caravans along that road unless something is done about these brigands. And if we cannot use that road, our businesses will be severely wounded."

Ahasuerus instantly made up his mind. "All of my subjects should be able to use all the Royal Roads without fear—and without having to pay bribes. I will see that this problem is taken care of."

It was a moment before the merchant realized that his request had been granted. His face brightened. "Th-thank you, my lord."

"I am glad that you called this problem to my attention. If

you will wait until this audience is over, I will see that you are reimbursed for the goods that were taken from you."

The merchant's eyes widened. "Thank you, my lord!"

Ahasuerus nodded and looked at Haman, who called the next petitioner.

That evening at dinner Ahasuerus told Esther about his interview with Akis the Merchant. "I am going to have to send a regiment of cavalry to the Persian Gates to clear out the Mardians," he concluded. "This is a situation I cannot tolerate."

They were eating in the small dining room of the royal apartments. Ahasuerus looked forward to these intimate dinners with his wife; he often even shared some of his problems with her. He liked to hear her comments; she was clear thinking and he could count on her telling him what she thought, not what she thought he wanted to hear.

He said, "I cannot believe that my father actually paid tribute to them!"

Esther sipped her water, regarding him over the top of the cup with her beautiful large eyes. "They must be dangerous, these Mardians. I do not think Darius was the kind to pay if he did not have to."

Ahasuerus gave a short laugh. She had perfectly captured his father in those few words. "That is certainly true."

Esther put her water back on the table and the page hurried to refill the goblet.

"Thank you, Niki," she said with a smile. The little boy's face lit up and he smiled back.

Ahasuerus was slowly growing used to the way his wife treated servants. He looked at little Niki's shining face, then back to Esther, who was now eating some lamb. He was relieved to see that her appetite seemed to be coming back. He had been waiting for weeks for her to tell him about the baby. He couldn't imagine why she was keeping it a secret from him.

His mind returned to the morning's session. "I cannot understand why so few people in Susa attend the Public Audience. In Babylon I always had a crowd."

"They are probably afraid to come." Esther patted her lips with a napkin.

He stared at her in astonishment. "Afraid? Why would they be afraid?"

Her eyes shimmered with amusement. "I saw you parading off this morning, my lord, all draped in purple and dripping with gold. You almost scared me."

He frowned. What did she mean? Of course he would properly dress for an audience.

She continued, "Then you probably sit on your golden throne and surround yourself with all your royal paraphernalia."

She looked at him for confirmation. "Of course," he said with dignity. "They have come to see a king, not a shepherd."

She nodded slowly. "You don't think that, under the circumstances, an ordinary person would find it a trifle intimidating to approach you?"

He began to feel a little huffy. "That is how my father always held his Public Audience."

"So I have heard. And how many people did Darius see?"

He liked it when Esther spoke her mind, but he liked it best when she agreed with him. "I held formal audiences when I was in Babylon and they were well attended," he informed her.

Esther ate another slice of lamb and looked at him. "I'll wager they were not as formal as the one you held this morning."

"I was not the Great King then," he retorted quickly.

"That is so. Now you are the Great King, and your people are so in awe of you that they do not feel comfortable coming to you with their problems."

He knew she was right, which irritated him a little. "Do you expect me to entertain them by sitting cross-legged around a campfire?"

Esther chuckled. "I should dearly love to see it."

A choking sound came from Niki. Ahasuerus ignored it.

Esther leaned toward him, the candlelight highlighting the warm glow of her skin. "I am not criticizing you, my lord. I am trying to explain to you why I think so few people attend your Public Audience."

He sipped his wine and thought.

"Perhaps you are right," he conceded after a while.

"Do you really want more people to attend? After all, you have more important things to think about than some trivial quarrel between a miller and his son."

"I don't like to think that my people are afraid to come to me."

"Darius might have needed all the trappings of royalty to appear a king. You do not." She smiled at him warmly. "Even sitting cross-legged around a campfire, my lord, no one would mistake you for other than what you are."

He smiled back. She had made him feel better. She always did. He watched as she cut up an apple and thought that it looked quite tasty. She saw his look and handed him a slice. He ate it with enjoyment.

She said, "This idea of a Queen's Guard seems to have gone over well with the younger eunuchs. I was talking to Hegai today and he sounded quite enthusiastic. They are all excited about choosing a uniform."

"They do realize they are going to have to acquire some military skills?"

"Oh, yes."

"And the older ones?"

"The older ones are mostly content as they are—as are the older women."

He shook his head in amazement. "A contented harem. You do not know how impossible that sounds."

"I am not saying that everyone is content, my lord."

She had no idea what a miracle she had created. "To have *most* of them content is wonderful."

"Well, we still have to find husbands for many of the younger girls. But we are working on it."

"We?"

"Hegai, Muran, and I."

"Excellent," and he extended his hand for another slice of his wife's apple.

CHAPTER TWENTY-FOUR

Ahasuerus had not traveled the Royal Road that went from Susa up the mountains to Persepolis since he was a child. He remembered it as being like the other Royal Roads in the empire, paved in all but the steepest parts with a packed gravel surface. During the good weather the caravans were able to travel daily from one staging place to the next, transporting their goods from one part of the empire to the other and then beyond.

Darius had always prided himself upon the internal security of his empire. Under his rule, ordinary citizens could travel the Royal Roads without fear of bandits, and even when silver was being transported in bulk, a guard of ten men was considered to be sufficient escort. This is why Ahasuerus had been so surprised when he discovered that his father had been allowing the Mardians to collect tribute for safe passage through the Persian Gates.

The Persian Gates was the name given to the impregnable pass on the Royal Road that led to Persepolis. Ahasuerus remembered a narrow gorge cut through the mountain rock, with cliffs soaring sheer above it on either side. It would not take a large party of men on the heights of those cliffs to render the road impassable.

Ahasuerus studied the maps that were available of the area and spoke to several people who were familiar with the road. When he decided what his course of action would be, he summoned the commander of one of his premiere cavalry regiments to give him orders. The commander's name was Cambyses.

Cambyses was surprised by the summons. He had just completed a successful tour commanding the cavalry at Sardis. He had only recently returned to court and had never met Ahasuerus. He dressed carefully in the cavalryman's uniform of embroidered full-sleeved tunic and leather trousers, and presented himself somewhat nervously at the small reception room where the king conducted business.

The king looked perfectly at ease as he sat in an intricately carved chair, his immaculate white robes disposed in perfect folds around him. He wore a thin gold fillet around his brow and the silken fall of his hair shone in the light from the hanging lamp.

The king came directly to the point of the meeting. "I have discovered that the Mardians have been exacting tribute from my subjects in order to pass through the Persian Gates. I have also discovered that my father allowed this. I, however, do not like the fact that my roads are not open to all my subjects. This problem must be dealt with."

Cambyses' heart sank. He looked as levelly as he could at his king, who was a beautiful creature, certainly, but the cavalryman doubted if he knew much about the logistics of mountain warfare. He devoutly hoped that Ahasuerus was not going to ask him to clear the pass with one regiment of men!

He did his best to explain the reality of the situation. "It is true that Darius paid tribute to the Mardians, but it was because that pass is a death trap, my lord. The Mardians have held all the high territory along that part of the Royal Road for years. Believe me, it is much simpler to pay tribute than it would be to try to flush them out." He added belatedly, "My lord."

Ahasuerus said, "It appears, however, that the Mardians

have grown greedier of late. I was told by one of our merchants that they have been taking the merchants' tribute money and then attacking and robbing the caravans as well."

Cambyses scowled when he heard this news. "I did not know that. Have they been attacking royal parties as well?"

"Not yet. However, I do not like the idea of paying tribute to vultures." The king's voice was perfectly pleasant. "It must stop."

Cambyses cursed under his breath. This was what he had been afraid of. "You will lose many men if you try to take that pass, my lord," he said bleakly.

"Perhaps not." Ahasuerus' face looked perfectly serene. Cambyses felt the muscles in his neck and shoulders tighten as he awaited the dreaded words. The king said, "I want you to take your regiment and scout that pass for me, Commander. See if you can get an idea of how many men the Mardians have in place."

Scout the pass. Cambyses began to feel a little better. "They are not just at the Persian Gates, my lord. They also hold the smaller passes that lead up to it."

Ahasuerus' graceful hands were reposing quietly on the arms of his chair. He lifted two fingers now, and his rings sparkled. "Find out exactly where they are," he said.

"Yes, my lord."

"And bring me some shepherds who graze their herds in the mountains around the Royal Road."

"Shepherds, my lord?"

"That is what I said."

The dread that Cambyses had been feeling since the king first mentioned the Persian Gates suddenly lifted. "Yes, my lord," he said, and now his voice had a lilt to it.

"Bring them back here with you."

"Yes, my lord."

"I do not want you to try to take the pass, Commander. Do you understand me? Pay the Mardians their tribute. There is to be no fighting. Just see if you can discover the Mardians' numbers. And bring me back some local shepherds."

Cambyses could not completely conceal his grin. "I understand, my lord."

Ahasuerus nodded in dismissal. "It will be best for you to leave as soon as possible. The snow is already piling up in the mountains."

"Yes, my lord," Cambyses said for the third time.

As the cavalryman left the king's office, he found Mardonius waiting for him in the court outside.

"What was that about?" the king's uncle demanded.

Cambyses, who was related to Mardonius through his mother, told the other man of his commission. When he had finished, Mardonius said, "I am going with you."

This was not good news. Cambyses, who had been with the cavalry that was evacuated from Marathon, was in sympathy with Mardonius' thirst for revenge on the Greeks, but he did not have a high regard for Mardonius as a commander. He said cautiously, "You are welcome to come, of course, Cousin, but I do not think you will find the outing interesting. I have specific orders from the king not to engage in any fighting."

Mardonius looked down his arrogant nose. "I have heard you, Cambyses, and I have said that I will come."

Since the king's uncle outranked him both in nobility and in military standing, the cavalry leader had no choice but to acquiesce.

Esther knew that she could not put off telling Ahasuerus about the baby any longer. Now that she was eating again, her stomach had swollen to the point where it was noticeable. She sat in her night robe before the mirror in her bedroom while Luara combed out her hair.

I will tell him tonight, she thought. Her hair spilled around her like glossy black silk. She smiled at Luara and said, "Remember what it looked like when I first came to the harem?"

Luara smiled back, but as she put down the comb she looked with concern into Esther's eyes.

"Is there anything wrong, my lady? You look sad."

Esther sighed. "Sometimes you can be almost too perceptive, my dear friend."

"I am sorry, my lady. I did not mean to intrude."

Esther shook her head. "You never intrude, Luara."

"Is it something I can help you with?"

"No, I will be all right. Truly."

Luara went to turn the covers back on the bed, then looked inquiringly to where Esther still sat at the dressing table. Esther shook her head. "I am fine. You may go, Luara."

As the door shut behind her maid, Esther stood up and walked to the window, which was securely shuttered against the cold. She looked up toward the sky and lifted her arms in the ancient Jewish attitude of prayer. Then she recited the *Shema*, the prayer that was the foundation of all Jewish faith: *"Hear, O Israel: the Lord our God is one Lord; And you shall love the Lord your God with all your heart, and with all your soul, and with all your might."*

"I believe that," she whispered. "Dearest Father in Heaven, I do believe that. And I will always pray to You in my heart. But I do not see how I will ever be able to worship You in public again. I came here at my uncle's command, and I believe now that Mordecai was right to send me. Because of me, he has become close enough to Ahasuerus to influence him about the Jews. I cannot do anything to risk my uncle's losing that position. If I tell Ahasuerus I am a Jew, he will surely connect me to Mordecai. He would be so angry, Father. My lie would hurt him far more than Vashti's disloyalty ever did. And I will not do that to him. I will not."

The clank of spears sounded as the king's bodyguards stationed themselves outside her door, and she walked to the bed and got in, pulling the covers up to her waist. Ahasuerus entered, closing the door behind him. His slippered feet made no sound on the thick carpet as he approached her.

He was dressed in a night robe made of the finest, whitest linen, having been ceremoniously undressed in his own bedchamber by the high-ranking lords whose turn it was to perform that nightly ritual. He got in next to her and Esther said softly, "You look tired."

He gave her a rueful look out of eyes that were definitely heavier than usual. Without replying he stretched himself flat upon the bed and yawned hugely. "I must be getting old. Two late-night parties in a row and my wife tells me I look tired."

"Those parties must be enjoyable. They would have to be in order to make up for your obvious wretchedness the following day."

"Tired and wretched-looking," he said. "I must be getting *very* old."

She tried not to smile but did not quite succeed.

"I can see that I'm going to have to work tonight to prove that my manhood is unimpaired."

"You have already proved your manhood to me," Esther said. "I'm going to have a baby."

It was out. Just like that. She didn't believe that she had said it. She held her breath and waited for his reply.

He reached out to lace his fingers into hers. "I was wondering when you were going to get around to telling me."

"You know?" Her voice was flat with disappointment. Of all the responses that she had imagined, this was not one of them. She raised herself on her elbow and stared down into his face, faintly affronted. "How can you know? Has someone told you?"

"I already have children. I know the signs." He lifted her hand to his mouth.

She hated the jealousy that always seared her heart when she thought of his children. It wasn't the children, she told herself. Surely she wasn't petty enough to be jealous of children! It was their mothers she disliked.

"That is true," she said in a subdued voice.

"This child will be special, however," he said. He was still holding her hand to his mouth and she could feel his lips brushing against her palm.

"I know. If it is a boy he will be the next Great King."

"I did not mean that." He moved her hand to rest upon his chest. His hair was fanned out around his head, as silken and fine as the Egyptian linen upon which he lay. He smiled up at her, and his face bore no sign of the fatigue she had noticed when he first came in. "This child will be yours. Yours and mine. That is what is special."

The ugly, jealous feeling vanished. "I feel that way too," she whispered.

He tugged on her hand. "Come here to me."

She slid close and nestled against him. His arms encircled her.

"I love you," she whispered. "I would love you even if you were a Mardian bandit."

He chuckled.

"Would you love me if I were somebody else?" she asked cautiously.

"Mmmm," he said.

She bit her lip. Had God given her this moment? Should she, after all— .

"Speaking of being somebody else," he said. "I had to dissolve Enshan's marriage today." Enshan was one of his half brothers.

Esther lay perfectly still, feeling the silkiness of his linen robe under her cheek. "Oh? Why?"

"His wife's family had led him to believe that they held the family estate near Ecbatana and that it would be part of her dowry. It turns out, however, that they misled him; the land belongs to another branch of the family."

"Surely Enshan has lands enough himself," she murmured.

"That is not the point, Esther. The girl's family definitely led him to believe that she would bring him those lands near Ecbatana. That is why he married her."

Esther could feel his breath gently stirring the hair on the crown of her head. She was almost afraid to ask the next question. "He does not care for her, then?"

"Actually, I think he has grown rather fond of her. But he says he cannot allow himself to look like a dupe, and I quite agree."

"Perhaps the girl did not know of her relatives' deception?"

"That is not the point," he repeated. "The point is that the marriage contract was based on a Lie. No marriage can prosper under those circumstances."

"I see," Esther whispered.

His voice changed, softened, his drawl becoming more pronounced. His hands moved caressingly up and down her back. "Would you really love me if I were a Mardian bandit?"

Esther hid her face against his shoulder and shut her eyes. "Yes," she said. "I would."

CHAPTER TWENTY-FIVE

C ambyses patted his horse's neck and surveyed the
ranks of men who were spread out behind him up
and down the snowy slopes of the high mountain
valley. Then he turned to look at what lay ahead. Not ten feet
from where his horse stood, the valley narrowed, the cliff walls
on either side soared steeply upward, and the road became
nothing but a stone gully cut through the mountain. He was
looking at the Persian Gates.

Cambyses lifted his eyes to gaze upon the men who
were standing on top of the cliffs on either side of the pass,

in perfect position to hurl rocks down upon any unwary soul who might venture into the canyon without their permission. He squinted into the gray winter sky and his lips moved as he began to count their numbers.

Mardonius pushed his horse up to stand beside Cambyses. "Bloodsuckers," he muttered, his gaze also raised to the men on the cliff tops. "It is a disgrace that the king's cavalry must pay tribute to bandits for the right to travel along a Royal Road."

Cambyses replied, "We have been doing it for years. Darius said that it was cheaper to pay a toll than it would be to lose men and horses in a fruitless fight."

"That was when we needed all of our forces for the war against the Greeks. Since Ahasuerus shows every intention of humiliating Persia by backing away from the Greek war, the least he can do is clear the roads!"

Cambyses finished counting before he said, "The king instructed me to pay the Mardians their customary toll for the use of the passes so that I could scout the road safely and come back with an estimate of their numbers." He turned to his cousin. "I had the definite impression that he plans to do something about removing the bandits."

This information did not sit well with Mardonius. His lip curled. "My nephew made one lucky military excursion into Egypt, and now he fancies himself a great general. All during the years that the rest of us were fighting Greeks, he sat in

Babylon and played at being a king. He knows nothing of military matters."

"You cannot deny that he was successful in Egypt."

Mardonius' red-brown eyes glittered with scorn. "A child could have pacified Egypt."

Cambyses did not hold Egypt in quite such contempt, but he refrained from saying so to Mardonius. There was sudden movement in the pass, and Cambyses' eyes picked up a horse and rider cantering toward them. "Ah," he said, "the tribute collector comes."

"Bloodsuckers," Mardonius repeated with contempt.

The horse, a sturdy hill pony, pulled up when it was still some twenty feet away. The rider, a swarthy-skinned man with a smile like a knife, said, "It will cost you twenty golden archers to cross the pass."

"*Twenty archers!*" Cambyses was livid. "Your usual fee is ten."

The man's smile never wavered. "The Great King is rich and we are poor. He can spare twenty archers."

Cambyses, who had already seen what he needed to see, said grimly, "He may be able to afford it but he is not going to pay it. My company is turning around and going back to Susa."

"As you wish." The man's dark face wore an expression of infinite disdain. "You will pay tolls for the passes on your way back, however."

"I have already paid the toll to use those passes."

"And you used them. If you want to use them again, you must pay again."

"I paid enough to use them twice!"

Bushy black eyebrows rose in amazement. "Did we say that the price covered two passings?"

"I gave you the customary price for two passings."

"Perhaps the toll collector neglected to tell you that the price has gone up."

Cambyses was so angry he could hardly speak. "I will not pay you any more money."

"Then you cannot use our passes." Casually, the Mardian picked his teeth.

This insult was the final straw for Mardonius. "You filthy, snot-dripping bloodsucker, get out of my sight before I sully my sword with your blood!" His hand, opening and closing, hovered dangerously above his sheathed weapon. For the first time in the encounter, the Mardian looked uncertain.

"You heard the lord," Cambyses snarled. "Get out of here."

After a moment's hesitation, the Mardian turned his pony and galloped back the way he had come.

"Scum," Cambyses said.

"They need to be taught a lesson," Mardonius said.

Still scowling, Cambyses nodded. He blew out through his nose, as if trying to expel the remnants of his temper, and said, "Let's go."

Mardonius stared in astonishment as Cambyses began to turn his horse. "You aren't going back?"

"Of course I'm going back. I have the information I was told to get."

"But what about these Mardians! You can't just let them think that they bested us."

"I have orders to obey," Cambyses said.

Mardonius suddenly whirled his own horse so that he faced the regiment, which was one of the most elite in all the cavalry. "Are we Achaemenids to be bested by a horde of dirty Mardians?" he shouted.

It needed no more to stoke the fire of fierce clan pride. The men had heard the exchange between their leaders and the outlaw, and they were outraged. They shouted back at Mardonius now, some raising their fists, others raising their swords.

"Let's ride through that pass and stuff it in their faces!" someone yelled.

Others took up the battle cry, and before Cambyses could stop them, the men began to gallop their horses toward the entrance of the treacherous gorge. Mardonius galloped with them, shouting as loudly as the rest. Cambyses struggled to contain his horse, to hold back from the charge so that he could secure the lives of the shepherds, who had been traveling at the cavalry's rear.

The horsemen were halfway through the pass when the

first rocks came smashing down. There was no precision in the way the Mardians threw, but the bounding, crushing, erratic shower of stone produced instant chaos in the pass. The horsemen were totally without protection; animals and riders went down under the relentless granite fusillade. Screams went up from men and beasts, and still the rocks rained down. Cambyses looked with horror at the scene before him, at the mangled bloody confusion of flailing hooves and limbs that choked the pass, and felt sicker than he had ever felt in a battle.

"God of the sky, what am I going to tell the king?"

It took Cambyses weeks to make it back to Susa, with the remnant of his once-proud regiment trailing behind him. The king received him in his office, the very place where he had issued the orders not to enter the pass. Cambyses did his best to keep his voice level as he recounted what had happened to one of the most elite regiments in the king's cavalry. He finished, "Mardonius fired them up, my lord. They charged before I could do anything to stop them."

The king's face looked bleak and hard. "How many men did you lose?"

Cambyses gritted his teeth and told him. Ahasuerus' silence was more than intimidating now. It was scary. At last he said, "I did not tell you to take Mardonius."

Cambyses fully realized that this had been his biggest mistake. He tried to explain. "He demanded to come and I did not feel that I could refuse him, my lord. He is a Grand Marshal, after all."

More silence from the king.

Cambyses said a little desperately, "Mardonius survived the attack, my lord. He is hurt, but we managed to get him back to Susa."

From the king's expression, Cambyses understood that Ahasuerus would have been far happier to hear of his uncle's demise.

"I am sorry, my lord," he said. "I did the best that I could. I am sorry it was not enough."

"He acted entirely contrary to my orders." Ahasuerus was furious, and Cambyses could not blame him.

"I told him that, my lord. I told him that my orders were to scout the pass and not provoke the Mardians." He added one more time, knowing it was futile since his career was in ashes, "I am sorry."

Ahasuerus stood and picked up his hat from the elegant desk he had been sitting behind. His mouth set into a thin line as he said, "Thanks to this debacle, I have reason to strip Mardonius of his military rank. It is a great pity that so many men had to die for such a thing."

"Yes, my lord." Cambyses bowed his head.

"But you did bring me some shepherds?"

"Yes, my lord." Cambyses' head came up. "I brought you two handfuls of shepherds whose flocks regularly graze the mountains that flank the Royal Road. And I made certain they are not Mardians."

There was a sharp line between Ahasuerus' brows. "Mardians don't need to graze sheep. They have found an easier way to earn their living."

"They have grown unbelievably arrogant, my lord. In order to get my wounded back to Susa, I had to pay them one hundred golden archers."

Ahasuerus' eyes widened with shock. Then he said, "Well, now they will have to deal with me."

At those words, spoken in that quiet tone, a chill ran up and down Cambyses' spine. Suddenly, and for no logical reason, he was convinced that the king would do it. Even Darius had backed away from the Mardians, but Ahasuerus would beat them.

"I would have liked to go with you," he said impulsively.

Thoughtful gray-green eyes regarded him for a long assessing minute. Then Ahasuerus said, "Why wouldn't you go with me?"

Caught up in that gaze, Cambyses felt his breath begin to come faster. He said with difficulty, "I failed you, my lord. I did not think that you would trust me again."

Ahasuerus looked at the hat in his hands. "Your mistake was in allowing my uncle to accompany you, not in the way you handled the rest of your mission."

Cambyses swallowed. The palms of his hands were wet with sweat. The king asked, "Have you learned from that mistake, Cambyses?"

"Yes, my lord."

"Then I do not think we need to discuss this any longer." Ahasuerus fitted the high cidaris onto his head. "You may return to your duties."

"I . . ." Cambyses took a deep breath and tried again. "Thank you, my lord."

Ahasuerus nodded. The young captain prostrated himself reverently before he backed out of the room.

The following day Ahasuerus went riding, and on his way back to the palace he paid an unannounced visit to his uncle's home in Susa. Mardonius was in bed, but his servants admitted the king.

Ahasuerus stood in the shadows inside the door of his uncle's room, trying to get his temper under control. This man had been his enemy ever since he was a child, and now Ahasuerus was going to destroy him. The next few minutes would feel very good.

Mardonius was propped up against his pillows but he looked terrible. When he saw the king in the door he said in a harsh voice, "Forgive me if I cannot greet you properly, my lord."

Ahasuerus crossed the floor toward his uncle's bed. The shutters were closed for warmth and the overhead lamp had been lit. It swung gently from its ceiling chain as the king passed under it. He reached Mardonius' side and said, his voice unusually clipped, "Others were not so lucky. They died in the Persian Gates because of you."

Mardonius' face was bruised and drawn with pain, but his eyes flashed defiance. "You are wrong. It was the Mardians who killed them, not I."

Utter contempt surged through Ahasuerus. *He is like a worm under my foot*, he thought. "What would it take, I wonder, for you to admit that something is your fault? For you to take responsibility for your own actions?"

"My life has not been as easy as yours, Nephew. My father worshipped you almost from the day that you were born. Nothing was too good for his royal grandson. He had no thought for me, his own son. Everything was for you, the beautiful Ahasuerus."

Abruptly the heat of contempt and disgust left Ahasuerus, leaving him cool and in command of himself. "My own father certainly did not worship me. Darius thought far more highly of you, and of Xerxes, than he ever did of me. He appointed you his Grand Marshal, Mardonius. He gave you command of half his army. And you bungled it—as you have bungled everything you ever set your hand to."

His uncle's fists clenched on the bedcover and his face

twisted with fury. "Darius was a greater soldier than you will ever be, and he trusted me. It is you who are the bungler, Ahasuerus. You fear taking on the Greeks. You have made Persia a laughingstock to the world."

The hotter his uncle became, the colder Ahasuerus felt. "I have been reluctant to take on the Greeks with my father's incompetent commanders in charge. However, I am about to get rid of the most incompetent of them all. You are dismissed from your position as Grand Marshal, Mardonius. In fact, you are dismissed from the army and the court as well."

"What?" Mardonius stared incredulously. When he realized that Ahasuerus was serious, he screamed, "You can't do this to me!"

Ahasuerus raised his brows. "I just have."

"I have my own following," Mardonius threatened. "They won't stand for this."

"Your following consists of Greek exiles who hate Athens and want to use Persia to get revenge. Your other cronies, Smerdis and Teresh, are dead. You have no following, Uncle."

"If I leave court, I will take Xerxes with me," Mardonius threatened.

"That will be his choice to make."

Mardonius pounded his fist upon the bed. "Gods! Why did Darius name you? *Why?*"

"Because, despite his paternal faults, Darius was a king.

Once you have recovered from your injuries, Uncle, you will remove yourself from Susa."

Mardonius opened his mouth to protest again, looked into Ahasuerus' eyes, and fell silent.

"Very wise," Ahasuerus said, his words dropping like chunks of ice. He turned and walked to the door, paused for a moment, then pushed it open with the flat of his hand. Without a backward glance, the king walked out.

Chapter Twenty-Six

Ahasuerus moved quickly once he had dealt with Mardonius. He interviewed the shepherds Cambyses had brought back to Susa and he spent long hours in discussion with his military commanders. Finally, after he was certain everything he wanted was in place, he gave orders for the Immortals, along with the Royal Guard, to prepare for a march up the mountain passes to the Persian Gates.

The king's intense involvement with military matters left Haman feeling as if Ahasuerus had forgotten him. Haman was jealous of the time the king spent with Coes. He was jealous of the time the king spent with the queen. Most of all, he was jealous of the time the king spent with Mordecai, as the two of them went over the costs of the campaign. Haman tried a number of times to get an appointment to speak to the king, but Ahasuerus kept putting him off. When finally he was summoned to the king's office, he was determined to make Ahasuerus understand that Haman was the person he could trust; that Haman was the person who was always looking out for the king's interests; that it was Haman who was his truest friend.

Ahasuerus was sitting behind his elegant desk when Haman came in. He had some papers in front of him, which surprised Haman, as the king did not read. Coming closer, however, Haman saw that the papers contained drawings and numbers. *Military matters*, he supposed grimly.

He halted in front of the desk. Ahasuerus was dressed in riding clothes and he looked up to give Haman a brief smile. "I know you have been trying to see me, old friend, but I have been busy. We are leaving in two days for the mountains, and there is still much to be done. I do, however, have a few things I must discuss with you before I go."

"And I have something to discuss with you, my lord," Haman returned.

Ahasuerus folded his ringless hands in front of him and said courteously, "I am listening."

"What I wish to speak about is directly related to the campaign against the Mardians, my lord."

A lifted eyebrow invited him to continue.

"I know you have been concerned with the military and financial aspects of the campaign, my lord, but I am concerned about the historical aspects."

"Historical?" Ahasuerus echoed, clearly bewildered.

"Yes, my lord. A king's reputation only survives through the concrete evidence he leaves behind him. I know the Persians are not as concerned about written records as are the Babylonians, but in this matter I think you must be attentive to the future."

The king said impatiently, "Haman, what are you talking about?"

Haman drew himself up. "It is my duty as your Grand Vizier to inform you, my lord, that when a Persian king moves against his own subjects, it is necessary for him to issue a proclamation stating his reasons for taking such an action. That is the law, my lord. You cannot take legal action against the Mardians without doing this."

Ahasuerus frowned. "I have never heard of such a law. My father certainly did not issue a proclamation every time he went to war!"

"This is the first time I have ever heard you cite Darius as a model, my lord," Haman retorted.

A rueful smile flitted across Ahasuerus' face. "That is so. But who would read such a proclamation, Haman? What is the point of it?"

Haman leaned forward, urgent to convince. "It will become part of the royal records, my lord. Believe me when I tell you that it *is* important. It will reflect on your reign and show to the generations to follow that you were a just and fair king." He straightened. "I am only concerned for *you* in this, my lord. I would never want your excellent intentions to be misconstrued, not now, not ever."

Ahasuerus waved a hand. "All right, all right. If you think it is so important, we will have a proclamation. You can write it yourself."

"I will be happy to do so, my lord. What do you wish it to say?"

Ahasuerus thought for a moment. "Say that my reason for moving against the Mardians is to rid the empire of a pack of bloodsuckers. I will leave the exact wording up to you."

Haman was hurt that Ahasuerus clearly wanted to get rid of him so he could return to military matters. He said stiffly, "Very well, my lord. I will draw it up and bring it to you tomorrow for your approval."

"As to that . . ." Ahasuerus opened the top of an intricately carved wooden box that stood on the corner of his desk and lifted out a cylindrical object. Haman knew the object well. It was the Royal Seal, made of lapis lazuli and capped on both ends with gold foil. The picture on the seal itself showed Ahasuerus standing beside a chariot and shooting arrows at a lion, which reared up on his hind legs like a half-human demon.

Two date palms framed the scene and in the sky between them appeared the symbol of Ahuramazda. The king's name and title, "Ahasuerus, Great King," were inscribed in Persian, Elamite, and Babylonian.

Ahasuerus said, "One of the reasons I wished to see you was to put my seal directly into your keeping. The business of the empire cannot simply grind to a halt while I am in the mountains. You know my mind better than anyone, Haman, and if there are decisions to be made, I know you will make them as I would wish you to." He smiled. "Your first action in my name can be to affix my seal to this proclamation you want so badly."

Haman's heart almost burst with pride at this sign of Ahasuerus' regard and trust. His own hand trembled as he received the precious seal from the king's slender fingers.

"Th-thank you, my lord. I will pray for your safe return."

"Thank you, Haman."

There was a pause while Ahasuerus looked down at his desk. When he spoke again, his voice was brisk and business-like. "There is one more thing I wish you to write down and sign with my seal."

"Yes, my lord?"

"Write that should I not return from this campaign, I name Xerxes as my heir."

Haman's mouth dropped open. "*Xerxes*, my lord?"

Ahasuerus' face was unreadable. "We must hope that he has grown up a little in the last few years."

"But . . . what of the queen's child?"

"I cannot name a baby to be Great King. It would be disastrous for the empire. Darius was able to put aside his personal affections and name the heir he thought would be best for the empire, and I must do the same. It has to be Xerxes."

Haman stared at him in consternation.

Ahasuerus smiled. "Come, Haman, don't look so dismal. I have every intention of returning to Susa. I am making this disposition only because it is my duty to cover all the contingencies. Now, give me your parting kiss and let me go. Coes is waiting for me in the stable yard."

Haman approached the king and touched his mouth to the cool skin that stretched over Ahasuerus' cheekbone. He began to withdraw, one pace, two paces, three paces away. At the door he said, "Do not worry, my lord. I will see to your commissions and safeguard your empire."

Ahasuerus smiled. "I know you will, my friend."

In the hallway outside, waiting his turn to see the king, was Mordecai. Haman could feel the blood draining from his face as he beheld the Jew. His fists clenched involuntarily, but Mordecai walked past him as if he were invisible and disappeared into Ahasuerus' office.

All of Haman's satisfaction fled as the door closed behind the Jew. As he walked down the corridor he was not thinking that the king had made him Grand Vizier and entrusted him with the Royal Seal; he was not thinking that his was the highest position in the land after the king himself, or that while Ahasuerus was on campaign he, Haman, would be the virtual Great King of Persia. In truth, Haman was not interested in the kind of power that drew most men.

What Haman wanted was quite simple: he wanted to be the most important person in Ahasuerus' life. Political power was only important to him as a sign of the king's regard; it meant nothing otherwise. Stewing in Haman's mind was the fear that his rival Mordecai was trying to insinuate himself into Ahasuerus' affections and that he might be succeeding.

All these years I have stood by him, Haman fumed. *I was his friend in Babylon when he was an untried youngster. I have always looked out for his interests, putting them above my own. And how does he repay me? He gives his trust and friendship to a Jew!*

As he continued to walk down the corridor, Haman's whole body shook as if he had been infected by a fatal fever.

Like everyone else in the palace, Esther had been shocked to learn about the men who had been cut to pieces by the Mardians, and she fully understood Ahasuerus' fury with Mardonius, although it frightened her a little. With her he was always so different.

If only she could rid herself of the dread that Ahasuerus would find out who she was! Yes, he loved her, but he thought that the person he loved was the daughter of a Babylonian mother, not a Jew. The image of Vashti was hard to dismiss from her mind. Ahasuerus was capable of great gentleness, but in the end, he was a king. He would not take kindly to being duped.

Then she learned that Ahasuerus was planning to lead the next attack against the Mardians himself and she panicked. Surely his presence was not necessary. He had thousands and thousands of soldiers; why could they not do the job without him? Why couldn't he send Coes? Why did he have to go himself?

When she poured all of these questions out to him, he patted her arm soothingly and said she was not to worry. He was not Mardonius and he would certainly not throw away his men by leading them into an impossible situation. They would be safe, and he would be safe, and she was not to worry. Then he buried himself in preparations for the coming campaign, evidently feeling that there was nothing more to be said on the topic of any possible danger to his life.

But Esther had a terrifying fear that God might take Ahasuerus from her to punish her for deserting her religion. She had been praying less and less of late. It was hard to pray; praying reminded her of her duplicity, and she was trying not to think about that. She was doing her best to live in the present, where she was happy. Thoughts of the future made her anxious and fearful. It was better not to let her mind go that way.

But Esther knew her scripture and she knew of the numerous instances where God had wreaked punishment on those who fell away from His worship. He had caused entire cities to be destroyed in some cases. One man would be as nothing to Him.

What if such punishment was about to fall on her and her innocent husband?

He had stopped coming to her bed because he was always so late he said he didn't want to disturb her. But her sleep was restless and her dreams showed her nightmare images of Ahasuerus lying dead on the cold mountainside. She would lie in her solitary bed, her heart crying out, *I cannot live without you, Ahasuerus. I cannot. I cannot.*

The evening before the army was departing, Ahasuerus sent her a message saying he would come to her that night. Esther waited in her bedroom, trying to summon up her courage. *I am a soldier's daughter*, she thought. *I must be brave. Ahasuerus expects that of me. I cannot send him away with the image of a weeping wife in his mind.*

The charcoal in the brazier had burned down and the room was cold when finally the bedroom door opened and Ahasuerus came in. Esther was sitting up in the canopied bed, with the covers pulled up to her chin, and she did not speak as she watched him close the door quietly behind him.

He said, "I was afraid you might have gone to sleep. I spent more time than I had planned with Coes."

She looked at him mutely.

He crossed the floor, sat on the bed next to her, and picked up her hand. "There is something I must tell you, my love. I want you to hear this from me and not from someone else."

Esther's heart began to hammer. The skin had tightened over his cheekbones the way it always did when he was worried. "What is it?" she whispered.

"I have left instructions with Haman that, in the event of my death, Xerxes is my heir."

The bottom dropped out of Esther's stomach at those words. *He has named his heir. He thinks he is going to die.*

She stared at him in mute terror.

He misunderstood the reason for her silence. "I am sorry, Esther, but I could not name our child. The one sure way to tear an empire apart is to put a child on the throne. Surely you can see that?" He leaned toward her, his hand tightening on hers. "Esther? You are always so clear-headed. Can't you understand that?"

Her voice came out as a hoarse whisper. "You told me there was no reason for me to worry. You promised me that you would come back from this campaign safely. You promised!"

His face relaxed. "Of course I will come back safely. I merely felt that it was my duty to the empire to name an heir."

Her heart was pounding in her chest.

"I should not have told you this." He was clearly annoyed with himself for distressing her. "Believe me, Esther, I have every intention of living long enough for our son to grow old enough to succeed me. I only told you because I didn't want you to hear about Xerxes from someone else and misunderstand my reasons for not naming our child."

She hardly heard him. She said out loud the words that were in her mind, "You think you are going to die."

He said slowly and clearly, "I do not think I am going to die. You are to put that thought out of your head."

All her good intentions of not burdening him with her fears had died the minute he had mentioned naming his heir. She pressed her free hand to her mouth. "Ahasuerus. I am so afraid. My father died in battle. Why shouldn't it happen to you as well?"

He swung his legs onto the bed to sit beside her against the pillows and cradle her in his arms. "Listen to me, my love. There is not even going to be a battle. I will come back safely— you have my solemn promise on that."

Her eyes clung to his. He was so calm, so certain. Comfort began to creep into her heart.

"No battle?" she whispered.

"No battle. We will all come home safe and sound. All of us. I promise."

She let out her breath and let herself begin to relax against him. He bent his head and murmured in her ear, "Do you think you might have enough energy left to give me a proper good-bye?"

She sniffled and managed a trembling smile. Her lips moved. "Yes."

Afterward, Esther pressed her forehead against his shoulder. "I love you so much. You could search the earth over and you'd never find anyone who could love you more than I do."

"I *did* search the earth over," he reminded her.

"That is so." She gave a husky chuckle.

His hand was gently stroking her long hair. "You are the very heart of my life. Always before, I was alone. Now there is you."

She lifted her head so she could see his face. "There are many people who love you, Ahasuerus."

His face was grave as he returned her look. "There are many people who love the image they have made of me."

Tears stung her eyes at this picture of his loneliness. He pressed her face against his shoulder once more and his cheek came down to rest on her head. "With you," he said, "I have come home."

CHAPTER TWENTY-SEVEN

The first part of Ahasuerus' expedition went with exemplary smoothness. Since it was not a time of year when armies usually moved, the Mardian bandits holding the lower passes were completely surprised by the king's appearance. The surprise, coupled with the sheer numbers of men who marched in the king's train, intimidated the bandits into allowing the king's forces to pass without paying tribute. So Ahasuerus and his attending army advanced without incident until they reached the impregnable Mardian stronghold at the Persian Gates.

The bandits at the lower passes had obviously sent word ahead to their fellow tribesmen that the king was coming, for the cliffs that towered above the treacherous pass were crowded with men, a sight clearly meant to daunt the king. The winter snow on the road was still as high as the horses' hocks, the air was frigid, and the way ahead looked impassable without paying off the Mardians.

Ahasuerus stopped his troops at the base of the pass and waited, with Coes and Cambyses at his side. As they had done before, the Mardians sent a man to collect tribute for the use of the pass. It was the same man who had come the last time, and Ahasuerus immediately ordered him taken into custody. There was some activity on the heights as the bandits watched their messenger being led away, but Ahasuerus merely ordered his men to make camp for the night at a safe distance from the heights. Then he waited for night to fall.

Under cover of darkness, a force of two hundred hand-picked men slipped away from the Persian camp and met with the king, who was waiting for them with two shepherds and Hathach. Coes, the commander of the small force, was the only one who knew what the king had planned.

Ahasuerus said, "These shepherds know a goat track that will take you up and around the mountain and bring you in behind the Mardians. You must go on foot; it is too steep and snow-covered for horses. It is vital that you reach the heights before dawn breaks."

The men looked at each other uneasily as they understood the king's intent.

"At dawn I will show myself at the pass," Ahasuerus went on. "I will have the Magi make libations, as if I were planning to attempt a crossing. Once I have their attention, you will attack them from the rear. Their weapons are simple; they should make easy targets."

"My lord!" It was Milis' voice rising from the lines of men in front of the king. "Can we trust these shepherds? What if they are Mardian sympathizers leading us into a trap?"

A rustle among the chosen troops greeted this inquiry. The men were worried about how the Great King would react to being questioned by a mere lieutenant and worried as well that perhaps the question was valid.

"Hathach?" Ahasuerus said quietly.

"The shepherds are to be trusted," the young eunuch, who had been born into a mountain tribe, reported. "The king sent me ahead with them to check the track. It is as my lord has said, steep and dangerous, but passable."

The heads of the shepherds bobbed up and down in vigorous agreement and smiles began to appear among the gathered men.

Coes said, "Let us make ready to depart. Everyone is to carry bows and plenty of arrows."

Following Hathach and the shepherds, the cream of Persia's cavalry took to the mountains on foot. The track was as difficult and dangerous as predicted, but the men forged on with grim determination, scrambling ever upward on their hands and knees through the snow-covered rocks of the bleak, frigid mountainside.

They reached the top of the cliff as the moon disappeared from the sky. The men drew up into firing lines and prepared their weapons, expecting that the Mardians would have sentries guarding their backs. There was no one.

"They're only bandits after all," Coes muttered to Hathach. "Don't even have the sense to protect their rear."

Hathach's teeth gleamed white. "That will make it easier for us."

And easy it was. As the first light began to stain the sky, Ahasuerus had the Magi pour libations to the rising sun. The Mardians on the cliffs watched the activity of the Persian army with riveted intensity, each man standing poised beside his pile of rocks expecting to have to use them shortly. The snow helped the men coming in on their rear to move silently, and it was not until the Mardians heard the cry of the first man with an arrow in his back that they realized they had been surprised.

Ahasuerus stood at the entrance to the pass and watched as the bodies of Mardians rained down from the cliff tops. In half an hour's time, Coes had built the agreed-upon fire signal on the heights, and Ahasuerus committed his army to the pass.

It took them four more days to clean the remaining

Mardians out of their strongholds. Those who did not die in the fighting, Ahasuerus sent under guard to Persepolis. When the snow had melted, he said, he would consider what would be their final fate.

Then the king turned for home.

Esther and Luara sat together in Esther's reception room, which over the last few months had gradually been transformed from an elegant, silk-hung chamber into a busy and untidy office. On Hegai's most recent visit, he had looked at the scrolls piled on the large table Esther had installed and said, his admiration mixed with amusement, "You have come a long way for a woman who wanted nothing to do with court life, my lady."

Esther and Luara had drawn even closer in the month since the army expedition had left for the Persian Gates. They both had someone they loved in danger, and it was a relief for them to have someone to talk to about their fears.

Today the two were engaged in looking at the fabrics and colors Hegai had suggested for the uniforms of the queen's new Eunuch Guard. They were sitting on the floor, surrounded by swatches of material and exchanging comments, some of them amusingly derogatory, about Hegai's extravagant taste, when Hegai himself tapped upon the door. Esther looked up from a swatch she and Luara had been giggling about and called, "Come in, Hegai."

The Chief Eunuch's face was grave as he stepped into the room. "My lady, your grandfather, Arses, requests an interview with you. He says it is urgent."

Terror struck Esther's heart and her hand gripped the fabric swatch so tightly that her knuckles showed white. "The king? Is he all right?"

Hegai hastened to assure her. "It is nothing to do with the king or the army. Arses was clear about that."

Esther started to breathe again. "All right, then." She put the fabric sample back on the floor next to the others and began to get to her feet. "I will see him immediately."

Hegai and Luara rushed to help her rise. "Where do you wish to meet with him?" Hegai asked when she was safely upright.

Esther gestured to the one empty divan. "Here in my office, I suppose."

Hegai's eyes swept with disapproval around the cluttered room. He looked back to Esther.

She sighed.

"All right, Hegai. I will not offend your sensibilities by entertaining my grandfather in the midst of such disorder. Bring him to the king's reception room and I will speak to him there."

Hegai did not even blink at her casual appropriation of the king's room. "Very well, my lady. I will do that."

"Do you want me to come, my lady?" Luara asked.

Esther gave her a reassuring smile. "It's not about the army, Luara. I had better see him myself, I think." She put a hand to her lower back, then moved to the door.

Ahasuerus' reception room felt desolate and empty as she walked in. All of the warmth of his presence had gone from it. She avoided looking at Ahuramazda's golden disk on the wall and walked to the window that looked out upon the cold winter garden. She had no idea what her grandfather might want, but she had a feeling she would not like it.

When Arses came in she turned and waited for him to kiss her cheek. "I am glad to see you, Grandfather," she said as he stepped back. "I hope all is well?"

His arrogant black brows were drawn together in a worried frown. She said, "Hegai told me Ahasuerus is all right. That is true, isn't it?"

"Yes," he replied. "Ahasuerus is safe, Esther. You need not worry about him."

"Then what is it? You seem . . . perturbed."

He reached under his wool tunic and drew out a rolled parchment. "Since I understand you can read, I think you had better read this for yourself. It is a copy of the king's decree that was proclaimed in Susa yesterday. One of your Jewish neighbors brought it to me and asked me to bring it to you."

He extended the scroll to Esther, who unrolled it and began to read:

The Great King, Ahasuerus, writes to the satraps of the twenty provinces from India to Egypt, and the governors subordinate to them, as follows: Know you that there is one tribe of bad will living among us, which by its laws is opposed to every other people and continually disregards the decrees of kings, so that the unity of empire designed by us cannot be established.

Having noted, therefore, that this most singular people is continually at variance with all men, lives by divergent and alien laws, is inimical to our interests, and commits the worst crimes, so that stability of government cannot be obtained, we hereby decree that all Jews living in our empire, together with their wives and children, must leave their present dwelling places and places of business and return to the land of their origin, as once was ordered by our father, Cyrus.

If they do not obey this decree by the fourteenth day of the month of Adar of the current year, then they shall be utterly destroyed by the swords of their enemies.

Esther's first thought was that this must be some kind of hoax, except that Ahasuerus' seal was affixed to the bottom of the page. She looked up at her grandfather in white-faced shock.

"Ahasuerus did not write this! He would never order such a thing! He has not even been in Susa for the last six weeks!"

Arses said, "We think this is Haman's doing, Esther. When the king went on campaign he left his Royal Seal in Haman's keeping and this is how Haman has repaid his trust. I knew he should never have appointed a Palestinian to such a high position!"

Esther looked back at the scroll, not believing what she had just read. Surely even Haman would not dare to do such a thing behind Ahasuerus' back.

Arses said, "Come and sit down, Granddaughter. You are as white as that scroll."

She allowed him to lead her to the divan facing the Ahuramazda disk. As soon as she was seated she turned to him. "No one who knows Ahasuerus will believe that he would order such a thing. There is no reason for it. It's the Mardians he was going after, not the Jews. Why did you come to me, Grandfather? It's Mordecai you should be speaking to."

"Esther . . ." Arses hesitated, then went on with slow gravity, "Haman has had Mordecai arrested on charges of embezzling gold from the Treasury."

"What?" She stared at him as if he were speaking a foreign language.

"I am afraid it is true," he said.

"It is not true. Uncle Mordecai would never steal anything!"

Arses held up his hand, as if to stop her rush of words. "I know that, Granddaughter. I may not like Mordecai, but

I would never doubt his honesty. You must see, though, that accusing Mordecai of such a crime gives Haman justification for moving against the Jews."

Esther pressed her hands over her eyes, trying to think clearly. At last she looked up, saying firmly, "Ahasuerus will never allow this to happen. Haman has overreached himself. Ahasuerus will be outraged that Haman dared to use his name to perpetrate such a monstrous deed. It is Haman who will find himself on trial, not Uncle Mordecai."

Arses picked up her hand and held it in a firm clasp. "The point is, Esther, Ahasuerus is not here."

The true horror of the situation dawned on Esther. The date set in the decree had been the fourteenth day of Adar and the month of Adar had already started. "He must come home immediately, Grandfather. You must send someone to get him." She gripped Arses' arm in her anxiety. "I cannot countermand the Grand Vizier. I do not have the power."

He put his hand over hers, a warm, solid grip. "I realize that, my dear. What you must do is send for the king yourself. He will listen to a message from you, Esther."

Esther shivered with panic. "But whom can I send? Everyone who would obey a commission of mine is with the king."

"Send Hathach," Arses replied immediately, clearly having thought this out. "He is a good horseman, and you can trust him. It must be Hathach."

"But Hathach is with Ahasuerus, Grandfather!" she cried.

Arses scowled. "I did not know that."

An idea finally stirred in Esther's shocked brain. "I know what we can do. I have my own guard now, who are sworn to serve me. I will send some men from my Eunuch Guard."

Arses' eyes narrowed. "I have heard nothing of a Eunuch Guard. What is it?"

Esther told him.

Arses shook his head emphatically. "I would not trust a task this critical to a bunch of untrained eunuchs."

"You wanted to send Hathach," Esther objected.

"Hathach may be a eunuch but he has the heart of a man. I don't know about these others. No, I will go myself." His fierce, dark eyes met Esther's. "Too many lives are at stake here, Esther, to take any chances."

She turned her fingers so that she could return his grasp. "Thank you, Grandfather," she whispered.

"It would be a black mark on Persia forever if such a thing were to be done to helpless people." He squeezed her hand and then released it. "Have you heard anything at all from the king? Do you know where he might be?"

"I have heard nothing. He could be anywhere between here and the Persian Gates. When was this decree published?"

"It was published yesterday in Susa, but I understand that riders left a week ago for the rest of the empire. That Palestinian weasel waited until he was certain the time would be too short for the Jews to escape."

Esther's breath caught in her throat. Haman had calculated well.

"Pray to that God of yours that I reach the king quickly," Arses said.

"I will," she promised. Then, as Arses got up to leave, she reached out to hold his arm. "Wait—what about Uncle Mordecai? Where is he now? Will he be safe until Ahasuerus gets here?"

"Mordecai is being held in Haman's own house. The weasel is taking no chances of losing his prey, but he must hold a trial before he can execute your uncle. Fortunately, the celebration of the vernal equinox is upon us and no trials can be held until it is over. I hope to be back with the king by then."

The vernal equinox was an important religious holiday for Persians. It was the time of year when the dark part of the day was surpassed by the light, and Persians saw in this change a symbol of the eternal struggle waged between Ahuramazda, god of light, and the Evil Spirit symbolized by the Dark. The celebration went on for three days. On the day before the equinox, the Magi rekindled the sacred fire in the temples outside the city. On the day of the equinox, there was a great royal banquet at the palace. The following day, the king concluded the religious ceremonies by making a visit to Ahuramazda's sacred spring in the mountains. A variety of rituals were held in ordinary Persian households during this three-day period also. Most importantly for Mordecai, during this holy period no public business could be transacted.

"If Ahasuerus is still at the Persian Gates, you will not reach him in time to prevent a trial," Esther said despairingly.

"Then for Mordecai's sake, we must hope that the king has finished his business with the Mardians and is on his way home," Arses replied.

Esther drew a deep, steadying breath. "If you have not returned, and if Haman calls Uncle Mordecai to a trial, then I will speak to the Head Judge myself and tell him that Uncle Mordecai is a friend of my family and that the king would not wish such a trial to take place in his absence. I think Sisames will listen to me and wait."

Arses nodded his approval. "I think he will too. It is common knowledge around the court that you have great influence with the king. No judge would dare to execute a man you favor without Ahasuerus' knowledge."

"I will pray for you, Grandfather," Esther said fervently.

Arses nodded and said stoutly, "I will do my best, Granddaughter. And with the help of the wise lord, Ahuramazda, I will succeed."

Two days before the vernal equinox, Arses, with three of his own men riding alongside of him, left Susa. Desperate to cover as much ground in as short a time as possible, he decided to take a shortcut through the hill country and pick up the Royal

Road at a point southeast of Susa. The track he chose was narrow and rough, but four men unencumbered by baggage could save a day by taking it. Neither he, nor anyone else in Susa, could know that the king was within a day's ride of the city and that Arses, in taking the shortcut, would connect with the Royal Road behind Ahasuerus, and never know that he had missed the king.

CHAPTER TWENTY-EIGHT

It was the day before the vernal equinox and the city was buzzing with news of the king's triumphant return. Ahasuerus had conquered the Mardians and the Royal Road was open again. There would be no more tolls. The citizens of Susa prepared to have the best vernal equinox celebration ever seen in the city.

Hathach rode into Susa early in the afternoon with a group of men from the Royal Bodyguard. They had left the king and some of the Royal Kin at Ahuramazda's sacred temple to the north of the city, where the Magi would rekindle the god's sacred flame. Ahasuerus would remain at the temple until tomorrow, when he would come into Susa for the feast that would celebrate the day of the equinox.

Hathach left his horse with a groom, something he rarely did, preferring to look after his pride and joy himself. Today, however, he was anxious to see Luara so he could tell her all about the king's brilliant plan and how well it had succeeded. Nor did he plan to hold back anything about his own part in the victory. Luara would be so proud of him.

Luara was in the queen's reception room. Hathach knew Esther would also want to hear all about the Mardian defeat, and he had a smile on his face when he knocked. The first thing he saw as he stepped into the room was the glint of Luara's bright hair. She was sitting on the floor with a pile of fabric next to her, and when she saw him she jumped to her feet and ran into his arms.

He hugged her, kissed her chastely on the cheek, and assured her that he was well. Then he looked at Esther, who was sitting at the scroll-piled table, a pen in her hand.

She was smiling at him, but her face looked tense and strained. He turned back to Luara and saw the same shadow in her blue eyes. "What is wrong?" he asked.

Luara told him briefly about the decree, then Esther picked up one of the scrolls from her table and read the exact words out loud to him.

Hathach could not remember ever being so angry. He

worshipped Ahasuerus, and for Haman to have done this . . . to have made it look as if the king would issue such an evil, merciless order! Even with the Mardians, who had attacked his own troops, he had made certain that the women and children were carried to safety.

Hathach choked back the language he would like to use and said instead, "Haman didn't think the king would defeat the Mardians in such a short time. I wish I could be there when that traitor has to explain himself to Ahasuerus!"

"I need to see the king first, Hathach." Esther was pale. "He is returning to the palace tomorrow for the feast, is he not? Hegai has brought me a note from the Jewish community in Susa. They write that if the decree is not revoked immediately, there won't be time to send couriers to Egypt to stop the massacre. They have begged me to try to persuade the king to revoke this edict."

Hathach wondered why the Jewish community would be writing to the queen, but it was not his place to ask. Instead he tried to explain to her why it would be impossible to see the king tomorrow.

"My lady, perhaps you do not fully understand the religious requirements of the equinox holy days. Followers of Ahuramazda are required to keep themselves separate from women during these three days. The king will return to the palace only to attend the royal feast. He will not come to see you; it would be against his beliefs to do so. He will not even sleep in his palace apartment, but will return to the mountains directly after the feast so as to be at Ahuramazda's sacred spring in time for the dawn."

Esther still had the decree in her hands and now she looked down at it, then returned her gaze to Hathach. "Do you mean I will not be able to see the king until the day after tomorrow, when he returns to Susa from the sacred spring?"

If he returns from the sacred spring. Hathach hesitated, then said, "My lady, the king has often chosen to go hunting for a few days when he is out in the mountains after the equinox. It is possible he will be away from Susa for another week."

Esther went so white that both Hathach and Luara stepped toward her. She waved them away. "Can *you* get to see him, Hathach?"

Hathach felt wretched. "I wish I could, my lady, but I am not a follower of Ahuramazda. I will not be allowed near their religious rites. I won't even be able to get a message to him when he arrives at the palace for the banquet. No one will deliver it."

Esther nodded slowly, her great dark eyes almost black in the pallor of her face.

"I can try, of course," Hathach said. "I will be happy to try, my lady. I am just afraid I will not succeed."

Esther nodded again. "Leave me, please, the both of you. I have some things I must think about, and you will want some time to yourselves too."

Luara took another step toward her. "My lady, you are so pale. Please, let me get you something to eat and drink."

"No, Luara. I am fine. You and Hathach go. I will send for you when I have decided what I must do."

"Yes, my lady," Hathach replied, took Luara by the arm, and steered her out of the room.

After her two attendants had left, Esther went into her bedroom. She was exhausted but she had to think. She lay on the big bed she shared with Ahasuerus and curled up in a protective ball around the baby in her womb.

So this was why all the seemingly impossible things that had happened to her had happened. There had been a reason all along. God had had a plan for her from the moment she had been born. She had not believed it when Mordecai had told her so. In fact, she had done everything she could to escape from it.

She had tried not to be chosen by the king.

Then she had tried to give up her religion. When Mordecai received his high appointment, she had thought that God's plan for her had been accomplished. She would be the wife that Ahasuerus wanted and her children would be brought up as followers of Ahuramazda. Her duty to her people was done.

And now there was this brutal reality. Even Mordecai was helpless against this evil. It was up to her to act—to save her people. She had to see Ahasuerus. Her own little life was as nothing compared to the enormity of what would happen if she did not act. But, even now, she was not strong enough to put her personal feelings out of her mind.

Once she told Ahasuerus she was a Jew, she would lose him. Her lie would be like a dagger in his heart. It would be a wound he would never forget, never forgive.

She pressed her hands against the swell of her stomach and whispered, "My little baby. I have no choice. Your mother has no choice. I don't know what will happen to us, but this is what God has called me to do. Me!"

The idea was unbelievable still. All the anguish she had endured while making the decision to choose Ahasuerus over her religion, all of it had been for nothing. The decision had never been hers; it had been God's all along. An evil force had been set loose in the empire and now the whole Jewish race was faced with annihilation. Unless she acted.

Her heart bled for Ahasuerus. Haman's betrayal would break his heart, and then she would have to tell him that she had been lying to him from the moment they met. She would give everything she had not to have to do this. But, for the first time since she had agreed to become a candidate for queen, she actually *felt* that she was an instrument of God. He had chosen her to save His people, and that had to come first.

Before her husband.

Before her child.

Before the anguish in her own heart.

She knew what she had to do. The only chance she had to see Ahasuerus would be at the palace banquet tomorrow night. She thought about the banquet scene and about what her own actions must be to get to him. The feast would be held in the Service Court, and she would have to get by the guards and enter that huge room, alone and unveiled, in front of the eyes of all the gathered men. She would have to go unveiled, because Persian law decreed that any unknown person who approached the king without his permission would be considered an assassin and instantly executed. It was crucial that Ahasuerus recognize her immediately and extend his golden scepter to grant her life. Then she would beg him to save her people.

She thought of what his face would look like, how the protective mask would come across it, and he would look at her as if she were a stranger. She began to cry and, once started, she couldn't stop.

When finally she was too exhausted to weep any further, she began to pray: *Dearest Father in Heaven, I didn't know it, but You were working through me all along; what happened to me was always part of Your plan.*

I once told Uncle Mordecai that I was no Moses, but You have called me to do as Moses once did. You have called me to save my people, not from slavery this time, but from extinction. I will do this humbly, knowing that I am but Your servant whom You have chosen to do Your work.

But . . . I am not Moses, Father. I am only a woman. A woman who loves her husband and her child. If it is possible, could You make Ahasuerus understand why I do this? Could You let him still love me . . . just a little? I know my broken heart is as nothing compared to the enormity of what my actions will prevent, but . . . please let him still love me.

After a while, she called Hathach and Luara into the room and told them what she was going to do. She ended by saying to Hathach, "Go to the Jewish community and tell them that they must gather all the Jews of Susa, even those who no longer follow the Torah. Tell them that every one of them must fast until tomorrow, at the time I go to the king. Tell them that I shall fast as well. And all must pray for me, that my mission to the king is successful and my people are saved."

It was a moment before the words *my people* registered with Luara. She stared at Esther and repeated them. "What do you mean, my lady?"

Brown eyes met blue. "I am a Jew, Luara. The Lord my God sent me here for exactly this action at this time. This was His plan, and I will execute it."

"My lady . . ." Luara's voice was trembling. "Think of what the king did to Vashti, and what she did by not coming at his command is as nothing compared to what you are planning to do tomorrow. It is . . . it is a sacrilege."

Hathach said, "Cannot I do this for you, my lady?"

Esther managed a smile. "You said yourself they would never let you in. They must let me in; I am the queen. No, Hathach, I thank you, but it must be I who does this thing."

Luara and Hathach looked at each other. Hathach spoke for both of them. "Then we will go with you."

When Haman learned of the king's presence outside Susa, he felt for one dreadful moment like a man suspended over an abyss who hears the *crack* of the tree branch to which he has been clinging. At any second he would find himself falling onto the cruel rocks below.

I must prove Mordecai guilty.

This was his only hope. If Ahasuerus could be convinced that the Jew had indeed betrayed the king's trust and taken gold from the Treasury, then he must understand the anger that had propelled Haman into issuing that infamous decree. Haman realized he had to move quickly. He would hold the trial immediately after the festival officially ended with the dawn ceremonies at Ahuramazda's sacred spring. Even if Ahasuerus didn't go hunting but came back to Susa, he wouldn't be in the city until late in the day. *I'll have Mordecai tried after dawn and then execute him immediately.*

No one at the court would quarrel with that course of action, Haman assured himself. Mordecai had his champions, of course, but they were all lower officials in the Treasury. Their protestations would not weigh against either Haman's powerful position or the evidence that he had manufactured and would produce at the trial.

I will not give him the honor of a beheading; I will have him hanged, Haman thought with grim satisfaction. He remembered all the times the Jew had refused to bow to him and his resolve strengthened. *I will get some of the Egyptian woodworkers to erect a scaffold. They don't follow Ahuramazda, so they won't mind working on the holy day. Then all will be in readiness once the judgment against Mordecai is pronounced.*

Ahasuerus would probably revoke the decree against the rest of the Jews, but at least Haman would have gotten the one Jew he hated most.

CHAPTER TWENTY-NINE

Luara begged Esther to eat something for supper, but she refused.

"Think of the child," Luara urged.

"I will drink some water."

She would do that much for the baby, she thought, but it would not harm him if she fasted for a day. By the time Luara had undressed her for bed, Esther was so exhausted that she actually slept.

When she awoke the following morning, the sun was shining. It was the day of the equinox, the day that the Light overtook the Darkness. Esther shut her eyes. *Please, dear Father in Heaven, be at my side today. Give me the strength I shall need to face my beloved husband and beg for my people. Help me, Lord. I beg You, help me.*

Luara brought her the water she had agreed to drink and stood by while she swallowed it. When Luara took the cup back, she said, "Hathach and I are fasting as well, my lady."

Esther looked into the beautiful face of her maid and tears came to her eyes. "You are so good to me, Luara," she said and held out her arms.

"You are the one who is good, my lady," Luara said, holding Esther tightly. "You have given Hathach and me a wonderful life. We would do anything for you. Anything."

The two women stood together for a moment longer, then Esther stepped back, wiping her tears with her fingers. "Would you get Hegai for me, Luara?" she asked, trying to sound normal.

"Of course, my lady."

Hegai presented himself quickly, his face grave. "What can I do for you, my lady?" he asked.

"I want you to tell Sisames, the Head Judge, that I desire to speak with him this morning. It is of vital importance."

His eyes flickered, but he said only, "I shall have to fetch him from his home. At what time do you wish him to be here?"

"As soon as you can bring him."

"Yes, my lady." Hegai bowed and left the room.

Esther awaited Sisames in the king's reception room, pacing up and down under the disk of Ahuramazda. She had to get Sisames to agree to her request. She did not trust Haman with her uncle's life. The Edomite had clearly been possessed by some demon and he might do anything. She had to secure Mordecai's safety if she could.

Hegai announced Sisames, and Esther arranged herself on the divan before he entered. He bowed deeply to her and she invited him to be seated. Then she said with as much authority as she could muster, "My lord Judge. It has come to my attention that a friend of my family, Mordecai, the king's Head Treasurer, has been arrested by the Grand Vizier, Haman."

Sisames eyes, enfolded in wrinkles, were looking at her warily. "Yes, my lady. That is so. Haman wishes the Head Treasurer to be tried for stealing gold from the Treasury."

"Have you set a date for such a trial?"

"The Grand Vizier has said he wants the trial to be held tomorrow morning, after the dawn ceremonies officially conclude the vernal equinox festival."

"I do not think that would be wise, my lord Judge," Esther said.

Sisames looked at her for a long moment. Finally, "May I ask why, my lady?"

Esther was sitting up as tall as she could, her back not touching the divan. "As I have explained, Mordecai is a friend of my family. He also was the man instrumental in saving the king from an assassination attempt. I believe you presided at the trial of Smerdis?"

"I did, my lady."

Esther made a conscious effort to relax the grip of her clasped hands. She did not want to appear nervous. "Considering Mordecai's ties to my family and his services to the king, I do not think the king would be pleased to find that he had been tried, and perhaps even executed, while the king was not present to hear the evidence himself."

All the wrinkles in the old man's face moved and then, to Esther's great relief, he broke into a smile. "I am in complete agreement with you, my lady. I see no reason why we cannot postpone the trial until after the king has returned."

Relief flooded through Esther. She had thought she would prevail, but she had never done anything like this before and she had been afraid she would not do it well. She smiled back at him. "Thank you, my lord Judge. You are a wise man."

Sisames rose slowly and creakily to his feet. "That Palestinian overreaches himself. I will be glad when Ahasuerus returns to put right the injustices Haman has done in his name."

"I will be glad as well," Esther returned. "Thank you for coming to see me, my lord Sisames."

"It was my great pleasure, my lady," the old man replied.

As soon as Esther returned to her own apartment she told Luara to send for Muran. "Tell her I must look beautiful today, as beautiful as I have ever looked in my life. I must look like a queen."

When Muran arrived and Esther told her what she planned to do, the Mistress was so upset she forgot to give the queen her title. "You cannot burst in upon the king in such a manner, Esther! It is not only contrary to court protocol, it is against the commandment of Ahuramazda for the king to see his wife on this holy day!"

"I understand all that, Mistress," Esther replied patiently. Then she explained to Muran about the proclamation and the reason she had to see Ahasuerus.

"You are a Jew?" The Mistress was horrified.

Esther held on to her fragile calm. "Yes. I am a Jew and Mordecai is my uncle. He wished me to become a candidate for the king's hand when he learned that Haman was an Edomite. My uncle was afraid that Haman would try to act against the Jews because our nations have always been enemies. I have questioned my uncle's plan many times, but, Mistress, now he has been proven right. Mordecai lies under peril of death and my people are threatened with annihilation. I have no choice; I must speak to the king."

Muran remained obdurate. "You cannot do this, my lady. You do not understand how unspeakable—"

Esther did not wish to hear any further about how unspeakable her actions would be. She cut into Muran's tirade. "Believe me, I understand perfectly, and my mind is made up. I would like you to help me dress for the banquet, Muran." She managed a slight smile. "It is important that I look my best, but even more, it is important that I look like a queen. The guards must be so awed by me that they will let me into the banquet. You can do that for me, Muran. I know you can."

Muran wouldn't give up. "You cannot go unveiled into that room of men!"

"I must. Ahasuerus needs to be able to see that it is I, and no other, who approaches him. Then he will raise his scepter and I will be safe."

Still Muran protested. At last Esther said wearily, "Very well, Mistress. I will not ask you to go against your own beliefs. Luara can help me. You may go back to the harem."

If the situation had not been so dire, Esther would have found the indignation on Muran's face comical. "Luara!" The Mistress almost spat the word. "She knows nothing about how a queen should look. If you are determined to do this, my child, then I will help you."

Esther felt tears prickle behind her eyes at this unexpected proclamation of loyalty. "Thank you, Mistress, you are a good friend. No harm will come to you because of this; I will see to that."

The Mistress raised her perfectly plucked eyebrows. "You may not be in a position to ... 'see to' anything, my lady. What you are planning to do is not something that Ahasuerus is

likely to forgive. He has already put away one wife; there is
nothing to stop him from putting away another."

The pain that Esther was trying so hard to ignore stabbed
once more at her heart. She waited a moment before she
replied, "It would be ironic, would it not? He put Vashti away
because she would not show herself before him at a banquet,
and now you are saying he may put me away for doing the very
thing that Vashti would not."

"Irony doesn't interest me. Your welfare does." Muran's
voice was tart, but real concern was in her eyes.

Esther blinked hard to hold back the threatening tears.
She picked up the Mistress's swollen hand and held it tightly.
"I thank you, Muran, but the lives of my people must outweigh
my own welfare. Surely you can understand that?"

The Mistress's great bosom heaved with a sigh. "I suppose
so. Now, my lady, let us start with a bath."

All during the long, tedious beauty session, Esther kept thinking about the day she had met Ahasuerus for the first time.
Today was almost a replica: the bath, the waiting women fuss-
ing over her skin and nails, the hours that Luara spent setting
pearls into the strands of her hair. She had been full of dread
on that first day, and she was full of dread today as well. Today,
she thought, was worse.

Luara had almost finished with her hair when Hathach brought word that the king had arrived back at the palace and was being arrayed in his state robes in a tent that had been set up in the Apanada. He would not even enter his own apartment today because the queen was present.

He was here. Soon she would see him. She had missed him so much, had longed for his return, and now . . . now she felt numb. This was good, she thought. It was better by far to feel nothing, to protect herself from the agony she knew was coming. But no, she must not think of that. Think instead of how long she had been sitting here, with Luara putting in those horrid pearls.

"Are you almost finished?" Esther asked fretfully.

"The pearls are in place, my lady. I just need to pull your hair back with these pearl combs."

Esther sat patiently as her maid worked, skillfully inserting the combs in a way that allowed the rest of the shining ebony mass to fall down her back to her waist.

Next came the robing. The tunic that Muran had chosen was ivory in color and the robe was ivory as well, sewn all over with the same precious pearls that sprinkled Esther's hair. Her soft leather slippers were encrusted with pearls as well.

Finally, after all the pleats had been arranged to Muran's satisfaction, the Mistress went to work on Esther's face. She outlined her eyes with kohl, making them look even larger and darker than usual. Then she dusted a light coral rouge on both her cheeks and her lips.

Muran had just pronounced her ready when Hathach came back into the room. "The king went into the Service Court half an hour ago. The food has not yet been served; they are still drinking the healths. It is time to go."

Luara moved to stand beside Esther. Muran raised her eyebrows. "You are risking the king's anger if you go with her, Luara."

Esther felt Luara step even closer. The girl said, "I do not care. I shall always go with my lady."

I should not let her do this, Esther thought. But she did not have the willpower to send Luara away.

Hathach spoke calmly. "Come, my lady. I will go first. All you need to do is follow behind me."

Esther knew Ahasuerus would be furious with Hathach if he did this. She said in a shaking voice, "You do not need to come, Hathach. I know my way."

Hathach turned and gave her a long, level look.

I can't cry, Esther thought. *I will ruin the eye cosmetics.* She attempted a smile, failed, and settled for a nod. Hathach opened the door and stepped out into the hall. Luara slipped on her veil, which she would wear until she reached the banquet room.

By the time Esther came down the steps that led from the living quarters into the King's Court, everyone seemed to know what she was going to do. As she crossed the court, a page suddenly darted forward and bent to kiss the hem of

Esther's tunic. "May the Wise Lord go with you, my lady," the little boy said.

"Thank you, Niki." She touched the top of his curly black head with her ringed fingers before she once again moved forward behind Hathach. And so the progress continued: Hathach first, then Esther, then Luara, coming behind as a proper maid should.

The first critical moment came when they reached the great double doors that led from the private royal apartments into the public part of the palace. The two eunuchs who stood guard there were obviously staggered to see the queen.

"My lady!" one of them protested. "You cannot go into the public rooms!"

Hathach answered, "The queen is going to the king. Step aside, please, and let her pass." His voice was pleasant but subtly loaded with authority.

Thank God for Hathach, Esther thought, as the eunuchs stood aside with obvious bewilderment to let her through.

The Household Court was busy with men coming and going about their business, and the shock of Esther's arrival ran through the place like an unexpected storm. Out of the corner of her eyes, Esther registered the aghast expressions, and for a moment her step faltered. Nothing anyone had said so far had made the offensiveness of what she was doing as clear to her as the stunned faces of the men in the Household Court.

Suddenly Luara moved forward and held out her arm. Esther closed her fingers gratefully around the support her maid was offering, and the two of them followed Hathach's long, slim back across the brick floor of the deathly quiet Household Court.

For a moment Esther's mind flashed back in time, to the day she had first followed Hathach, the day she had first come to the harem.

I thought I would die if Ahasuerus chose me to be his wife. And now I feel as if I will die if he puts me away. She drew a deep, steadying breath. *I must stop thinking this way. I must only think of what I have to do.*

They were entering now into the passage that led from the Household Court to the Service Court, where the banquet was being held. When they reached the door to the Service Court they were stopped by the two guards who were posted there.

After staring at Esther in disbelief, one of them said to Hathach, "You can't go in there. The king has not sent for you."

Luara removed Esther's veil and Hathach said, "The queen may go where she chooses."

"Not into a religious banquet she can't," the other guard said deliberately.

Esther looked at first one guard, then at the other. She lifted her chin. "You cannot stop me."

The first guard stepped forward, as if he would physically bar her way.

"If I tell the king that you have laid one finger on the queen, you are a dead man," Hathach said coldly.

The man hesitated and the two guards looked at each other. Hathach used the moment to push open the door into the Service Court and walk in, holding it open for Esther. She followed, still clutching Luara's arm.

Ahasuerus saw her first. He was seated on his golden throne at the far side of the court, a golden coronet on his head, the golden scepter in his hand. His purple robe was embroidered with gold and the hand that grasped the scepter was covered in golden rings. The expression on his face was incredulous.

A hush swept across the room as the men seated at the banquet tables turned to follow the king's eyes to the doorway where Esther stood. The room was suddenly filled with a tension so overpowering that the air seemed to vibrate. Esther felt it with every nerve, every vein, every fiber of muscle in her body. She dropped Luara's arm and forced herself to take one step forward into the room, then another, and yet another still.

The pearls in her hair and on her robe shimmered, making it seem that she moved in a circle of luminous radiance. Still she walked on, slowly, gracefully, her back straight, her hands hanging loosely at her sides. Ahasuerus didn't move but she could see the grim set of his lips, the tightening of the skin across his cheekbones. He lifted the scepter in his hand to extend it toward her and, looking at him, she knew that he was angry.

Suddenly his face began to blur and go out of focus. She blinked, trying to clear her vision. Dots began to dance before her eyes and her skin felt cold and clammy. She shook her head, with all its shimmering pearls, trying to clear it.

"My lady!" Luara ran forward to grab Esther's elbow to support her. Her knees buckled and she felt herself beginning to sway.

Stupid! she scolded herself, blinking furiously over and over. *You can't faint now.* She swayed dangerously and thought in panic, *I'm going down!*

Then strong arms caught her and lifted her up. Her head fell onto a familiar, beloved shoulder and she closed her eyes tightly. She felt him walking with her and heard his voice say, "Pull those curtains closed, Hathach, and bring me some water." Then she was being lowered into a chair.

"Esther!" He sounded worried. "Are you all right?"

She opened her eyes. He was sitting on his heels in front of her and the taut, angry expression was gone. When he saw that her eyes were open he ordered, "Put your head down, Esther. You will feel better more quickly that way."

She obeyed.

"Breathe slowly and deeply," he said.

She breathed slowly and deeply.

"Here, my lord," came Hathach's voice. "Water."

"Drink some of this," Ahasuerus said. And Esther lifted her head and let him hold the golden cup to her lips. She swallowed.

"I am sorry, my lord," she whispered. "It was important that I see you and I did not know how else to do it."

"What could possibly be so urgent that you felt you had to create a public spectacle?" he asked.

She looked at the mixture of concern and bewilderment on his face and thought wildly, *I can't tell him now—he is in the midst of a religious banquet. I cannot tell him such dreadful news and then expect him to be able to fulfill his religious duties. I am going to destroy enough in his life as it is.*

She replied in a low voice, "I will not keep you from your banquet, my lord, but if you will come to me tomorrow, as soon as you return from the mountains, I will tell you then." She leaned toward him. "It is important that I see you, my lord. Please don't go hunting. Come back to the palace so we may speak."

His eyes narrowed a little. "Why can't you tell me now?"

She shook her head. "It is a long story and I do not want to keep you from your religious duties, my lord. But I must speak to you tomorrow! As soon as you return! Can you do that?"

"You are making no sense," he said impatiently.

"I know, but I will make sense tomorrow, I promise you."

He blew an impatient breath out through his nostrils. "All right. I will return to the palace when the ritual is finished."

She drew a long, shaky breath. "Please bring Haman with you, my lord."

He frowned, clearly irritated by her reluctance to speak, but then he glanced at the drawn curtain. He stood up, rising easily from his heels. "If that is what you wish. You are right, I must get back to the banquet."

"I am feeling better now." She bit her lip and looked wildly around the small curtained enclosure that was screening her from the Service Court. "My lord, how am I going to get out of here?"

The grim look reappeared around his mouth. "Send your maid to get a veil."

"I have one here, my lord," Luara said.

"Put it on the queen." As Luara did as he instructed, Ahasuerus turned to Hathach. "Take the queen back to her apartments by way of the Apanada. That way you will not have to pass through the Service Court again." The look he gave Hathach was not friendly. "You have made enough of a sensation for one day, I think."

The young eunuch said respectfully, "Yes, my lord." He did not apologize.

"I am ready," Esther said.

Ahasuerus stared at his wife, whose face was now properly hidden. "You are quite certain you don't want to tell me now what this is all about?"

"I think it will be better if I tell you tomorrow, when you will have the time to consider what is to be done. But you must come tomorrow, my lord!" Her voice was full of urgency.

"I will come the moment I return from the sacred spring," he said. The grim look was back around his mouth.

She looked at him imploringly.

"And I will bring Haman."

"Thank you, my lord," she whispered.

"If you are indeed ready, my lady, then we will go." Hathach's voice as he spoke to Esther was gentle and the king shot him a quick, speculative look.

"Take my arm," Luara said, using the same tone of voice as Hathach.

"Put her to bed," Ahasuerus said abruptly. "She needs to rest."

Luara looked directly at him, something servants were never supposed to do. "Do not worry, my lord. I will take good care of her."

He nodded and turned to go back into the banquet.

CHAPTER THIRTY

The scaffold was ready. The Egyptians had begun work on it Thursday evening, immediately after the king had left the palace banquet to go out to Ahuramazda's sacred spring in the mountains. Now Haman stood in the first light of morning regarding the huge, grim structure with satisfaction. The Egyptians had built it according to his instructions, and it was twice as high as the scaffolds commonly used to execute convicted thieves. Haman had ordered it to be erected just outside the walls of Susa, in close enough proximity to the palace to make it easy to transport

Mordecai quickly from his trial to his place of execution, but high enough so all in the city could see what happened to a thieving Jew.

When Haman arrived at the palace, he went immediately to his office to gather together the evidence that he would produce against Mordecai. The trial and execution must take place this morning, while Ahasuerus was still in the mountains.

Haman's activity was interrupted by a visitor, one of the lesser members of the Royal Kin, who was bursting with the news of Esther's sensational entrance into last night's banquet. Haman, who did not worship Ahuramazda, had not been there. As the young man recounted his story, Haman listened in stunned silence. When his informant finally ran out of scandalous details, Haman asked in horror, "But why would the queen do such an outrageous thing?"

The young man shrugged. "The king did not say, and, of course, no one would dare to ask him. He spoke to her in private for a few minutes and then he returned to the banquet as if nothing had happened."

Haman felt the first stirrings of uneasiness. "And no one has any idea what was said between them?"

"You know Ahasuerus," came the breezy reply. "He keeps his own council, as usual."

"And there was no message to me before he left the palace?" Haman asked anxiously.

"None, my lord."

As soon as his informant had left, Haman picked up his copy of the decree against the Jews and read it through. His scalp prickled as his eyes moved across the words. Ahasuerus could be back in Susa by this evening if he did not go hunting. What would he say when he saw what Haman had done in his name?

Perhaps I was overzealous, Haman thought. *Perhaps I should have been content with the life of Mordecai.*

With crystal clearness, he saw in his mind's eye the face of the king. *I did it for you,* he thought. *I did it to save you from the clutches of an evil people.*

But for the first time, this rationalization rang hollow in his ears.

It is the king's fault that I was driven to this, he told himself next. *If Ahasuerus had not let himself fall under the sway of Mordecai . . . if he had paid more attention to me . . .*

Sweat broke out on Haman's forehead. He shut his eyes and rubbed them with his long bony fingers. With Ahasuerus so close, the jealous mist that had obscured Haman's vision was beginning to lift, and he was frightened by what he saw.

Mordecai was frightened also, but unlike Haman, he had no questions about his own righteousness. For five days and five nights, he had been held a prisoner in Haman's house. He had eaten none of the unclean food he was offered, consenting only to drink the water. He had prayed constantly, not for himself, but for his people, whom death was staring in the face:

O Lord God, almighty King, all things are in Your power. You made heaven and earth and every wonderful thing under the heavens. You are Lord of all, and there is no one who can resist You. Lord God, King, God of Abraham, spare Your people, for our enemies plan our ruin and are bent upon destroying the inheritance that You gave to us. Do not spurn us, whom You redeemed for Yourself out of Egypt. Hear my prayer; have pity on Your people and turn our sorrow into joy; thus we shall live to sing praise to Your name, O Lord. Do not silence those who praise You.

And he prayed also for his niece, Esther, in whose fragile hands lay the fate of an entire people.

Esther slept fitfully that night and woke early to prepare for Ahasuerus' visit. The first thing she did was send Hathach to see what was happening in regard to Mordecai's trial. The young man returned with good news.

"There will be no trial, my lady. Sisames told Haman that he would not try Mordecai until he had instructions from the king himself to do so. He said the trial must wait until Ahasuerus' return."

A huge weight rolled off Esther's heart. She had trusted

Sisames when he told her he would postpone the trial, but it was a great relief to know that it had actually been done.

"Haman was livid, I hear," Hathach added. "But with the king so close by, there was nothing he could say that would move the judge."

Esther said, "Thanks be to God, Mordecai is safe."

"He is still under guard in Haman's house, but I don't think Haman will dare to do anything to harm him now," Hathach agreed.

"What about Haman? Is he still in the palace?" A crucial part of Esther's plan was to have Haman present so she could confront him personally with what he had done.

"Yes, my lady. He is in his office. Raging about the Head Judge's obstinacy, I expect."

Esther bit her lip. "I hope he does not go home before the king gets here."

"He rarely leaves the palace before midafternoon, my lady," Hathach reassured her.

"Good." Esther turned to Luara. "I want the table in my dining room set for three. The king has promised to return immediately after the ceremonies and he will be hungry."

While the dining room in the Queen's Apartment was prepared, Esther dressed in her simplest robe and tunic. She refused all of the jewelry Luara offered. "I don't need to look like a queen today, my friend. I need to look like a petitioner."

Finally, after what seemed an eternally long morning,

Hathach brought the news that the king had just ridden into the palace courtyard. Esther's whole body felt rigid with stress. *The time has come. Soon it will be done.*

Hathach cracked the door slightly and the threesome in the queen's reception room stood in total silence, listening intently for the sound of footsteps. It was not very long before they heard them. Then they heard Ahasuerus say, "Send for Haman and tell him to attend me in my reception room. But first I need a bath."

"Yes, my lord."

The door across the corridor closed and there came the sound of a single man walking back down the corridor. The messenger going for Haman, Esther thought. Hathach softly closed her door all the way.

"Courage, my lady," Luara said. "The most dangerous part of this whole affair was your intrusion into the banquet, and that is behind you. The rest will be easy. Once the king hears what Haman has done, he will be thankful for your intervention."

She means well, Esther thought, and sent her maid the flicker of a smile. She thought of having to tell Ahasuerus that one of his most trusted friends had betrayed him and she quaked. He would not only be angry, he would be devastated. And then, to add to his pain, she would next inform him that his wife had been lying to him ever since they first met.

Oh my dearest love, I would do anything to take this agony from you, but I cannot.

They moved into the small dining room to await the king. Luara urged Esther to take a sip of wine, but she shook her head. "It will make me dizzy."

They continued to wait.

More time passed. Then there came a soft knock upon the door. Hathach opened it and a page announced the arrival of Ahasuerus. The king came in, followed by Haman.

Hathach slipped out the door to go inform the kitchen that the food could be served and Luara followed him.

I will not faint, Esther told herself as she greeted her guests and asked them to be seated at the table. She flared her nostrils and inhaled deeply. *I will not faint.*

Ahasuerus scanned her face. "You are too pale and the shadows under your eyes look like bruises. Are you feeling well enough for this, Esther?"

His concern is so sweet, Esther thought. Would he ever look at her this way again? "I am well, my lord," she replied quietly. "If you will be seated, I will serve you and your Grand Vizier some wine."

She poured the wine into the golden goblets with the dexterity and grace that she had learned from Muran. Ahasuerus' eyes were a darker gray than usual as he accepted the cup from her and there was a line between his brows. Haman looked wary.

The king put the cup down decisively. "If you want me to eat, Esther, you are first going to have to tell me what this is all about. What could possibly be so dire that you had to violate my banquet last night?"

The moment had come. Esther turned from the wine table and faced the two men. To her great relief, she felt perfectly steady as she spoke the words she had rehearsed over and over again in her mind. "My lord, I have an urgent request to make of you. That is why I wished to see you—to ask you to grant me this request."

He frowned. "A request? Of course I will grant you a request." He glanced at Haman, clearly puzzled as to the necessity of his attendance.

Esther straightened her already straight back. "My lord," she said in a formal voice. "I ask you that my life be spared, and I beg that you also spare the lives of my people. For my people and I have been delivered to destruction, slaughter, and death."

At Esther's words, Haman had gone deadly white. He made as if to rise from his chair, then, realizing the futility of escape, he slumped back down again.

Ahasuerus did not notice Haman's movement; his eyes were all for his wife. His voice was clipped. "I do not understand you, Esther. Who dares threaten your life?"

"You do, my lord," Esther said quietly, "although I do not think you know anything about this decree."

"What decree?" Ahasuerus slammed the flat of his hand down on the table, making the golden cups and plates jump. "Esther, what are you talking about?"

She flinched at the noise of his hand crashing upon the table, but her own hands were steady as she withdrew a roll of parchment from within the folds of her robe. "This decree, my lord."

The sweat began to pour down Haman's face.

Esther went on, "This is a decree that was sent out under your Royal Seal, my lord. May I read it to you?"

He nodded impatiently.

Esther unrolled the parchment and began to read from it. Ahasuerus made an abrupt movement and she looked up. "Go on," he said tersely, and she continued until she got to the relevant point:

We hereby decree that all Jews living in our empire, together with their wives and children, must leave their present dwelling places and places of business and return to the land of their origin, as once was ordered by our father, Cyrus. If they do not obey this decree by the fourteenth day of the month of Adar of the current year, then they shall be utterly destroyed by the swords of their enemies.

She stopped reading. The silence in the room was terrifying. Haman sat in frozen stillness, his gaze glued to the scroll in Esther's hand.

At last the king said in an ominously quiet voice, "I never caused such a decree to be written."

"I never thought you did, my lord. It was promulgated after you left Susa to deal with the Mardians." She moved to stand next to him and held the parchment out for him to look at. "However, you can see that it is signed with the Royal Seal."

Ahasuerus looked down at the familiar symbol. Slowly he lifted his eyes, slowly he turned his head. "Haman," he said, "is this your doing?"

Terror looked out of Haman's dilated eyes. "Yes, my lord," he whispered.

"You were going to issue a decree against the Mardians." Ahasuerus was as bewildered as he was angry, and Esther felt her heart go out to him. "What is *this*?"

Haman heard the bewilderment also and a gleam of hope flickered in his golden stare. "My lord, the queen has not told you that I found evidence that Mordecai was stealing from the Treasury. It made me so angry, my lord, that a Jew would so betray your trust that I . . . that I let myself get carried away."

"Carried away?" The note in Ahasuerus' voice was terrible. "You have authorized the murder of thousands of men, women, and children—in my name—and you say you were carried away?"

"My lord. I am sorry. I was so angry at the Jew's betrayal. I did not think . . ." Haman's eyes fell before the look in Ahasuerus', and his voice trailed off.

Fury swept through Esther. "This accusation of Mordecai is completely false, my lord. Mordecai is as honest as you are yourself. The evidence Haman speaks of was manufactured by him. It is merely an excuse for ordering the extermination of my people." She could feel her face flush with her anger. "Yes, Haman, *my* people. I, too, am a Jew, and this proclamation applies to me as well as it does to the thousands of other innocents whom you would slaughter in the name of racial and religious hatred."

The only sound in the room was the harsh ratchet of Haman's breathing.

Ahasuerus said abruptly, "I must get messengers on the roads immediately if they are to reach their destinations before the fourteenth." He pushed the chair out of his way and, brushing past Esther, he walked to the door. They heard his voice outside in the corridor telling a page to bring him a scribe and the captain of the Royal Messenger Service. There came the sound of a door closing, and Esther realized that he must have gone into his own apartment.

She looked at Haman. He was ashen. "My lady—" he began, then stopped, silenced by the look in her eyes.

"He trusted you," she said bitterly. "He made you his Grand Vizier. He gave you his seal."

"I was trying to protect him! He trusted all the wrong people!"

"He trusted you." Esther's voice was hard and pitiless as she repeated the words. "When they told him that you had poisoned his medicine, he never hesitated. He drank it all down. Do you remember that, Haman? What was that, if not a sign of trust? And then you did this to him."

Haman whimpered, "Oh my dearest lord, what have I done?" and he buried his hands in his face.

A flicker of pity stirred in Esther's heart and she pushed it down. She would not feel sorry for Haman. "What have you done with Mordecai, my uncle?"

Haman dropped his hands. "He is under guard in my own house, my lady. He is safe, I promise you."

All of Esther's anger came rushing back. "You were going to kill him. You made up lies about him and you were going to kill him."

"My lady." Haman pushed back his chair and, before she knew what he was going to do, he had rushed across the floor, flung himself at her feet, and clutched her robe. "Please, my lady, I am sorry, I did not mean—"

"Take your hands off my wife!"

Haman and Esther froze.

Then Haman scrambled to his feet. "My lord, I did not mean . . ." His voice trailed off as he saw who had come into the room with the king.

"Arrest him," Ahasuerus said to the Eunuch Guardsmen he had brought. "I never want to see his face again."

Ahasuerus and Esther stood in silence as Haman was removed. He did not struggle or attempt to appeal to the king, but, haggard-faced, walked in the midst of the guardsmen with the profound calm of utter despair. Then a small, big-eyed page announced the arrival of one of the palace scribes.

"Sit at that table," the king said to the rotund man who had entered behind the page, "and write down what I am going to say."

The scribe hastened to do as he was asked, moving one of the untouched golden plates so that he could unroll his parchment and find room for his ink and freshly sharpened quills. He dipped a pen into the ink and looked expectantly at the king. Ahasuerus dictated:

Ahasuerus, the Great King, to all the twenty satraps and governors of provinces in the Empire of the Persians: Greetings.

Some men become more ambitious the more they are showered with honors through the bountiful generosity of their patrons. Not only do they drive out gratitude from among men; with the arrogant boastfulness of those to whom goodness has no meaning, they suppose they will escape even the judgment of the All Wise Lord.

For instance, Haman, son of Hamedatha, a Palestinian, certainly not of Persian blood, and very different from us in generosity, was hospitably received by us. He repaid this generous trust by weaving intricate webs of deceit by which he plotted the destruction of Mordecai, our savior, and the whole race of Jewish people who are our loyal subjects.

You will ignore the letter sent by Haman, for he who composed it has met with our most bitter displeasure and punishment. No Jewish blood is to be spilt on the

fourteenth day of Adar, nor of any other month. Instead
this day shall be turned from one of destruction into one
of joy, which you shall celebrate by feasts and by rejoicing,
so that both now and in the future it may be, for us and
for all loyal Persians, a celebration of victory, and for those
who plot against us a reminder of their inevitable fate.

When the last word had been taken down, the scribe
looked up at Ahasuerus, who said, "The royal messengers are
waiting for copies of this decree, which are to be sent throughout the empire as swiftly as possible."

"Yes, my lord." The scribe blew on the parchment to help
dry the ink. "We will have the copies made within the hour."

"Bring them to me when they are finished and I will affix
my Royal Seal."

"Yes, my lord."

"You may go."

"Yes, my lord." The little man looked anxiously at his pens
and ink, clearly wondering how he was to take them along with
the parchment, which had to be held open as it had not yet
dried.

"Leave them," the king said impatiently as he saw the man's
dilemma.

"Yes, my lord!" Unable to perform the prostration with the
parchment in his hands, the scribe contented himself with a
deep bow before exiting through the door.

Alone in the room, Esther and Ahasuerus looked at each other. His face was still and reserved, but Esther saw that the hands at his sides were clenched.

He said, "You told me you were a Babylonian."

She had never actually told him that, but she had certainly allowed him to believe it. She said, "My family did come to Susa from Babylon, my lord, but they are Jews. Mordecai is my uncle."

"And you did not think it worthwhile to tell me this?"

His voice was so cold, so distant, that she wanted to weep. "My lord, may I tell you how this came to be?"

He replied in that same cold voice, "I would be interested to hear such a tale."

They were standing with half the width of the room between them. Esther thought fleetingly about asking him to sit, but his expression warned her not to. She clasped her hands together and began to tell him about Mordecai's dream and his fear that something terrible was going to happen to the Jews.

"There were so many girls more beautiful than I, my lord. I never expected you to choose me. But you did. And then I came to love you so much, and I was afraid to tell you the truth."

"You thought I would reject you if I knew you were a Jew?"

She took one step toward him in her anxiety to make him understand. "I never thought that. I thought you would be angry with me because I had lied to you."

The still expression on his face never changed, but his eyes darkened. "You were right," he said.

Cold despair washed through Esther. She couldn't reach him. Her betrayal, on top of Haman's, was too painful. Still, she continued to try.

"I had made up my mind never to tell you the truth, to separate myself forever from my religion. I told Uncle Mordecai that I would not do his work anymore, that now it was up to him to be the Jewish advocate at court, that all I wanted in this world was to be your wife." Her voice quivered, but his expression didn't change. "Then *this* happened, just as Uncle Mordecai had dreamed."

He said nothing.

"God put me here for a reason, my lord, and I had to act. I never wanted such a thing to happen, but when it did, I could keep silent no longer."

"I see." He opened his hands, then slowly closed them into fists again, the only sign he gave that he was not as composed as he appeared to be. "The Royal Messengers will leave Susa within the hour. I am sending two riders on each stage of every road so that if something should happen to one, the other will be able to continue on. There is no reason for them not to make their destinations in time to stop this massacre."

"Thank you, my lord," she whispered.

"I have ordered Mordecai's release."

"Thank you, my lord."

"You look tired. I suggest you get some rest." And without another word, he turned his back, walked to the door, pushed it open himself, and went out.

Esther stood staring after him, her eyes dry and burning. The grief she felt was too terrible to find a release in tears.

CHAPTER THIRTY-ONE

Early in the afternoon, Filius, the Deputy Treasurer whose recommendation to Hegai had allowed Esther to be presented as a candidate, received a summons to attend the king in his business room off the Court of the Royal Kin. When Filius presented himself, Ahasuerus was sitting behind his desk. The Deputy Treasurer had never been this close to the king and he found himself trembling with a mixture of nervousness and awe.

Ahasuerus was not a big man and he was dressed in the same simple white robes that many aristocratic Persian men wore. The only sign of his kingship was the thin, golden fillet on his head. Even his hands were bare of rings. But Filius had felt his power the moment he walked into the room. There was something about him . . .

The king regarded his Deputy Treasurer. "Was Haman planning to call you as a witness at this trial for Mordecai?"

Filius couldn't get his answer out fast enough. "No, my lord! He has never once spoken to me about the charges against Mordecai."

"Do you think the charges are valid?" was the next question.

Filius had come determined to tell the truth, no matter the cost. He summoned his courage and replied, "I have worked with Mordecai for over ten years, my lord, and I would stake my life upon his integrity. I do not believe that these charges can be valid."

A small silence fell as the king's light eyes studied Filius' face. Then Ahasuerus said, "The lord Haman tells me he has evidence that Mordecai was stealing from the Treasury."

Filius started to clasp his hands behind his back, then quickly changed his mind. One did not hide one's hands before the Great King. "As I have not been allowed to see this evidence, my lord, I cannot say how it came into being. Perhaps the lord Haman is mistaken; perhaps he has misread some of the accounting. I can only repeat that I would stake my life on Mordecai's honesty."

The king's face was unreadable. "Did you request to see the evidence?"

"Yes, my lord, I did."

"And the lord Haman refused to show it to you?"

"Yes, my lord."

The king looked down at his hands, which were clasped together on the top of his desk. He said, without looking up, "The lord Haman produced evidence against the last Head Treasurer as well. Did you think that evidence was in error also?"

"No, my lord." Filius had not expected this line of questioning and once more he had to restrain himself from putting his hands behind his back, a position he had always found comforting.

The king's quiet inquisition continued: "Had you suspected that Otanes was stealing from the Treasury?"

Filius was in despair. There was no right way to answer this question. "I . . . I might have had some suspicions, my lord."

"Yet you did not think this information would be of interest to me?"

Filius was caught and he knew it. He fell back on the truth as his only possible answer. "My lord, I am but a Dadian and a clerk. It was not for me to accuse an Achaemenid noble."

Ahasuerus raised his eyes once more to Filius. "Do you know of any reason why the lord Haman would wish to harm Mordecai?"

Filius was silent.

"Answer me." Ahasuerus' even voice was infinitely more terrifying than shouting would have been.

Filius blurted, "I know that Mordecai would not bow before the Grand Vizier, and this lack of respect enraged Haman."

Ahasuerus lifted his brows. "Why wouldn't Mordecai bow?"

"Because Haman was an Edomite, my lord. Apparently there is longstanding enmity between the Jews and the Edomites." Filius shivered. "Indeed, my lord, the air fairly crackled with hatred every time the two of them met."

"I did not know that." Ahasuerus sat for a moment in silence, his eyes once again on his hands. Filius waited anxiously for the next question. Then, without looking up, the king said, "That is all, Filius. You may go."

"Thank you, my lord." The Deputy Treasurer prostrated himself and backed out of the room, desperately hoping that he had not just lost his job.

The next person the king asked to see in his office was Coes, whom Ahasuerus had sent to Haman's house to order the release of Mordecai.

"He is safe, my lord," Coes reported with satisfaction. "Haman's servants were guarding him and they were more than willing to let him go upon my command." Coes started to add something about Haman, then decided it was unnecessary. The circumstances could not have made it clearer to Ahasuerus what a snake Haman was.

"Mordecai was not hurt?" Ahasuerus asked.

"He looked somewhat haggard, my lord, but he said that was because he would not eat Haman's food."

The king nodded. His face looked still, but the skin across his cheekbones was taut and the look in his eyes would freeze the rivers. Coes, who knew him well, could see that Ahasuerus was enraged.

Coes said, "I learned a few things from the guards who remained in the city, my lord, that explain why the queen felt it necessary to intrude upon the banquet. Had you waited even until tomorrow to return to Susa, you might have been too late. Haman had the Jew's trial and execution arranged for this morning. The queen rightly thought that Mordecai was in imminent danger of death. Fortunately, Sisames refused to proceed unless he heard from you directly."

Ahasuerus said, "I see."

Coes took a step closer to the desk. "And there is one more thing, my lord. Haman had a scaffold built just outside the city walls. I spoke to some of the workmen who were still there, and they told me it was for the Jew who had embezzled money from the king."

"A scaffold? He was going to *hang* my Head Treasurer?"

"Yes, my lord. And the scaffold is at least twice as high as those we use to execute common criminals."

"His audacity surpasses all belief," the king said, his soft voice sounding eerily dangerous.

"Yes, my lord." Coes waited for his orders.

Ahasuerus said, "Coes, you will take this ungrateful Palestinian and hang him upon the very scaffold he built for an innocent man."

Coes repressed a smile. "I will be happy to do so, my lord. When do you wish it done?"

For the first time there was the flicker of emotion in the king's cold eyes. "Today," he said.

"The city is still celebrating the festival, my lord. Are you certain you don't want to wait until tomorrow?"

"Haman's very existence is an insult to the Truth. To destroy him is to destroy the Lie. What could be a more fitting tribute to Ahuramazda?"

"Very true, my lord," Coes said heartily. "All who love the Truth will rejoice at the destruction of such a traitor."

There came a tap at the door and a page came in. "My lord, the decrees are ready for you to affix your seal."

"Bring them here," Ahasuerus said.

Coes left and the scribes came in with the king's new decree.

The interminable day passed and Esther waited, but Ahasuerus did not come to see her. She sent Hathach to tell Coes that someone had better go after Arses, who still might not realize that the king had returned to Susa. Hathach reported back to Esther that Coes would take care of it.

It was late in the afternoon when Hathach told Esther that her uncle wished to see her. She and Luara were in the queen's reception room, looking over a marriage offer for one of the harem girls. Esther told Hathach to bring her uncle to her.

Mordecai had bathed and eaten before coming to the palace, but even so Esther was appalled by his haggard looks. She took two steps toward him and cried in distress, "Uncle Mordecai! You look terrible! Are you certain you are all right?"

"Yes, Esther." His face was grave. "Thanks to you, I am all right."

Her lip quivered and tears filled her eyes. "I am so glad to see you! I was afraid that monstrous man would kill you before I could speak to the king."

"My brave girl," he said tenderly and held out his arms.

He had sheltered her for almost all of her childhood. For years, his arms had been her safety and her refuge, but even as she huddled against him, she knew that he could not help her now. It was not her uncle's arms she longed for.

She said into his shoulder, "Ahasuerus has promised me that there is nothing to fear. He has sent two messengers on every stage of the road and there is still time for them to reach their destinations. None of our people will be hurt."

Mordecai patted her back. "This is all because of you, Esther. You have saved your people—Israel."

She pressed her forehead deeper into his shoulder. "What is happening to Haman?"

"The king has ordered him to be hung from the very scaffold he erected for me." Mordecai sounded pleased.

Esther stiffened and backed away from her uncle's embrace. "How awful all this is for Ahasuerus," she whispered.

"Yes. He trusted that Edomite snake. This must have come as quite a shock."

Esther nodded mutely.

Mordecai scanned her face. "You look distressed, Esther. Why? What is there to worry about now?"

She tried to explain. "Ahasuerus is . . . upset . . . with me. He trusted me like he trusted Haman, and I, too, have deceived him. I let him believe a lie about me; I never told him I was a Jew."

Mordecai gestured dismissively. "Surely that cannot matter now? He should be grateful to you, Esther! You saved his name from infamy."

"I don't think he is feeling grateful right now, Uncle Mordecai," Esther said shortly. "I think he is feeling betrayed."

"Not by you, surely!"

"By me, because I lied to him. By you, because you lied to him. By Haman, of course. By Haman most of all."

Mordecai was full of confidence. "He will get over it, chicken. I can understand that right now he may be feeling a little annoyed, but once he has a chance to assess the situation, he will be grateful to you. There is no need for you to worry."

Esther stared at her beloved uncle.

How insensitive he is, she thought. He would die for her, of that she had no doubt. But he would never understand her feelings. Once she had thought that all men were like that. Now she knew differently.

She didn't bother to attempt an explanation; she merely said, "I hope you are right, Uncle Mordecai."

A smile lit up his thin, drawn face. "Think about it and you will see that all has turned out for the best. I know that you are fond of Ahasuerus, and now that he finally knows you are a Jew, you will be able to follow your religion and remain married to him as well."

There was nothing she could find to say in the face of such blind optimism.

Mordecai squeezed her hand. "Ahasuerus will not stand in the way of your religious practices, Esther. I'm sure of it. He may not be a Jew, but he is a good man. He has impressed me."

Esther regarded her uncle's face and a flicker of humor curled her lips at his unconscious arrogance. She thought of how Ahasuerus would look if she told him that he, the Great King of Persia, should feel deeply honored that he had made a good impression on his Jewish underling. She said, "Thank you, Uncle Mordecai."

"He is a good king." Mordecai added an additional approbation.

"I think so too," Esther said.

"So, then. You will be restored to your proper identity,

and we will have gotten rid of Haman, who would always have been a threat to Jewish interests. Things could not have worked out better." Mordecai beamed at her. "You have been the means by which the Lord worked His will, Esther. I am so proud of you."

She said, "Uncle Mordecai, has it ever occurred to you that if you had not provoked Haman by refusing to bow to him, he would never have done this terrible thing?"

The smile left Mordecai's face, leaving it grave. "Esther, it is just not in me to bow to an Edomite."

She shook her head at the hopelessness of men. "And of course it was not in Haman to ignore your taunt."

"They want a seaport, Esther, and they will not be content until they have pushed us out of the way to get one. If we regard them as anything less than enemies, we will be making a grave mistake."

Esther sighed. "It seems to me such a pity that we cannot all live together in peace." She looked at her uncle's hawk-like face. "But I suppose that is a woman's dream."

His expression softened. "It is a splendid dream, chicken. Keep it always in your heart."

Unfortunately, that is where it will stay, she thought sadly.

"Don't look so downcast! Smile and be glad! You are a heroine, Esther." Mordecai grinned at her, a light-hearted, youthful grin, and she found herself smiling back. She was happy that her uncle was safe.

"Have you heard that Grandfather was ready to come to your rescue?" she asked.

"No. What do you mean?"

Esther told him what Arses had done.

Mordecai looked a little chagrined. "I have never liked Arses, but I always thought him an honorable man."

"He said much the same about you," Esther returned with amusement.

"Hmm." Mordecai ran his finger up and down his nose.

"Grandfather probably still does not realize that he missed Ahasuerus. We have sent messengers to bring him back. When he does return to Susa, Uncle Mordecai, I think you must go to thank him."

Mordecai looked gloomy. "I suppose I must."

"He was outraged at the proclamation. He said it would be a blot forever on the name of Persia if such a massacre were allowed to occur."

"Any honorable man would feel thus," Mordecai said, but he looked more cheerful. "Certainly I will go to see him, chicken. Now that your whole heritage is known, it would be foolish of us to continue to be at odds with each other."

Esther smiled. "It would make me happy if you and Grandfather could become friends."

"Friends might be a little too much to ask, Esther," Mordecai replied cautiously.

"Not even to please your heroine?"

He laughed and leaned down to kiss her on the forehead. "To please my heroine, I will even try to become friends with Arses."

She reached out and gave him a brief, fierce hug. "I am so glad to see you, Uncle Mordecai!"

He looked down at her, his expression suddenly concerned. "You look exhausted, Esther. I want you to get some rest."

"I will try," she said.

"Don't worry about Ahasuerus. Blame everything on me. It doesn't matter if I lose my position as Head Treasurer. You are the one who is important now."

She smiled mistily. "Thank you, Uncle Mordecai."

He nodded, kissed her again on the forehead, and left the room.

They had offered to allow Haman to see his wife and children, and he had refused. He knew they would be all right. Ahasuerus was not one to seek revenge upon the innocent. And there was nothing he wished to say to them.

He was already dead. His life had ended in the queen's room some five hours earlier. Deprived of the light of Ahasuerus' regard, he was destroyed as surely as a plant would be destroyed without the life-giving warmth of the sun. Not even the sight of the enormous scaffold caused his heart to

hurry its heavy rhythm. It plodded dutifully onward—*thump,
thump, thump*—not realizing yet that the organism it sought to
sustain was already dead.

There was a crowd gathered around the scaffold and it fell
oddly silent as the execution procession approached from the
palace. Haman walked in the midst of his guards as if he saw
and heard nothing.

Coes himself had taken charge of this duty, and he sig-
naled now that the prisoner should be brought ahead. Haman
scarcely felt the guards' hands upon his shoulders as he walked
forward steadily and climbed the high ladder to the top of the
scaffold.

When they put the rope about his neck, he did not close
his eyes, but stared unblinkingly toward the Eastern Gate of
the palace, clearly visible to him from his high perch. Then the
trap door beneath him gave way, and he fell to his death.

CHAPTER THIRTY-TWO

That night Esther lay alone in bed, her hands folded over her rounded stomach. She was exhausted, but she could not sleep. She had been waiting for hours, but still he had not come.

The easy tears filled her eyes. What was going to happen to them? Ahasuerus might put her away, as he had Vashti. He could also let her stay but erect a barrier between them, the same protective barrier that kept him safely separated from everyone else. And that she could not bear. The loneliness of living with him and being shut out from him would be almost as terrible as not seeing him at all.

She had heard the courtiers who undressed the king leave long ago and so she knew he was there in his bedroom. Her heart had been bleeding for him ever since Mordecai had told her of Haman's execution.

Father in Heaven, she prayed. *He has just executed his closest friend. I do not want him to bear this alone. Please. He cannot be left to bear this alone. Send him to me. I beg You, send him to me.*

With every particle of her being, she longed to cross that hallway and go to him, but she knew that she could not. Because of her deception, she could not be the one to go to him. It was he who must come to her, and he had not done so.

The small oil lamp that she had told Luara to keep lit was still burning. Esther blinked her tears away and stared at it. The minutes went by and the lamp began to flicker. Was this how their love was going to end? Was it going to flicker out, like the lamp? She shut her eyes so she wouldn't see it happen.

There was the murmur of voices in the corridor outside her room and Esther's eyes flew open. She stared at the door, almost forgetting to breathe, she was willing so hard for it to open. Finally it did, and Ahasuerus came quietly in. He closed the door behind him, glanced at the flickering lamp and then at the bed. He said softly, "Esther? Are you awake?"

"Yes." She pushed some pillows behind her back and sat up. "I couldn't sleep."

"Nor could I." He did not come over to the bed, however,

but went to sit upon the stool in front of her dressing table, putting the whole width of the room between them.

"He is dead," he said in a curiously flat voice. "I killed him."

"I know, Ahasuerus," she said softly.

"I didn't even give him a trial."

"It wasn't necessary. He admitted his guilt."

"I liked him so much." He was still speaking in that same flat voice. He clasped his hands between his knees and stared down at them. "When I was newly appointed king in Babylon—I was so young, Esther, only eighteen!—Haman made himself my friend. He helped me, guided me through the intrigues the satrap set to catch me out. It was largely because of him that I was able to be successful there."

"He revered you," Esther said.

"I thought he did." The note in his voice wrenched her heart. "Obviously I was wrong."

"You weren't wrong, Ahasuerus," she said gently. "I remember the expression on his face when you drank the medicine that Xerxes told you Haman had poisoned. Love shone out of his eyes when he looked at you that day, my lord."

"It wasn't love." His voice hardened slightly. "How can you say he loved me when he did such a terrible thing to me?"

She was quiet for a moment, thinking of how she should frame her reply. Finally she said slowly, "I think he was jealous, Ahasuerus. And jealousy can make a person do terrible things, things they would not normally dream of doing."

"He had no possible cause for jealousy." Ahasuerus raised his face so that the lamplight flickered off his hair and skin. "I made him my Grand Vizier, Esther! I gave him the highest post in the empire. Whom could he have been jealous of?"

"I have been thinking about this ever since I learned of his plan, my lord." She rested her arms on her up-drawn knees and leaned toward him. "He was jealous of me, for one. I never understood why he disliked me, but now I think it was because he saw that you cared for me, and he was jealous. I think he came to be so jealous of Uncle Mordecai that he was pushed into doing this dreadful thing."

She could see his puzzlement from all the way across the room. "Why would he be jealous of Mordecai? Because I made him my Head Treasurer? But Haman was still his superior, Esther."

"I don't think Haman was interested in political power, my lord. It was Ahasuerus the man he cared about. He saw that you liked Uncle Mordecai, whom he considered his enemy, and he was jealous."

"By all the devils in the underworld, was I to like no one but Haman?"

She sighed. "I think that is exactly what he wanted, my lord. He wanted to be the sun in your life, the only one you trusted. And Uncle Mordecai's being a Jew made it that much worse. There is no trust between the Jews and the Edomites."

"But to send out such a decree! He must have been mad."

"I think he probably was, my lord," she said somberly.

For a long moment he said nothing. Then, abruptly, he put his face in his hands. His aching voice came from behind his cramped fingers. "He was the last person I would have ever thought would betray me."

The pain in his voice broke her heart. She got out of bed and crossed the distance between them to stand close before him as he sat there on her dressing table stool. She didn't touch him but searched for words that might bring him some measure of comfort. "He wouldn't have seen it as a betrayal, my lord. He would have thought he was protecting you. I think right and wrong were all twisted up in his mind." She looked down at his bowed, burnished head and said quietly, "Ahasuerus, none of this was your fault."

He reached for her blindly, wrapping his arms around her waist and pressing his face into the hollow of her neck. "I killed him, Esther," he groaned. "I killed him."

He was shivering. She held him close and rested her cheek against his smooth hair. She felt his anguish and his sorrow resonate in her own being, but all the while a part of her rejoiced. He had not turned away from her in his hour of need, and that knowledge was ineffably sweet.

She felt something hot and wet soak into her nightgown and gathered him even closer. "There was nothing else you could have done. He had committed an unpardonable crime."

"That doesn't make it feel any better."

"I know, my love. I know."

The baby kicked. He felt it and lifted his head, heedless of the tears streaming down his face. "What was that?"

There were tears in her own eyes, but she smiled through them. "Your son. Or daughter, as the case may be."

He reached up a hand and laid it gently on her stomach. The baby kicked again, and Ahasuerus smiled. "Life," he said.

She put her hand over his. "Yes."

"Esther . . ." He looked up into her face.

"I am so sorry, my lord. I did not want to continue to deceive you about my identity, but I was afraid to tell you. I was afraid you would be so hurt, so angry that I had lied, that you would turn away from me."

They looked at each other, their hands still clasped on her stomach. "I could never turn away from you," he said. "I could not bear the loneliness if I did that."

"I feel the same way," she whispered.

He closed his eyes and rested his head against her once more. "Hold me, Esther," he said.

As she wrapped her arms around him and buried her lips in his hair, she closed her own eyes and thought, *Thank You, Father in Heaven. Thank You for giving me back my husband.*

Author's Note

It is always a challenge when an author takes a familiar
story, whether it be myth, legend, or well-known biblical material, and decides to turn it into a novel. Most of
the time, in order to produce an effective novel, it is necessary to rearrange some of the original material. I have long
thought that the Book of Esther would make a wonderful
love story. The elements are all there: the exotic setting of
the Persian Empire; the Cinderella story of this little Jewish
girl becoming the queen of the Great King of Persia; the
amazing conclusion where she intervenes with her husband

to save her entire people from annihilation. What could be more romantic?

But novelists have rules that do not govern other kinds of writing. A novel must create believable, reasoning characters who drive the action. As E. M. Forster famously put it: *"The king died and then the queen died is a story. . . . The king died and then the queen died of grief is a plot."* To turn the Book of Esther into a novel, I had to give the characters humanly understandable reasons for acting as they did. Haman had to have a reason for hating Mordecai so much; Mordecai had to have a reason for sending his niece to the King of Persia's harem; Esther had to have reasons for doubting her uncle's dream; Ahasuerus had to have reasons for picking such a socially unsuitable girl to be his queen. For all of the above reasons, I felt it necessary to tinker a bit with the Esther story as it is presented in the Bible.

Another thing a novelist must be cognizant of is pace. A plot needs to keep moving, so in some places you will find that I have telescoped time in order to achieve a more dramatic and suspenseful effect.

Then there is the issue of the historical background of the novel. Historically, there is no king called Ahasuerus. The king who followed Darius was his son by Atossa, Xerxes. The years of the beginning of Xerxes' reign, which lasted from 486 BC–465 BC, is the time setting for Esther, when the vast Persian Empire stretched from India to Turkey. Xerxes took the throne four years after the Persian defeat at Marathon in

Greece, and I used this historical background to give motivation to some of Ahasuerus' actions. Ahasuerus, you will have noticed, is a far more admirable character in the novel than the king in the Bible. Since I was writing this story as a love story, clearly the hero had to have some good qualities that would make Esther fall in love with him.

Where the Bible story and the novel come together is in the underlying premise. God has a plan for the world, and He works His plan through the actions of humans. The big question is, will we allow God to work through us? God wants us to be His partners, but we have the free will to accept or refuse His challenge. In the Judeo-Christian tradition, all of God's people must listen to His voice and open their hearts for Him to use us for His purposes.

ACKNOWLEDGMENTS

I am tremendously indebted to my wonderful agent, Natasha Kern. Her faith in this book was so strong that it empowered me to keep working on it. I must also give thanks to my editor at Thomas Nelson, Ami McConnell, whose suggestions helped shape the character of Esther. Finally, thanks are due to my wonderful husband, Joe, who has always been the wind beneath my wings.

READING GROUP GUIDE

1. The king's banishment of Vashti is the catalyst for the contest that brings Esther to his attention. How does the shadow of Vashti hang over Esther for the remainder of the book?

2. Do you think Mordecai can really love his niece and at the same time ask her to do something that is so opposed to everything she believes in?

3. It takes a long time for Esther to accept the role that has been thrust on her. What are the steps she must take before she arrives at her decision to stand up for her people?

4. Esther finds herself caught between her love for her husband and her responsibility to her God. Can such a struggle happen in today's secular world?

5. In the Bible, Haman stands for pure evil. His only motivation is his hatred of the Jews, which is never quite explained. It is a given. How does the novel try to expand Haman's motivations to greater complexity? Do you think Haman's actions are believable, given the context of the novel?

6. Does Haman in any way pre-figure Judas?

7. At the beginning of the Book of Esther, the Jews have become in danger of assimilating into the Persian culture and forgetting their special mission from God. Is that happening to Christians today?

8. For Jews the celebration of Purim reminds them that with the gift of survival comes responsibility. Wherever injustice and hatred exist in the world, Jews are called to speak up and lead the call for justice. Does the same call apply to Christians?

9. Does Haman's plan to destroy the Jews remind you of the Holocaust? Why do you think the Jews have been the target of such hatred over the centuries?